A DARK, DARK TRUTH

A Lake Pines Mystery

L.L. ABBOTT

WELCOME TO LAKE PINES

Where the scenery is beautiful, but the secrets are deadly.

A fictional small town in Northwestern Ontario that's home to both year-round residents and summer cottagers. Hidden secrets, private lives, and tension lay the groundwork for treacherous crimes. But there are more than secrets buried in this small town.

LAKE PINES MURDER MYSTERY SERIES

Murder at First Light

Death at Deception Bay

Murder of Crows

The Dead of Winter

The Night is Darkest

Conspiracy of Blood

Deadly Past

Echoes of Guilt

Dead in the Water

A Dark, Dark Truth

Last to Die

A DARK, DARK TRUTH

A GRIPPING, SUSPENSEFUL MYSTERY

L.L. Abbott

Cover designed by Warren Design

L.L. Abbott
Visit my website at www.LLAbbott.com

eBook ISBN-978-1-989325-98-8
Paperback ISBN-978-1-989325-99-5

Hemlock & Ash
reading made real

Do you ever read book dedications?

Well, I guess you're reading this one.

Most people open a book, skim past the dedication in hopes that they find their name but never do. Over the years, I've dedicated my books to my two wonderful sons, supportive husband, father, friends, and family who have encouraged me through their own perseverance, and (my favorite) my dog. Which is probably the best dedication in the history of all dedications. Am I right?

Yet, what about ***YOU,*** *my reader?*

You've never brought me tea or talked me through a late night. But you ***HAVE*** *offered kind words of support, and lovely comments on social media and book-selling sites, and you keep reading my books.*

Even though I don't know all of your names, I think of my readers fondly every day when I sit down to write.

This book is for ***YOU.***

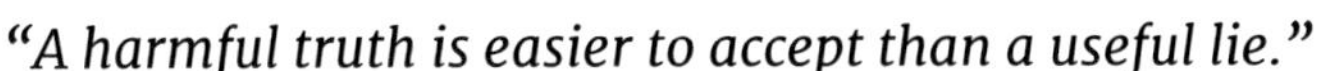

"A harmful truth is easier to accept than a useful lie."

– *Good advice that most people don't take*

A DARK, DARK TRUTH

CHAPTER 1

The sky over the lakefront glowed with the wriggling reflection of bright orange and red lights. A normally quiet lane behind Main Street was awash with emergency personnel, as rain-soaked officers swiftly diverted traffic and evacuated nearby structures.

Screeching sirens overpowered the cacophony of alarms that rang from nearby shops, signaling both the loss of power and the impending threat to their businesses. The emergency weather alert blasted through cell phones, warning Lake Pines residents of the approaching storm.

Emergency alerts shook several people from a deep slumber at twelve-fifteen. Leaving many confused and afraid. While the stabbing alarm thrust anyone who was already awake into a frenzied panic.

The storm was more forceful than the national weather service originally predicted. Seasonal forecasting and stratospheric modeling combined with satellite images had promised that the eye of the storm would veer south of the populated areas around Lake of the Woods. Except for heavy rain, Lake Pines was supposed to be spared the worst of the storm.

But those were computer-based modeling programs and held no accountability for what had happened during the darkest point of the night.

Even though the eye of the storm veered south of Lake Pines, the edge of the storm swept over the town. Building up force as it grazed the edge of the thirty-sixth largest lake in the world. Resulting in catastrophic wind speeds and destructive flooding in low-lying areas.

Shattered windows, torn shingles from rooftops, and collapsed structures marked the storm's path.

Kerry almost ignored the text alert when her phone buzzed and shook across the surface of her night table. However, the repeated sounds of incoming texts, not only to her phone but to Simon's, jolted them both out of bed.

Tumbling in a half stupor, she haphazardly searched for her clothes. She yanked a sweater from the oversized ottoman at the foot of the bed and pulled it over her head. Kerry rushed across the room and into the empty hall, pulling on a pair of mismatched socks. Leaping awkwardly as she rushed into her father's room, shaking him from his deep sleep when she realized the magnitude of the emergency.

As they ran down the stairs, the pelting rain echoed a haunting tapping sound through the ordinarily quiet house as the howling wind knocked an oversized branch against the roof. Had it not been for the emergency call, Kerry would've crawled deeper under the covers, wrestling Raven for space among her pillows.

Instead, she followed Simon down the stairs, where Oliver was waiting with their coats when he realized an emergency was calling them away from the safety of their home to the bitter storm that raged outside.

When the weather service predicted the severe storm, Oliver opted to sleep in the house as opposed to in his small apartment above the garage. Kerry was grateful for his decision as she looked down at Dominique, who was now cradled in his arms as Raven scurried around his feet. The dog tucked his tail tightly under his belly and pulled his ears back, reacting to the potentially dangerous situation that was bearing down on their town when the high-pitched echoing wind drew forth a primal warning. In a few minutes, Oliver would bring them below ground, taking shelter in the supportive structure of the stone foundation. Just in case the storm worsened.

All Kerry wanted to do was to wrap her arms around her daughter and her loyal, protective dog, promising them both that everything was going to be alright. Simon tugged at Kerry's elbow, pulling her away from their daughter and the dog, and guided her out the door and toward his truck. Their commitments were calling them away from their family, away from where they really wanted to be, and it made Kerry want to scream in protest.

It was pouring when they rushed from their house and drove to the location where emergency crews gathered sixty feet away from the building in question.

No one spoke.

Everyone waited and watched, understanding that anything that could be done, had already been attempted.

But at least no one was hurt. Those were the mumbles that came from several onlookers. The incongruousness of the comment seemed glaring among the devastation that littered the roads around town. In fact, so much had been harmed, and Kerry wondered if the town could survive what had happened.

Rising smoke struggled against the vigorous downpour, forcing the gray billowing clouds to twist toward the ground as the fire raged inside the building. Sparks shot forth from the broken windows, snapping and singeing the damp air.

Police and ambulance attendants eventually halted their efforts to remain dry as they fought against the burgeoning flames. Some even stood back, realizing there wasn't much they could do beyond what the initial fire crew had achieved shortly after they arrived.

Simon was busy directing police officers to different areas of town, hoping that the storm wouldn't leave their community vulnerable to the already frightening rise in break-ins. The unpredictable thefts instilled fear in the town, prompting business owners to shutter their shops and stores before dusk. Customers felt unsafe in the shopping district and had avoided late-night dinners in town, worried they may end up in the middle of an altercation. Fear had settled on Lake Pines, dispiriting the town's morale, and impeding the economy.

Among the crises that preoccupied the police were reports of downed power lines, toppled trees, and broken windows. Sally had rushed to the station once Simon enacted the emergency protocols after the storm's electrical surge cut power to half of the homes in Lake Pines. With her wavy blonde hair held back with a large clip, and the remnants of smudged mascara in the corner of her eye, she was on her second cup of coffee by the time Josh arrived at the station to help her field several emergency calls.

Simon was doing his best to direct everyone from under the protective tarp that shielded him from the blowing rain. Surrounded by police, fire, and ambulance personnel, Simon coordinated the entire emergency operation, unfazed by the storm that swirled around them. Never once did he display irritation that the emergency alert shook him awake after two hours of sleep.

Everyone knew that the hospital and the assisted living facility were a priority for the power company. While firefighters throughout town attended to fires just like the one Kerry watched engulf the small brick building on Main Street.

She looked on as sprays of foam and water arced from hoses. Axes shattered doors and windows as fire personnel slowly reached the source of the blaze inside the building.

As her raincoat trapped the humidity against her skin, an itch crawled across Kerry's back, making her regret her choice of the wool sweater she grabbed in the dark. Pushing the irritation aside, she focused on the situation that was unfolding in front of her, and her mind raced with what the next few days would entail.

Dragging the back of her hand across her forehead, she wiped the rain from the edge of her bangs as she tucked her long brown hair behind one ear. For the next three hours, she absorbed the commotion, forcing down any emotion that would detract her from a calm, level-headed reaction.

Over several hours, the wind slowly calmed, and the rain petered to a drizzle and then, eventually, a mist. Before she realized it, a soft glow from the east settled over the bay. It was a new day, in what seemed like a different town.

When the storm had moved beyond Lake Pines, pink splashes brushed across the light blue morning sky. The beauty could have deceived everyone into thinking the events of the previous night were a dream, but the destruction that littered the streets told another truth.

The dark side of Mother Nature had thrashed the small lakeside town. Her atmospheric beauty was all that remained from the violent storm that pushed across the waterfront as it relentlessly struck buildings, tore across forested parks, and battered the iconic statue that had greeted visitors to the picturesque town for over fifty years.

Everyone was talking about the forty-foot statue that had overlooked the bay since the mid-60s; dazzling tourists who ventured into the recreational region throughout the year.

Witnessing the changing tides, the twisted fish was resolute against the stark brightness of the sun bouncing off the frozen lake in winter and standing watch on a warm summer night when the lake absorbed the sinking darkness into blue-gray waters.

The iconic statue stood proudly on the shoreline of Lake Pines, and within hours of the violent storm's approach, destructive wind gusts had destroyed the aging structure.

Gapping holes trailed along the hull, with branches and debris clinging to the uneven metal edges. Boughs with wilting leaves drooped from sharp daggers, resembling the afterthought of a monster's meal. Light filtered through the holes as water dripped out of the structure, collecting at the muddy base, as streams refracted random rays of light.

Kerry slowed her Jeep as she drove past the statue the next morning. Crowds had already assembled in the adjacent park as residents surveyed the damage caused by the intense storm. Photos would soon flood social media, spreading the news across town and the country that the storm destroyed the iconic Canadian structure.

She didn't stop. Her presence would only bring questions that people should direct to the police department. But more and more, her arrival at crime scenes and accidents gave the impression that she was a police officer, as well as the town's medical examiner. Lately, it was getting hard to separate her job from Simon's in the eyes of the residents of Lake Pines.

Continuing along the road, she veered around fallen branches that blocked her path. Kerry raised her hand in a sympathetic wave to shop owners who were balancing large boards against the blank spaces in walls that held glass panes a day earlier.

Almost everyone reported some level of damage that the storm had caused. It would be several days before the town maintenance crews cleared debris from the walking paths as they triaged their clean-up efforts.

Kerry parked in the same familiar spot next to the curb and stepped out of her Jeep. She took a few steps and paused, surveying the landscape that had drastically changed over the last twelve hours. A faint scent of burnt wood, dampened ash, and melted plastic caught her by surprise.

Although, it shouldn't have.

Kerry was familiar with fire-related incidents, and the distinct scents could linger in the air for days. She walked around the structure with the fire inspector, assessing the damage.

Fire crews preserved as much evidence as they could for the investigator. Which wasn't easy, considering the intensity of the blaze. After an exhaustive two hours, everyone was confident in their assessment.

A spark started the fire after lightning damaged the central generating station, causing power to surge through the grid, knocking out electricity, and damaging circuits. There was nothing anyone could have done to avoid the disaster.

Kerry clutched the report in her hand as the fire inspector guided her back to the road. Away from the zone that was deemed unsafe.

Safety crews were standing by and moved forward when the fire inspector gave them the signal. Kerry watched as they knocked down the east wall, sending the last remaining section of the building crashing to the ground.

Pieces of brick disintegrated, and a cloud of red dust shot into the air, obscuring the sidewalk that had once led to the front door of the building.

Her building. Her lab.

Kerry wrapped her arms around her body as she stumbled back, grasping the side of the Jeep, steadying herself against the shock—and trying not to scream.

CHAPTER 2

A bright white arrow pointed to the west side of the parking lot. A row of trees surrounding a six-foot wooden fence obscured the hospital from the road. Boards that were splintered and cracked from the storm separated the lot from the adjacent forest. A security fence divided the parking lot into two main sections. One for visitors and patients and another for staff. The lot couldn't accommodate the regular complement of nurses and doctors, let alone the extra people who were now using rooms in the building.

Over the last year, the hospital's administration attempted to promote alternative modes of transportation to all staff members.

Financial incentives for staff who didn't drive to work lasted only as long as the warm summer months did. The return to five-foot snowdrifts, ice-covered roads, and icy winds jolted most people back to their cars. Three doctors, four nurses, and one technician were the only remaining staff battling the elements for the sake of the environment and bonuses.

Kerry tucked the hand-drawn map, which outlined her assigned parking area, under her sun visor. She shared an unlit area of the lot with the EMS Ambulance and two security guards. The faded yellow lines outlined three spots, but everyone did their best to squeeze and angle four vehicles into the corner space in the lot.

Kerry wiggled out of the Jeep, closed the door, and walked sideways until she was free from the cramped space. She arrived early, hoping to miss most of the hospital staff, and had been completing some reports when Simon's text lit up her phone.

Peter is heading over to the hospital. Couldn't keep him from heading your way. Sorry.

Simon stopped short of adding a smiley face emoji or a row of x's and o's, prompted mostly because of the Superintendent's clampdown on interdepartmental relationships.

One week ago, Peter distributed a province-wide memo to every law enforcement employee outlining the expected conduct for coworkers who were also involved in a personal relationship. The edict was in response to a follow-up investigation in the wake of several anonymous complaints from within a Toronto police detachment. The inquiry revealed that two lead detectives overlooked a crucial piece of evidence, putting the outcome of a murder investigation in jeopardy.

Talk of arguments on crime scene locations or ineffectual sharing of information proved to be more than just random rumors when the detectives in question finally admitted they were in the process of a messy divorce. The interdepartmental review ruled that their actions inhibited the transparent and judicial process of the investigation.

In fact, it not only exposed the department to potential lawsuits, but their indolent approach to the investigation almost resulted in a killer evading a first-degree murder charge. Since then, Superintendent Peter George enacted a strict policy he referred to as *Departmental Professionalism*.

Even though Kerry and Simon never let their marriage interfere with any investigations, they knew with Kerry as the town coroner and Simon as the Chief of Police that other people may scrutinize their actions. Because of that, they avoided any public, or texted, displays of affection.

Kerry glanced around the windowless room, unsure where she would seat Peter when he arrived. She and Peter were friends before she became the town's coroner and before he received his promotion to Superintendent. But friendship aside, if Peter was showing up unannounced, his visit was purely business.

She had been working in the small ten-by-ten space for eight days. Thankfully, the funeral home collected Cody Jesper's body from the lab a day before the blaze. A remote server stored her files, reports, and diagnostic tests, which ensured there wasn't any loss of important information. However, in a town as small as Lake Pines, it left only a few locations that Kerry could use as a temporary office.

Her make-shift desk, built from unattractive but sturdy framing boards, barely had enough room for the second-hand computer the hospital gave her. Thomas offered to build a workstation for her when he heard about Kerry's unplanned change in an office setting. However, when he arrived at room 24B, the restricted space allowed only for a thick piece of paneling balanced on two filing cabinets. One on each end.

After he removed the cheap Formica table with two mismatched chairs, Thomas used the leftover wood to build the desk and two floating shelves that ran the length of the room, giving Kerry e some storage space for her files and containers.

Which only left room enough for one chair, two stacks of boxes, and a mini fridge. As it was, Kerry couldn't bring Raven to work because of the hospital's policy on animals in the workplace. Not that she would've been able to find space on the floor for his bed, but she missed having him around. Especially with her father and Elin recently taking Dominique and Lucia on a brief vacation to British Columbia.

While Kerry waited for Peter to arrive, she added her comments regarding the toxicology analysis in Cody Jesper's file in the note section on the report. She shook her head. At least Elaine Jesper made it easy to solve her husband's murder. The increased levels of chemicals and toxins in his blood ranked higher than any Kerry had seen before.

His wife hadn't even disposed of the empty pill bottle or the box of rat poison when two detectives arrived to search their home. Both were covered with her fingerprints and stashed under the counter in their bathroom. That, along with her inability to use a consistent alibi with any of the officers who questioned her, pointed the finger of guilt squarely in her direction. The police arrested Elaine Jesper, but Kerry's final report and toxicology findings were due to be submitted to the lawyer by the end of the day.

Normally, Kerry didn't fall behind with paperwork. However, her recent move to the hospital basement was making it difficult to remain organized.

Another change to her routine was the requirement to share an examination room and lab with another doctor. Room 19B sat on the opposite end of the hall and had largely been the sole domain of Doctor Varanus' research study.

There were several small rooms in the hospital basement, and staff members labeled their offices with hand-stenciled signs. Some wrote their names on paper and taped them to the doors, while other rooms had more utilitarian uses. Such as room 23B which was simply identified as 'morgue'.

The hollow walk through the faded mint green and baby blue painted hall deadened the faint buzzing of the suspended fluorescent lighting. Making the walk from Kerry's office to the examination room seem longer than it probably was.

She felt disjointed as she coordinated her movements through the hospital. Twice, as she was rushing from 24B to the room with the shared printer and then the examination room, Kerry pushed into other rooms, frightening staff who had grown accustomed to working undisturbed. One thing was becoming increasingly clear. Each day she was away from her own space, she became more disorganized.

Kerry tried not to become exasperated by the situation and she refocused her attention on the final report. The knock came on the door just as Kerry submitted the file and closed her email.

Even though she could have just reached out and pulled the door open, she stood and opened the door, knowing it was Peter on the other side. Greeting him with the level of respect and professionalism that their friendship and his position merited.

"I'd invite you in, but as you can see, I don't have a lot of room or a second chair." Kerry joked as she opened the door, revealing the restricted space.

"That's okay, Kerry. What I have to say won't take long." Peter took off his hat and stepped into 24B. "Actually, that's what I wanted to talk to you about."

She closed the door and leaned against the wall. "I'm glad to hear that. I was worried that you weren't returning my calls because there was a problem with the reconstruction of the lab."

Peter pressed his lips together and folded his arms across his body. Normally, Peter's warm caramel smile and welcoming eyes reminded Kerry that he wasn't just her boss, he was also one of her closest friends. But there was a tinge of concern lining the edges of his temple as his brow crinkled forward, and he tilted his chin toward his chest. "There isn't a problem. Just a change."

"What do you mean '*a change*'?"

Peter lifted his gaze and offered a feigned smile as he explained, "You know that most coroners work out of the local hospitals in their district. At least the ones in smaller towns." Peter leaned back, shifting his body quickly when he realized the desk that he was leaning on was only a piece of wood balanced on two cabinets. "Anyway, the department heads have decided that you should permanently work in the Lake Pines Hospital. You could share the diagnostic equipment and examination rooms, which would cut down on expenses."

"Next, you're going to tell me I'm going to have to pick up a shift in the emergency room." Kerry regretted her terse remark but didn't take it back.

"I know it's going to be an enormous change since you have had your own separate building for so many years, but I think once you think it over, you'll realize that it's the best decision."

"For your budget, maybe. But not for my productivity." Kerry waved her arms around the small room. "Look at the size of this space. I'm not sure what the original use for this room was, but I sensed a faint odor of cleaning products when I moved in and there's a drain in the middle of the floor."

Even though there was no record of the room being used as a janitorial storage closet, no one in the hospital denied it either.

"I promise to find a larger space. This obviously isn't an ideal setup for you."

Kerry let out a sigh and rolled her eyes. "Thanks."

Peter offered a slight nod, but a nod wasn't a yes or an agreement to give her a new office.

As he stepped into the hall, he turned around, offering Kerry a sympathetic smile. "Everything is changing Kerry. It was just a matter of time before Lake Pines felt the sting of the budget cutbacks. The damage from the fire just pushed things along."

Kerry stood in the hall, watching Peter until he disappeared around the corner. When she heard the metal door at the end of the hall slam shut, she closed her door. Unaware that at the opposite end of the hospital basement, a shadowy figure waited, watching Kerry's every move.

CHAPTER 3

Michel pulled the faded black baseball cap down to the edge of his brow. The cap, like most fishing-themed items of clothing, was popular among the residents of Lake Pines and ensured that he would fit in with the crowd moving along Main Street. Dressed in clothes that were the opposite of what the paparazzi normally photographed him wearing, meant he would remain invisible while moving around in plain sight.

He shielded his well-groomed features behind a jumble of beige, green, and blue as he moved through each store, disguising his true physique. His cropped hair, stylishly trimmed to the same length as his beard, itched below the thick polyester strap he tightened at the back of his head. He wanted to rip the cap from his head and loosen the top button of the plaid shirt to rescue himself from the prickly heat building below the fabric. *Who had told him plaid was the uniform of cottagers at the lake?* Since he donned the disguise, he hadn't seen a single person wearing an outfit that involved the patterned design in any form.

Michel wished he was wearing the custom-tailored Loro Piana shirts he purchased in Italy. Over the years, he restricted his splurges to fine clothing, wine, and food. Except for the island in Haven Bay, Michel eschewed exorbitant spending. He knew it would be more difficult to conceal his secret if he intertwined himself in elite social circles.

Everyone liked to ask questions, and most people craved a scandal. Both of which Michel meticulously avoided.

He never invited fame or global recognition, and in fact, he would've preferred to avoid the limelight. He had worked hard to change everything about himself.

Casting away his identity was his only chance at living a normal life. Events that were out of his control had molded how the world viewed him, and that alone angered him. The only way to survive was by changing into what the world could accept and what people were comfortable being around.

Michel always believed it was best to conceal his identity. But something deep inside of him changed last spring, and he wanted to do the right thing. It was Henri Badeau, his partner, and friend, whom he credited with helping him find his own voice.

"A harmful truth is easier to accept than a useful lie." Henri had mumbled when, during a late night sharing an exquisite bottle of Rémy Martin XO, Michel explained his past. Henri was understanding and supportive and assured Michel that he did nothing wrong. Many years his senior, Henri ran his business the same way as he lived his private life. With direct honesty and with brutal criticism. It's what made him a successful restauranteur and a business force to admire. It's also what made him a great friend.

That was the moment that Michel wanted to stop hiding the truth. No matter how dark or painful it was. He just had to make it to the end of the summer, and Lake Pines was the place that could offer him the solace to do that peacefully.

Michel rushed across the road, avoiding a crowd walking in his direction. They were holding signs and shouting as they protested the exorbitant funding that was being spent on the shoreline statue that was damaged in a recent storm.

Led by an older man wearing cargo shorts and sandals, they chanted in unison, unveiling their discontent. A wiry charcoal and silver beard covered the old man's face, extending from his cheekbones to below the collar of his white T-shirt. Mostly shrouded from the sun in an oversized Tilley hat, the man's narrow eyes were barely visible under the brim.

Tens of thousands of dollars were being spent on architectural landscapers that were hired to enhance the waterfront park and forested trail leading up to the statue. Including everything from widening the path with an extra thick cedar chip walkway to adding benches and photo platforms for tourists.

The primary source of the crowd's displeasure involved the amount of money that was needed to repair the damaged hull of the statue and repaint the exterior.

Embroiled in the fish statue melee, were the town councilors who had agreed to contribute to the local fundraising efforts, matching each donation dollar for dollar. However, caught up in the save-the-fish excitement, the councilors neglected to set a cap on their funding match, and they were now on the hook for double the amount that they'd budgeted for the project.

This Michel gathered from the many signs in storefront windows and the heated conversations he overheard between individuals in shops. Everyone was eager to share their opinion, and no one was immune from hearing either side of the story.

This was one example of why he rarely came into town when he arrived in Lake Pines for his vacations on his private island. It was the one place he could be alone with his thoughts, locking the outside world away and listening to what his heart really wanted. Buying the island several years ago was the best decision he made, but whenever he arrived, he adhered to a few strict rules. He invited no one to his island, and he rarely came into town.

However, this time there were a few items he needed over the next few days, and when he couldn't reach the woman that he hired to shop for him, he made a quick trip into town.

His list was short, which meant he only had to visit a few stores to purchase the supplies he needed. Once he was done, he could avoid coming into town for the rest of his vacation.

He knew that if he was going to be recognized anywhere, it would be while he was at the grocery store. His agent advertised his books and network show in food stores across North America. Which is why he sent Tanya Foley an email with a shopping list a few days before he arrived.

It was especially difficult to avoid celebrity recognition in Canada, where most people referred to him as the Canadian who made it big in the global restaurant scene.

The unknown talent from an unknown town. The Ryan Reynolds of the culinary realm.

He still cringed when he recalled the paper's headline the morning after he won the national contest. He thought it demeaned his talent, and because of that, he avoided being in the public eye. Using only cash, Michel purchased the last items on his list and slipped them into his tote as he left the hardware store.

A thin film of sweat coated his brow as the heavy cap shielded the lake breeze from his skin. He loved the warmth of the sun, which is why he and Henri were opening a small bistro in Bandol, a fertile wine region in the South of France. But before he could move on to the next stage in his life, Michel had to correct the damage made by the lies he perpetrated throughout most of his adult life.

As he rushed down the street, Michel's stomach growled in protest at having missed breakfast. His day of overseas travel, combined with the nervousness about what he was planning to do, suppressed his normally robust appetite.

He spotted a café across the street and dashed through a line of parked cars as he headed toward the front door. He caught the faint sounds of Shawn Ogilvie's latest song wafting from a car stereo as a car rushed by, bringing about a smile when he recognized his favorite Canadian artist.

The rich aroma of freshly ground coffee cascaded through the door, which was propped open with a wooden doorstop. He could almost taste the buttery richness of warm croissants as the intense aroma wafted through the early morning air. As he looked up at the sign, Michel couldn't remember the café being here the last time he visited Lake Pines. He was almost sure that it wasn't there the year he bought the cottage.

But then again, he couldn't say for certain.

Lake Pines provided all that he hoped for. Storm Island in Haven Bay was away from the regularly traveled boat routes and the appropriately named bay offered Michel the privacy he desired.

Except for his neighbor, who had an irritating propensity for dropping by his cottage unannounced, Michel could spend weeks alone on his island with no one knowing he was there.

But this summer everything would change.

Guided by the powerful aroma of the baked treats inside the café, Michel rushed toward the front door. He peered through the expansive café window and noticed every table was full. It was a good sign for the small town, which he heard had felt the economic stress of the pandemic and then a rash of robberies that forced shop owners to close their businesses before dark.

He decided that the scent drifting from the café was worth the risk of being recognized.

The clanging of cutlery on plates and laughter intermingled with conversation invigorated Michel's mood. It brought a feeling of friendship and warmth that became his bastion of protection when he needed one many years ago. Finding a place in France where he could blend his passion with a profession was a blessing, but he built it on a lie that he was now planning to shed.

He was about to step through the doorway when he came to an abrupt stop and leaned toward the window. Arranged on an antique table were a pile of cookbooks, a collection of hand-painted pottery, and scented candles. Pushed between the books and giftware was the promotional tabletop book release image that he and his agent approved last month. But the only problem was, the book wasn't supposed to be released until the end of August.

Michel specifically timed the book's publication day to coincide with the same week he'd be posting his revealing interview. The benefit of accessing several social media platforms without a producer was that Michel could tape and upload the video when he was ready. And until then, only he knew the information it contained.

He stepped away from the café and turned around. He hesitated and glanced nervously toward the dock at the bottom of the hill where another group of protestors was disembarking from a large boat and making their way up the ramp to join the crowd at the waterfront fish statue.

As he lumbered toward the dock, he leaned his body away from the force that threatened to pull him toward the cement. Michel panted as he reached for his phone and dialed Camille's number, getting her voicemail on the second ring. His message was brief, but Camille would know what he was calling about.

How could she not have said anything? He just spoke to her moments ago.

Even through his heaving breaths, he made his point and no matter how much she helped his career, she had no right to disregard his decision.

A few minutes later, Michel reached the quiet seclusion on the east side of the public dock, and he stepped into his boat. He pulled away from the waterfront, drove through Safety Bay, and headed directly for Storm Island. If his agent didn't understand the potential harm that she unleashed by releasing his book early, she soon would. As would anyone else who he harmed, or shielded, with his lie.

CHAPTER 4

It was a little past six when the sharp ringtone exploded in the small room. The ringing continued, growing louder and more persistent as Kerry searched through her bag for her phone. The sound seemed to bounce off the walls and reverberate through the small room, creating a sense of tension and unease where none existed.

No one had asked Kerry where she thought she could work after the fire destroyed her lab. In fact, she thought of two other locations that would be preferable to the windowless space in 24B.

She had only planned to work until four, but somehow, the hours had slipped away. Kerry couldn't believe that she had been working for two extra hours without even realizing it. She checked her phone again, hoping that maybe it was just a mistake, but the time remained the same.

Oliver's image flashed across her screen, and she smiled, relieved that it was her father and not Peter. She didn't want to deal with another excuse, explaining why she should work in what amounted to a forgotten closet space in the hospital basement. And lately, any conversation regarding her office space turned into an argument justifying her job.

She answered the video call, leaning her phone against her empty coffee mug, and her father's face came into focus. The sunset brushed across the water's surface, artistically tinting the water from a steely blue to a light purple. A light breeze tousled Oliver's silver hair, which had grown over the top of his ears, and the gentle lapping sound of the waves cascaded in the background.

"Dad," Kerry shouted into the phone. "How was your flight?"

Oliver tilted the phone and an image of Dominique and Lucia came into view. "We landed about an hour ago and came right here after we got the rental car."

"Are you at Jericho Beach?" Kerry asked, recognizing the North Shore Mountains, and the ships anchored in Burrard Inlet in the background.

"Yeah, Elin wanted to stop by before we checked into the hotel. It's been years since she was in Vancouver." Kerry caught a quick glimpse of Elin crawling over the rocky beach in her tan pantsuit and cream knit sweater and wondered if she was like that when Thomas was a small child. Oliver turned the phone back on himself. "We're going to catch the ferry to Victoria tomorrow afternoon after we take the kids to Granville Island."

Kerry heard Dominique laugh as she and Lucia played on the beach, feeling the sting of missing her daughter instantly. It was the first time Dominique had been away from them for any huge length of time, but Kerry knew with Simon's heavy workload at the station, and the recent fire in her lab, that they wouldn't be home as much as they wanted to, anyway.

Still, it hurt to be so far away from her daughter.

"How are *things* going?" Kerry emphasized the word things, knowing that Oliver understood she was referring to his time spent with Elin and not the toddlers.

He couldn't control his reactionary grin. Even with the glare shining down on Oliver's face, Kerry noticed the corner of his right eye dip toward his crooked smile as a faint blush rose to his cheeks.

"Great," was all her father offered.

"Call me tomorrow after dinner, and I'll make sure I'm with Simon so he can say hello to Dominique."

"Will do," Oliver said. "If you see Josh and Thomas, tell them that Elin will call them before Lucia goes to bed. Love you."

Oliver ended the call before Kerry could respond and the image of Dominique's smile faded as she waved into the camera.

Kerry turned her phone over and leaned back in her chair. She wiped her eyes and stretched her arms over her head. The absence of natural light made it impossible to judge the time passing throughout the day, and she felt more tired than she thought she should. She sent Simon a text, telling him she was on her way home, eager to see both him and Raven.

Should I pick something up for dinner on the way home? Kerry typed.

No need. Simon replied. This time, he added a heart emoji, which meant he was already waiting for her at home.

Kerry gathered the file on her desk, stored it in the filing cabinet, and locked the drawer. She grabbed her coat and purse, turned the short distance to the door, and grabbed the doorknob.

Through the gap at the base of the door, a sliver of light edged across the tile and the small yellow corner caught Kerry's eye. She opened the door and the stark fluorescent beam pushed through the darkness, illuminating the uneven white and black speckled floor tiles, and threw strands of excessively bright artificial light into her small room.

Kerry's eyes drifted down to the folded piece of yellow paper, wedged against the edge of the door frame.

She reached down and unfolded the paper. Probably another missive from the hospital administration reminding staff to lock the doors and turn off the lights when they left for the day. Apparently, the expense of paper and the plethora of memos she received during her short time working in the hospital basement didn't count toward the departmental cutbacks. She stifled her anger, reminding herself that this was just a temporary situation.

She scooped the paper up from the floor and was about to toss it onto her desk when she unfolded it.

But when Kerry read the two neatly typed lines on the page, she knew it wasn't a note from the hospital administration.

You can't hide your deep, dark secret any longer.

Kerry glanced into the hall, craning her head in each direction, and realized it was empty.

It arrived under a veil of secrecy. The sender marked the ominous note with only two lines of text. It was unclear who left the note, but they obviously intended it for her.

On its own, the note proved nothing. She received threats in the past, mostly to do with autopsies that gave insurance companies the loopholes they needed to deny policy payouts. They came from disgruntled family members who disagreed with the cause of death, or lawyers that would pick apart every word and line in her reports, but she never felt as if she was in danger.

A wide range of emotions surfaced during the grieving period, and for most people, just getting their opinion out in the open was enough.

But this felt different.

It was the second sentence, the underlined word, and how it collided with the secret from her past that frightened her.

This time, no stone will remain unturned.

CHAPTER 5

Kerry settled into the oversized chair next to the fireplace and closed her eyes as Raven lifted both paws and climbed onto her lap. With her eyes closed, she leaned into his head, ripe with the scent of fresh grass and decaying leaves. Raven crammed every joyous moment of an entire afternoon after spending only twenty minutes outside in the yard.

One deep breath was all it took to relieve the tension that had built up in her neck and shoulders since she left the hospital. The dog sensed Kerry's unease, the way he normally did, and leaned into her chest. She rubbed the back of his neck, and his tail thumped against her leg. His rhythmic breathing and low groan were the tranquility she needed, and they settled into the chair in an awkward cuddle.

Simon entered the room carrying a tray with an assortment of tapas plates and rested it on the ottoman next to Kerry's chair. Raven snapped his head away from Kerry's body and pushed his nose toward the warm pita bread, and Simon gently nudged him away.

"I swear, this dog has gotten worse since Oliver's been gone."

"My dad only left this morning," Kerry leaned forward, wrapping her arms around the dog's neck. "I think it has more to do with me not being able to take him to the office."

Simon gently tugged on the dog's collar and guided Raven to his bed, pointing toward the floor.

"That won't work," Kerry laughed, just as she tore off a piece of warmed pita bread and tossed it up in the air. "Give him a small piece and he'll leave us alone."

Simon shook his head and grinned. "I guess there's no chance we'll be able to train him as a police dog."

"I don't think with all the cutbacks that Peter wants to put into place that there would be any funding for it anyway," Kerry snapped.

"I still can't believe that they might not rebuild your office."

Kerry shrugged her shoulders and scooped some food onto a small plate, enjoying the rare luxury of eating dinner without a toddler. She pulled her legs up on the chair, resting the plate on her lap, and reached for the glass of wine in Simon's outstretched arm.

"Unless you have a better idea, I'm not sure what I can do to change his mind about permanently placing me in the hospital basement."

"Josh said Thomas tried to build you a decent office."

"He tried, but if a builder with his expertise can't make it work, then there's not much hope."

"By the way, thanks for getting the Jesper case report off to the court."

"No problem," Kerry stabbed her fork into a falafel ball and dragged it through a dollop of hummus before popping it into her mouth. "Did you get the picture that my dad sent with the girls playing on the beach?"

Simon nodded, "I'm still trying to get used to the fact that your dad is dating Thomas' mother."

"How does Josh feel about his mother-in-law getting cozy here in Lake Pines?"

"He said Elin is acting like her old self since she's been spending time with your dad, so he's rooting for the match." Simon noticed a distracted gaze in Kerry's eyes. "What's up? Are you uncomfortable with your dad dating Elin?"

"No, nothing like that. I just miss Dominique."

"So do I."

Simon leaned back in the chair and stroked the edge of his jaw as he held Kerry's eyes with his calm, focused stare. There was a peacefulness that Simon always seemed to find, even when difficulty surrounded him. It's what made him a great boss and what initially attracted Kerry to him.

The corner of his mouth lifted, and the hint of a small dimple peaked through the auburn shadow that was thickening on his face. Kerry was still getting used to seeing Simon with a beard, but despite the change in his appearance, the affectionate and reassuring gesture was recognizable. Even if Simon didn't know it, the smile was everything she needed at that moment.

"Do you like it yet?" Simon pushed his chin forward and rubbed the side of his face.

"I've made peace with it," Kerry joked, but in fact, she loved the way it looked, and he knew it.

Raven, not fully satiated with the small pieces of bread Kerry tossed in his direction, crept forward on his belly until he was beside the ottoman, letting out a low, rumbling whimper. They both laughed as the large black dog pulled his ears back on his head and widened his eyes.

"Why don't we take Raven for an extra-long walk tonight after we finish eating? Then at least we won't be ignoring all our kids," Simon suggested.

Raven jumped up, tilting his head at a sharp angle at the mention of a walk. "See, he's trainable." Kerry laughed as she tossed him another piece of bread.

Relaxing in the dimly lit room, they finished all the food Simon arranged on the tray and then drained the last of the wine into their glasses. And when they couldn't ignore Raven's impatient whimper as he nudged his leash on the floor, they cleared the dishes and slipped into their shoes.

The normally chilly spring was warmer than anyone expected, and the fragrant scent of freshly cut grass and lilac buds sprouting on the hedge at the end of their driveway filled the air. Without the distraction of the note or missing Dominique, the night would've been perfect.

Simon rambled on about their summer plans, and how he wanted to explore the caves on Sultana Island as Kerry's mind drifted back to the folded piece of paper that someone had slipped under her door.

Before she realized it, they had walked the long, winding distance to the lakeside statue poised at the entrance to the small town. They both stopped, letting Raven explore the muddy path deep in the forest nestled next to the small park with the statue. Looking at the current state of the gigantic structure, it was impressive that the monolithic conception made it to the point it had.

A forty-foot, hollow, twisted metal fish graced the most scenic mound at the entrance to town. Situated just beyond the fork in the highway, the statue welcomed travelers to Lake Pines for over fifty years.

Kerry understood the fervor of the fundraising committee to rescue the iconic monument. Looking past the grime and rust, they remembered the importance of the proud symbol that was reflected in the waters of Lake Pines Bay.

They clung to the memory that the statue represented a magnificent moment in their town's history. Back when the economy was strong, tourism was at its peak and the population of Lake Pines was bursting at the seams.

Returning the statue to its original glory may prompt a re-emergence of better times and a more positive outlook.

The note that was surreptitiously slipped under her door forced Kerry to revisit a time in her past when she was full of positivity and ambition. But unlike the planned renovation of the statue, the note didn't bring about pride from her past, but shame because of what she did.

Despite the ominous tone of the note, it wasn't a threat that needed to be made. She understood the seriousness of what could happen if someone revealed the truth. Fighting to have her own office would be the least of her concerns.

The note she received under her door was direct, and she wondered when she should tell Simon the truth about what happened so many years ago. Or if she should continue to maintain the lie.

No matter how much she tried to erase the memory, the image of Vivienne Strong flashed across her mind. She recalled the horrifying scene in the parking lot, where she died, alone, so many years ago.

As Kerry thought about the note, the nightmare of her actions swelled around her, stealing the peace in their walk.

She believed that what she had done had ended the injustice that occurred.

However, the delivery of the note made her realize it was the beginning of the worst that was still to come. Someone knew what happened, and they were watching her.

CHAPTER 6

Lisa completed the renovations to her café in January. Customers could now appreciate the full extent of her vision, which was to encourage more residents to sit, lounge, and connect with each other. The combined café, restaurant, and artisan shop had an upbeat, modern style with a traditional, local feel.

Tourists could enjoy their meal or purchase a souvenir from Joe Blacks, while locals often strolled into Lisa's café when they craved a treat. If she could encourage more customers to shop and eat at the café, this year could be her most profitable yet.

Every day, Lisa welcomed regulars and newcomers into her café with the enticing aroma of her coffee and baked treats, along with the promise of a congenial environment. Even though Lisa fought the suggestion, several customers continued to persuade her to rename the café to reflect the warmth and kindness of the owner. Lisa's Place, Lisa's Coffee Lounge, and even just Lisa's were among the top suggestions for a new name. There wasn't a day that went by without someone offering an unsolicited suggestion.

Lisa hurriedly cleared the last few cups and plates from the breakfast rush, thinking about next week's menu items, when Kerry walked into the café.

"Do you have time for a break?" Kerry asked, as she greeted her friend.

Balancing an armful of dishes, Lisa nodded and grinned as she walked into the kitchen. "Be with you in a sec."

Kerry was wearing a yellow sweater and a matching coat, and although she tried, she failed to disguise the bright blue rain boots emblazoned with pink butterflies that peaked out from beneath the black pants she pulled down over them.

Lisa returned from the kitchen, noticing the boots for the first time, and laughed. "Are you expecting a storm today?"

"Ha, very funny," Kerry glanced down at her feet and tilted one boot in the air. "Simon bought Dominique and me matching boots as a joke. Raven chewed the toe on my shoes, and these were all I could find as I was rushing out the door."

"Isn't he kind of old to be chewing shoes?" Lisa waved to a couple when they paused outside her café to glance at the display on the table next to the window.

"I think he's feeling ignored," Kerry said. "My dad left yesterday with Dominique, and I haven't been able to take him to work with me."

"Sorry to hear that. I'll get us some coffee and you can tell me all about it."

The aroma from the freshly ground beans, combined with the hissing sound of the espresso machine, reminded Kerry why she enjoyed coming to Lisa's café. And judging by the number of customers that lingered over their tables long past breakfast, many other people did, too.

"Have you given any further thought to changing the name of your café?" Kerry asked as she pulled off her coat, tossing it over the back of an empty chair next to the window.

"I don't think so." Lisa carried two mugs of hot coffee to the table and sat across from Kerry. "Everyone expects to see the black and gold sign at the end of Main Street. I don't want to brag, but I think it's become a bit of an iconic landmark. It's a good thing I got the sign back. The storm blew it into the lane behind the pharmacy."

"At least it didn't end up like the lakeside fish statue."

Their conversation veered to the protests surrounding the large muskie that had recently undergone a fundraising campaign to mix reviews from both residents and cottage owners. Many had hoped the storm that damaged the tail section of the statue would signal its removal. Instead, the local supporters of the iconic fish rallied together and started a campaign to raise funds that would pay for the repairs.

A Lake Pines blight, some had called it. But to those that supported its placement, it was akin to an Egyptian obelisk. Rising with unyielding allegiance as it surveyed the bay through heavily misted mornings and clear crisp nights.

The image graced everything from postcards to street signs. A local craft brewery even named a beer in honor of the statue. City maintenance workers and specialized metal fabricators rushed to complete the repairs to the hull before a group of young artists could repaint the exterior. Even though the town council approved the work, the controversy hadn't faded.

But today, it was Lisa's display on the table next to the window that grabbed Kerry's attention.

"Are you having a book signing here?"

Lisa glanced at the table displaying the white hardcover books with crisp images of sliced avocados, mint leaves, and a bowl with flakes of parmesan cheese and grilled asparagus spears tossed among thick strands of pasta. The cookbook's title was simply 'pure', all in thick, bold, lowercase text.

"I'm hoping to convince the chef who wrote the book to swing by the café. He's usually at his cottage at some point each summer and I was hoping to have him autograph them. Even if he doesn't want to hang around and speak with any of the customers."

"Why wouldn't he want to meet his fans? Don't most authors like the idea of meeting the people who read their books?"

"Yes, but Michel Lalonde isn't like most chefs or authors," Lisa explained. "He doesn't boast about his achievements, and he only makes the news when another restauranteur reveals he created a specialty dish. He rarely gives interviews, and when he does, they're only in print. There aren't even that many photos of him online. Not clear ones anyway."

"Is that the young chef from the east coast?" Kerry asked, recalling a story about a film producer who discovered a young chef when he dined in a small Halifax bistro.

"That's him," Lisa said. "He bought a cottage several years ago and when his publisher dropped off the books, she mentioned he'd be in the area this summer. I figured if I could track him down, then I could get some books autographed. It would be great to let everyone know I'll be selling them here in my café. Unfortunately, he avoids public appearances. But if I can get a few minutes alone with him, I might be able to convince him to come to the café. I just need to find him first." Lisa motioned to the table with her eyes, "They cost me an arm and a leg since I had to pay the publisher four months ago."

"Why don't you add a book to my bill? With Dominique and my dad out of town, Simon and I can try a few more adventurous recipes."

Lisa jumped up, excited to ring up the first sale of the book.

"Are you sure you don't want to wait for a signed copy?" Lisa wiggled her eyebrows and waved the book. "It may become a collectible one day." Lisa teased.

Kerry shook her head. She reached for her wallet and then asked Lisa to add a second one for Josh, who she knew was a fan of the Canadian chef.

If there was one thing Kerry was certain of, people who didn't want to be found were good at remaining hidden. And unfortunately for Lisa, Chef Lalonde was probably no exception.

CHAPTER 7

The basement wing of the hospital had a separate entrance tucked along the back side of the building. Entering the hospital through the small brown steel door meant swiping two security passes, descending two flights of stairs, and then walking the length of the building until Kerry reached her office on the far side of the building. However, the labyrinth had its advantages since she rarely passed anyone on her way to room 24B.

Kerry tossed the cookbooks and the bag containing her new shoes on the small table in her temporary office. After she pried her sweaty feet out of the thick rubber boots and slipped on her newly purchased footwear, she turned on her computer and sat down at her desk.

She pulled the cryptic note from her pocket and read it as her computer fan whirred to life. The screen flickered as the machine struggled to load the updated operating system and Kerry made a note to at least ask Peter for a new computer.

There was something different about the composition of the stationery. Something that stood out from ordinary notepaper found in shops around town. She sensed it the moment she picked it up off the floor.

The soft, yellow paper had a distinct feel. Different from even the fancy note paper she had at home and that she used for special messages or to add to gift bags.

Even in the poorly lit office, Kerry could tell the paper was expensive.

She brushed her fingers over the raised and indented swirls embossed on the surface. The top edge was stylishly frayed with light brown flecks embedded in the layers.

Not exactly the paper of choice for threatening secretive notes.

Still, it wasn't something she thought she should ignore.

Kerry held the paper in front of the small lamp on the edge of her table, examining the typed font and searching for any inconsistency in the letters. She knew she could access the police database and search for similar notes, but that would entail bringing it to the attention of Simon to get his approval to use Jamie's equipment. The note wasn't part of an ongoing investigation or something she could connect to a cold case, and until Kerry was certain what the note meant, she wasn't ready to tell Simon what happened. Not yet anyway.

However, there was one person she could tell.

Kerry pulled up Jean's information in her email contacts and wondered what she would write. Her hands hovered over the keyboard as she searched for the right words.

How could she begin an email like this? Did she even want to?

Jean Lamont was the only person who knew what happened during the first year of Kerry's career. If he hadn't run interference with the police and backed up Kerry's version of the events, she would have lost her job and the police could have charged her with obstruction of justice.

Her future would have ended before her career even began.

A phone call was the other option, but she knew that hearing the disappointment in Jean's voice would be too difficult to handle.

She attempted three versions of an ambiguous message, but the number of years that had passed between the time Kerry stepped over the line until now was too great. Even if Jean understood what she was trying to say, she wasn't sure it was fair to involve him for a second time.

After all, it had been her decision, not his.

Kerry never forgot Vivienne Strong's name. It was the first time she was involved with a murder investigation and the stinging memory of almost being the reason her killer walked free hid in the corners of her mind. Where all embarrassing memories and guilt live until someone forces them into the light.

She typed the woman's name into the search bar. There was almost no information online. Social media sites were in their infancy stages at the time of the murder and memorial or tribute pages were uncommon.

A vague reference to her obituary was all Kerry could find. The local paper had scanned the blurry image onto their website and Kerry could barely read it. However, she didn't need reminding. She remembered every facet of the murder and the subsequent investigation and didn't need to be reminded of the gruesome story that the journalists printed in papers across the country. Kerry typed the woman's husband's name into a search field along with the date of the trial, and it was as if the crime didn't take place. There was nothing online.

Newsprint was the medium of choice for reporters during those years and although the news spread quickly, once readers discarded their papers, they quickly forgot about the woman's murder. Kerry closed the browser window on the computer and thought about her current situation.

At the same moment that she faced the prospect of losing her office, the cryptic note arrived, and Kerry felt an overwhelming need to disappear. She wanted to run away.

Everything was closing in on her.

Before she could focus on her future, she needed to figure out who was threatening her with her past. She couldn't include Simon in her quest, so the only option was to deal with the situation alone.

Requesting a leave of absence was one decision that made sense. The stress of dealing with the province's budgetary constraints in rebuilding her lab and wondering if the person who wrote the note would go public had stolen her focus from her work, anyway.

The second stage in requesting a leave of absence was for the province to designate a replacement to take over her role in Lake Pines. Considering her current work environment, they would either send a retired coroner or a recent graduate. Neither of which she thought Simon and Josh would be excited about, but she felt she had no other choice.

Attached to Kerry's request was a comment asking Peter to give her enough time to explain the situation to Simon before he submitted the paperwork.

Kerry would then join Oliver and Elin on their west coast adventure, and hopefully, by the time she returned home, the nightmare that was her current life would have faded back to normal.

CHAPTER 8

Felicity Brightwater and the two junior councilors glanced up at the tattered and worn façade of the statue and wondered who had decided on its initial installation. Facing the harshness of the icy winds in the winter, the scorching heat of the summer sun, and the piercing winds of the fall, the iconic fish had little chance of withstanding the elements.

The force of the spring storm and the flying debris battered an already frail exterior, causing extensive damage to the tail segment of the hull. Unleashing a torrent of polemic proportions in the small lakeside town.

The focus of the current controversy was centered on a jut of land barely larger than its sculpted metal base. Even a greedy land prospector couldn't imagine a building of any investment value being constructed on the outcrop of land. Which is what brought the mayor and her two most ardent supporters on the council to the dilapidated mound of earth.

Although the view was spectacular, the rocky lake bottom, uneven shoreline, and unpredictable winds would make it an unpleasant place to live or work.

Instead, almost half a century ago, the town pulled together with the shared vision of a statue. Something that could represent the lakeside town. After a much-heated town hall debate, the town erected a larger-than-life statue.

The initial critics of the project foresaw the potential concern for maintenance costs. However, no amount of number crunching and protests could stave off the small town's desire to be represented by a symbol that would be uniquely theirs.

And after plebiscites, school contests, and an assembly of business owners, the town of Lake Pines decided that the ideal representative of their town should be a massive muskellunge.

Initial sketches and models presented the model of a fish caricature adorned with handprints of every child in Lake Pines. However, they abandoned the design idea after they realized gathering every child would be more problematic than obtaining the funding for the project.

Frustrated, but still inspired by the concept, the exhausted artists returned to the drawing board. On their third and final appeal, they presented an idea for a sculpture that resembled a prehistoric reptilian monster. With some slight tweaks in the paint scheme and an agreement to reduce the size of the teeth, the sculpture became less ominous and more welcoming to tourists.

By the end of that summer, the muskie joined the iconic ranks of Mac the Moose, the Wawa Goose, and Manitoba's collection of bronze bison statues that were spread across the province (and which no one could be quite certain what their names were).

Benji Young, the initial dissenting voice of the project, resurfaced when the renewed fundraising campaign was underway. In his seventy-eighth year, his rage against the project hadn't diminished, and he made everyone aware of his discontent with the mayor's office. Felicity could still hear the resounding echo when Benji slapped his most recent petition on her desk.

Three days into the current fundraising campaign, Benji arrived at the mayor's office and presented the unsuspecting city official with a list of over three hundred names, hoping to put a stop to the proposed repairs.

Unbeknownst to him, the town council unanimously voted to approve a funding match campaign when a small, but enthusiastic, community group proposed the idea to raise money for the repairs. Caught up in the excitement, no one on the city council thought to cap the dollar amount so the fundraising efforts wouldn't push the town's budget into the red. Which it was perilously close to doing by the end of the second day of canvassing the residents of the town.

Being the mayor of the small town had been a dream of Felicity's since she was a teenager. Previous city officials failed to understand the plight of the ordinary residents of the town, mostly because of their age difference. It took some imagination on their part to understand what mattered to the residents of the town. Felicity, on the other hand, lived and breathed Lake Pines.

She learned in her second year as mayor that what looked like a straightforward job was actually a lifestyle committed to not just the town, but every individual who lived there. For Felicity, being the mayor was more than a career. It was her calling. And every day, something new reminded her this was the most beautiful place on earth.

Felicity turned around just as a loon call reverberated through the air. The distinct flapping sound rebounded off the surface of the water as the loon drifted above the lake, before coming to a splashing stop. And then silently, it drifted out of the trail of the sunlight that danced across the surface of the water and came to rest by a rocky outcrop near the shore. The long slender body and spear-like beaks were a favorite silhouette for photographers at dusk. The haunting call was synonymous with summer and Lake of the Woods and the diving bird graced several paintings, souvenirs, and signs.

As the speckled loon drifted close, it was as if it was paying homage to the fallen fish, dipping its beak toward the land. Then, ruefully, it pierced its blood-red eyes in Felicity's direction just before it plunged below the surface of the water.

Felicity wondered why a large loon wasn't the choice for the tourist statue over fifty years ago, and then with a sigh, she resolved herself to the fact that they'd be in the same position no matter what the iconography choice had been. They'd either be repairing the hull of a fish, or the broken beak of some species of waterfowl.

She shielded her eyes from the glare of the water and twisted her face up at the forty-foot statue. "How in the world did we get ourselves wrapped up in this mess?"

Neither Miranda nor Martin, the two councilors lovingly referred to as Thing One and Thing Two, responded. Every person involved bore the shame of jumping onto the save-the-fish campaign and, like it or not, they committed the town for the long haul.

"Think of it this way," Miranda eventually offered. "We created a lot of jobs with this project."

"And," Martin jumped in, rescuing his twin sister, "With the contest to rename the statue underway, you have most of the town excited about the project."

Felicity knew from reading several reports that the storm's damage not only ruined the exterior of the statue but threatened the stability of the structure. For safety reasons alone, it left them with two choices. They either had to repair the statue or remove it.

A gaping hole was visible from below the base of the patchwork of tarps that were wrapped around the cracked and broken hull. Although the city maintenance crew did a decent job keeping water from filling the rusty cavity, the damage was impossible to disguise.

"Do you think we should get a security guard to protect the area at night?" Miranda asked. "Anyone can just walk up to it."

Felicity wiggled her head back and forth with indifference, "How much more damage can be done?"

She turned around and surveyed the weed-filled lawn and worn-down bench near the water's edge. They couldn't ignore the deterioration of the once-grand waterfront promenade. "I know we'll have Benji in my office until we complete this project, but I think sprucing up the waterfront and repairing the statue is what this town needs right now. A little local pride can't hurt, especially with everyone so afraid because of the break-ins."

Miranda and Martin nodded in unison, which they often did. It was a mannerism that they contributed to being fraternal twins, but Felicity wasn't altogether sure they didn't do it just to irritate her.

They both glanced up at the statue, shoulders touching, nodding their heads in disturbing harmony. The twins garnered stares whenever they were together. Their conspicuous features were noticeable not because of what people saw, but what everyone sensed when they looked at the twins for any length of time. In a theatrical setting, they'd be mistaken for characters from a spine-tingling horror film. With their translucent skin and pale blue eyes, they resembled apparitions more than the kind-hearted volunteers they were.

Felicity was one of the few people who saw past their unsettling glazed-over stare and recognized the altruistic nature that sat at the root of their personality.

They were a fixture at the animal shelter, adopting two dogs and one cat, as well as fostering several other animals. Miranda and Martin gave their time freely to causes they believed benefited the town, and the restoration of the statue was no exception. Felicity knew that with Miranda and Martin on her side, she'd weather the storm of detractors like Benji Young, and together, they'd ensure the project was a success.

Her job as mayor encompassed more than ensuring the operation of the town offices. Felicity's responsibilities extended to the promotion of the town's economic growth beyond the borders that edged the highway and the waterways.

The recent robberies posed an additional challenge to the local tourist economy. Felicity was vocal about putting a swift end to the robberies and even promised to push for extended jail time, considering the widespread fear the burglaries caused.

A national travel magazine had always ranked Lake Pines among the top ten locations to visit in Canada. However, the rise in crime forced businesses to close early, creating a vein of fear that spread through the town, and then eventually throughout the hospitality community. It didn't take long for Lake Pines to disappear from the list of regularly recommended tourist towns. Leaving vacancies in lodges and hotels and empty seats in restaurants.

All Felicity could hope for was that the police would find the criminals responsible and restore the calm and serenity that everyone associated with Lake Pines. Until then, she would lead the repair project for the effigy that stood next to the main road into town.

Felicity stepped over the uneven, rocky surface, carefully placing her foot on areas of flattened soil, uninterested in repeating her fall from earlier that day when she climbed out of her boat near the path. Her shoes offered almost no traction on the rocky ground, and judging by the twin's awkward gait, neither did their sandals. The trail snaked from the small dock near the construction office and through the trees, leading them along an unnavigable route that made the dilapidated park around the fish statue look pristine.

They pushed through the bristle of branches, making the path difficult to walk. Felicity stumbled through the thicket of growth, scraping the base of her leg, and tearing her pants. She was growing tired of the arguments with government officials and defending the need to beautify the town that many people, including herself, saw as the jewel of Lake of the Woods.

As mayor of the small town, Felicity committed her tenure to ensure that Lake Pines didn't fall any lower on the list of recommended travel zones, and she'd fight Benji Young and a flotilla of government officials to do just that.

"Let's get a barricade set up on the path here," Felicity shouted to the twins trailing behind her. "The last thing we need is for the area to become an accident zone."

Like the statue, the people of Lake Pines faced pressure from unforeseen exterior forces. It was obvious their combined fates were inseparable from the moment they erected the muskie icon in the small park next to the road.

The diverse group of people living in Lake Pines stood as a sentry to the stories from the past and steered the dreams of their future. Together, the people and the muskellunge lived on the edge of the lake as they confronted the storms and survived against all odds.

And like the haunting call of the speckled loons that drifted into the bay, more than just the eyes of the town were upon Felicity as she spearheaded the repairs. She felt as if the eyes of the entire country were upon Lake Pines, wondering what they would do next.

CHAPTER 9

Michel gazed across the calm waters of Haven Bay, frustrated by the poor positioning of the dock on his island. That would change once he began his renovations, even though he was sure that his neighbor would protest that project too. Spending numerous summers on Storm Island confirmed to Michel that it was where he wanted to spend most of his downtime.

Global travel was overrated. At least that's what he thought. And the calmness and the serenity he enjoyed in Lake Pines was rarer than anything he had ever experienced. Lake of the Woods had stood the test of time and outranked the wonders of the world, and he understood why cottagers and locals wanted it to remain that way.

The island across the bay was visible from the tip of his dock and he shifted his chair, awkwardly positioning himself so he was slightly out of view. It wasn't likely that his neighbor could see him over the distance that spanned between the two islands, but he at least wanted to give himself the illusion of complete privacy.

He needed the time to think about how he'd approach the next few months leading up to the eventual release of his book. His summer in Lake Pines was supposed to be a reflective time as he prepared for yet another monumental shift in his life. Camille warned him he would risk everything he worked hard for if he moved forward with his memoir, but Michel didn't care, and he begged her to accept his decision.

At even his young age, he was growing tired of the shroud of lies he lived beneath. He wanted to be free to live honestly. After all, it wasn't his crime he was hiding. There was nothing he had done wrong, and somehow, he felt like a culprit or a silent accessory to the horrid crimes.

No. Camille was wrong. If anything, the truth would help his career and give strength and support to the true victims.

Swallowing the last drops of coffee, Michel rested his cup on the arm of the Adirondack chair and leaned back. The sound of the lapping water beneath the dock moved rhythmically to the building breeze rustling the reeds along the shore.

A slow-rising heat was replacing the faint chill and dampness that had been present in the early morning air, revealing a clear, warm day. Michel had removed the uncomfortable fishing cap the moment he reached dock and was still enjoying the breeze on his skin.

At five thirty that morning, Michel had plunged into the dense fog that hovered above the dead calm water, beginning his lake day in the same manner he did every time he was at his cottage. He ignored the danger of diving into the water when the fog hindered visibility. Preferring privacy from his nosey neighbor over his safety made the risk of hitting the bottom worth taking.

Every self-help book, online forum, as well as his own therapist, explained that Michel's risky endeavors were a silent cry for help. It was his way of skirting danger and punishing himself for what happened several years earlier.

Nevertheless, it was how he coped.

Soon he'd be free from the pressures of concealing the past, and only then could he move forward with the future. But most importantly, he could move forward with Henri and their restaurant. A smile inched across Michel's face. The relief and realization of what he needed to do were clear.

The early release of the cookbook was a problem, but not an insurmountable one. He'd deal with Camille and figure out whether he would move up the release of his own memoir or stay the course and set out to do what he had initially planned.

He tried to relax. Turning his head to the side, he watched the tips of the reeds as they swayed in time with the breeze and slowed his breathing.

Yes, everything would work out just as he had planned. It would just take slightly more work.

The morning chill had left a light scent of the woodsy mist in the air, and he relished in these small moments. They reminded him of what was real in this world and what wasn't. He didn't want to rush through his day, but he needed to deal with what he saw in the small café on Main Street. He needed to speak with his agent and find out why the publisher jumped the gun on the release of his cookbook.

It seemed like an insignificant issue, but Camille was aware of the manuscript that Michel wanted to publish first, and her mistake might have jeopardized his carefully organized plan.

Michel's phone buzzed, and he pushed his thick hand deep inside his pocket and pulled it out. Answering it before it was close to his ear.

He recognized Camille's contact info before he heard her voice and the calm that was restored since returning from town quickly disappeared. Michel clenched his jaw as he pushed the phone against his ear. He jumped up from the chair and climbed the steep stairs leading to his cottage. Michel grunted, still upset by what he saw in town, as he yanked the door open and stepped inside.

"Michel, your message sounded so urgent," Camille screeched into the phone. Screeching was how Camille Scott often spoke to

Michel. It was a tactic she employed, giving the impression that she was too busy to be having the conversation at all. This, her secretary admitted, she only did with her highly profitable clients.

"Imagine my surprise, Camille, when a coffee shop in Lake Pines had a stack of my cookbooks pushed up against the window. Books, that I'll remind you, weren't supposed to be printed and distributed until the end of August."

"Are you sure?" The screeching had stopped, and Camille stuttered into the phone. "There has to be some mistake."

"I think I know what my own cookbook looks like!"

"Yes, yes. Of course, you do," Camille sighed. "Let me call the publisher and find out how a mistake like this could've happened. Every approval needs to come through my office before the publisher sends anything to print. Even the reprints."

"I don't need to remind you that the timing of my manuscript needs to be perfect. If anything goes wrong—"

"I know," Camille blurted out, interrupting Michel's warning. He had made the threat enough times over the last year that Camille was having nightmares about it.

"Justice was denied once Camille, I won't let it happen again."

Michel ended the call and dropped his phone on the desk. His eyes drifted to the four-hundred-and-fifty pages that were printed and neatly bound in the middle of his desk.

Michel placed his hand on the manuscript as if to summon the strength that was contained in the words. If anyone had seen the manuscript inside the famous chef's cottage, they wouldn't have believed it belonged there. Authored by a name reminiscent of past horrors and with a title that was not in keeping with his popular cookbooks.

He repositioned the yellow note paper, resting it on the cover, and drew a line through Camille's name. His timeline will need to be moved up if he was going to do everything that needed to be done before he uploaded his video.

Michel reached for an empty crystal glass, a bottle of Rémy Martin XO, and the manuscript and climbed the stairs. It was early in the afternoon, but he needed to steady his nerves as he completed his final review of the book.

As Michel retreated to the second-floor sunroom, a shadowy figure moved beyond the trees, shifting near the open window.

The shade shrouded their features. Remaining perfectly still, as if frozen in time, concealing their presence from Michel as they listened in on his phone call.

As Michel stepped out of the room, the intruder moved out of the shadow and stepped back into the dense forest. Realizing the danger themselves, long after Michel was gone.

CHAPTER 10

After Tanya Foley picked up the last of the supplies from Lisa, she tucked the boxes along the seat in the front of her boat and secured them with straps of bungee cord. Crates of vegetables from the farmer's market, apples and pears from Kenny's fruit stand, general grocery items, and, of course, coffee beans and baked goods from Lisa's café.

Tanya knew that she should have been honored to get the surprise email from Chef Michel Lalonde. However, in addition to the substantial fee, the last-minute job also came with his expectation of confidentiality. After she dropped Sam off at daycare, she dashed from one shop to the next, purchasing the requested items from Chef Lalonde's list.

Under strict instructions to purchase the items and to remain secretive about where they were being delivered, Tanya spent the entire morning running in and out of several stores. If anyone questioned her bulk purchases, Tanya said she was preparing for another catering job.

But every time she checked a store off her list and thought she was almost finished, she'd receive a text from Chef Lalonde requesting something else. Typed in full caps and marked with exclamation marks, his texts only added to her mounting stress.

Eventually, Tanya turned off her phone and pushed it to the bottom of her bag. She had to get Sam from daycare by five and if she made any more stops before heading out to Storm Island, she'd never make it back in time.

If Tanya doubted her decision to quit working for the celebrity chef, this morning's antics convinced her otherwise. When the moment was right, she'd let him know that he'd have to find someone else to run his errands during the time he was in Lake Pines.

She was growing fatigued and distracted when she reached the last shop. Tanya hadn't divulged who was behind the massive shopping trip until she reached Lisa's cafe.

Under the weight of exhaustion, his name slipped from her lips. No matter how hard she tried, Tanya couldn't take it back. She watched helplessly as Lisa's unbridled excitement propelled her into an excited frenzy as she jumped toward the table, pointing at the pile of his cookbooks.

Tanya pulled Lisa to the side, quieting her excitement, and she explained that Chef Lalonde didn't want anyone to know he was in town. Lisa swiped her fingers across her closed lips and vowed to keep the secret.

Tanya didn't think Lisa would be able to, but she brushed her concern to the side as she left the café.

It didn't matter, anyway. Tanya would arrive at Storm Island in the next twenty minutes, deliver the boatload of food, and then return home. After that, she didn't care if Chef Lalonde learned she let someone know he was in Lake Pines.

How much of a celebrity did he think he was? Actors and actresses, along with some of North America's most successful business owners, vacationed and purchased cottages in Lake Pines. Not only were they approachable and friendly, but none of them acted as if they were above the locals in Lake Pines. Which contributed to the friendly relationship between cottage owners and the residents of Lake Pines for generations.

When Chef Lalonde's agent contacted her several summers ago, she was beyond excited to be hired to assist the well-known chef while he was in Lake Pines. The chance to work alongside the Canadian talent who had garnered attention from restauranteurs around the world was a dream come true. However, her dream soon turned into a nightmare when she realized she would be nothing more than a glorified errand girl. Whenever Tanya would offer to help in the kitchen, Chef Michel Lalonde would respond with clenched jaws and eye rolls.

By the third day, it became apparent that she would get no further than the front porch and that he would restrict her duties to random shopping trips. Whenever the temptation to quit hit, she would think of the exorbitant fee she received to shop for him.

In two weeks of running errands and putting up with the temperamental chef, Tanya earned the equivalent of four months of catering jobs. This, Tanya convinced herself, was the price she'd pay to save up enough money to start her own restaurant. Only then would she refuse to take on jobs like the one she was doing for Chef Michel Lalonde.

Tanya picked up speed as she drove south. Drops of rain drummed on the front windshield and the canvas roof of the boat, increasing in tempo as a medley of clouds drifted above her. She reached for her raincoat, pulled the red slicker from behind her seat, and slipped it over her arms as she steered the boat through the intermittent rain. Glancing up, she knew it would be a temporary storm burst as rays pierced through patches of blue sky that surrounded the islands in the distance. From her experience living on the lake, the weather would probably clear by the time she reached Storm Island.

The aptly named Haven Bay sat just outside of the edge of the normal storm winds. Protected by high cliffs and a convex bend in the shoreline, Storm Island faced the brunt of the westerly storms on one side, while the cottage and dock remained sheltered on the other.

Holding up to its reputation, the wind eased as Tanya reached Haven Bay and pulled into the empty slip in the boathouse. Just as she was instructed.

After securing her boat to the cleats on the edge of the dock, she unloaded the boxes, bags, and crates of supplies and stored them in the extra-large fridge in the boathouse. Many cottagers had a fridge and food storage areas in their boathouses. However, the units she was more familiar with were usually cast-off appliances from their homes in the city and not industrial-sized units that were normally found in restaurants. But then again, most cottagers weren't globally recognized chefs.

The whirring fridge motor muted the echo of the lapping water inside the boathouse as it struggled to keep cool against the rising heat and humidity. Steeped in darkness, the small room had always given her an uneasy feeling. She constantly felt someone was about to pounce on her when her back was turned. The original owners built the storage room as an afterthought at the back of the boathouse. The only light in the space came from the small lightbulb inside the fridge.

When she pulled the door open, a blast of cool air slapped her in the face as the internal glow of the fridge illuminated the room.

Her skin was damp from the humidity under the canvas boat roof, and the chill from the refrigeration unit was painfully uncomfortable. The early signs of arthritis flared up on rainy days on the lake, and the icy air tightened around each joint in her hand as she stocked items on the door and in the cupboards. She worked quickly as she organized the groceries and then, after one final glance, she pushed the door closed and rushed out of the room.

Once she was done, she left the invoices and receipts on the counter, collected the empty boxes, and tossed them in her boat. With any luck, this would be her last visit to Storm Island.

She was just thinking how lucky she was to avoid a conversation with Chef Lalonde when the sound of rushing footsteps resounded above her, quickening in pace as the strides narrowed and grew closer. She closed her eyes and swore. She was within seconds of jumping into her boat and driving away from Storm Island and the wrath of Chef Lalonde. But as the steps neared the boathouse door, she realized she had missed her opportunity to escape.

Tanya dropped her chin and let out a sigh. She gathered the tiny amount of energy that remained and headed out of the boathouse and onto the dock, ready to meet Chef Lalonde and deal with the criticism that would inevitably come.

CHAPTER 11

Hugo Lawson folded his arms across his chest, pushed his shoulders back, and glared at the bylaw offer standing on the end of his dock.

"Do you *see* what I *mean*?" Hugo asked, pointing to the images he printed of the recent construction plans. His crooked finger jabbed at the pages as he peered through the square, blue-tinted frames that were slipping down his sharply angled nose.

Cindy Dawes received Hugo's complaint a day earlier, and after losing the battle with her supervisor, booked an appointment to visit Hugo Lawson at his cottage.

"How did you come by these plans, Mr. Lawson?"

"I don't *think* that's the *question* you should be *asking*."

"No, I bet you don't," Cindy mumbled under her breath. She pushed her glasses, repositioned them on the bridge of her nose, and continued to compare the plans Hugo captured on his phone camera to the plan that was included in the building permit she had on file.

"I'm not sure what you want me to do about this."

"Get over *there* and stop *construction*!" Hugo stretched his arm out, pointing directly west toward Storm Island. His habit of randomly yelling every third word was losing its intended effect. Cindy felt like Hugo had watched Scarface a few too many times and now took to mimicking the famous actor without realizing it.

In general, she was just tired of dealing with Hugo Lawson. At first, she found his gruff, throaty tone oddly charming when he'd launch into animated explanations of his complaints. Lately, he was simply annoying.

Still gripping the printed images that Hugo handed her the moment she climbed out of her boat, she dropped her arms in frustration and shook her head. Today, more than ever, she realized how much she hated her job.

When she first graduated with a city planning degree, Cindy hoped she'd be creating plans for new neighborhoods. She wanted to create viable sustainable models for residents and businesses to combat greenhouse emissions. Instead, she was fielding complaints from residents and cottage owners and reviewing building permits.

"There isn't any work taking place right now," Cindy explained. "I drove around Storm Island on my way here," Cindy unfolded her fingers as she listed off what wasn't happening on the island. "There are no workers, no heavy machinery, and no lumber stacked on the dock."

Hugo jabbed his finger toward the paper in Cindy's hand, "Then why does that plan differ so much from the one that was submitted to the planning department?"

"I don't know, Mr. Lawson. Why don't you tell me where you got it and then maybe we'll have a better idea?"

Hugo paused, carefully considering how he should respond. He didn't want to incriminate himself, but he was also worried about what would happen if he let the matter drop.

"I got them from Lalonde's cottage," he reluctantly admitted.

"Chef Lalonde invited you to his cottage?" Cindy asked. She couldn't refrain from laughing. "You and he can't even spend a summer on the lake without getting into an argument."

Hugo glanced off to the side, avoiding Cindy's stare, and she realized why he was so edgy about her question.

"He didn't invite you. Did he? Were you trespassing?" Cindy took enjoyment in asking a question that seemed to cause Hugo a fair amount of embarrassment.

"Those plans go against the sixty-foot frontage rule and not to mention he's flagrantly ignoring the size requirement for the septic field!"

Cindy thrust the crumpled page toward Hugo's chest. "Here. Take this and pretend that you weren't dumb enough to call and make a formal complaint after you broke into Lalonde's cottage and stole these images."

"Stole?" Hugo asked, taken aback by the accusation.

"Yes. Stole." Cindy turned around and jumped into her boat, no longer feeling obligated to spend one more minute entertaining the irrational musings of Hugo Lawson. "And you'd probably be smart to remember that I'm a town official and I can easily report the theft of those plans from Michel Lalonde's cottage. As a matter of fact, I'm probably obligated to contact the police."

"These are just photos, not the actual plans," Hugo said in defense of his actions.

Cindy tilted her head and glared over her glasses. Having reached her breaking point, all it would take is one more idiotic comment uttered by the Scarface wannabe, and she'd call Simon.

Sensing an end to Cindy's patience, Hugo raised his hands in the air and apologized.

Without a farewell, Cindy pulled her boat away from Hugo's dock and sped toward town. Once her boat rounded the tip of the island, Hugo grabbed his raincoat, jumped in his boat, and started the engine.

The bylaw officer may not be interested in forcing Michel Lalonde to follow the rules like everyone else. But unlike the excited cottagers and shop owners in town, Hugo wasn't impressed with his presence in Lake Pines, nor was he easily bullied by the arrogant celebrity. As he steered his boat toward Haven Bay, he promised himself that he wouldn't leave Storm Island until he forced the fancy chef to back down from his illegal building plans. And this time, he wouldn't take no for an answer.

CHAPTER 12

The rumble of the two-hundred horsepower engine pulled Michel from the focus of his manuscript. He peered over the second-floor deck railing and into the bay and cursed the interruption. The dark blue boat slowed as it neared his dock and Michel suddenly recalled the appointment that Thomas reminded him of two days earlier.

He called out from the balcony, instructing the man to wait in the boat. Michel stashed the manuscript under a sofa cushion and rushed down the stairs before bursting through the doors of the cottage.

Michel completely forgot about the lumber delivery, distracted by his conversation with Camille. Never one to forget an appointment, he grew angrier as he neared the dock.

"Where do you want me to stack these?" The young man, probably in his twenties, asked as he sprang onto the dock with ease. He wore a tight blue t-shirt revealing a full-sleeve tattoo on his right arm and an outline of a cross inching up the left side of his neck. The shirt, although a size too small, bore the emblem for the design and construction firm Michel hired to build an updated cottage on the island.

The young man brushed his shoulder-length curly hair behind his ears, fidgeting with a loose strand that fell forward on his brow, as Michel rushed down the steps.

He bounded down the stairs, swinging his arms heavily by his side. Michel was involved in every step of the design. He chose the material and paint colors and was adamant about the construction crew following a strict timeline. He offered a slight nod, and then immediately turned around to inspect the load on the boat.

Narrowing his eyes as he squinted, he snapped, "This isn't birch!" Michel leaned forward and under strained gasps, he squinted at the label on the board. "The design expressly stated we would use birch."

The young man flipped through the pages of the invoice and turned the pad of paper around for Michel to read. "These are the ones you signed off on. Isn't that your signature?"

Michel recognized his trademark signature at the bottom of the invoice. He had a vague recollection of adding his signature to the invoice PDF and emailing it back to Thomas, but it wasn't like Michel to make such an egregious error.

"Well, this isn't the wood I wanted to use," Michel waved his hand. "You'll have to take it all back. Don't even bother unloading it."

Noah tightened his fingers into a fist and held his arm next to his body. All it would take would be one more screw-up and he could lose his job. He wouldn't let some high-flying celebrity push him around.

This would be the third mistake this month, and if Noah pulled into the construction site with the same load he just collected, then someone else would smugly step in and take over his routes.

Noah handed the invoice to Michel. "This is your signature on the bottom of the invoice. Isn't it?"

Michel momentarily glanced at the sheet, rolled his eyes, and muttered that it was.

"Well, the cost might not be a big deal for you, but I'll get dinged the delivery fee if I show up back at the construction site with this load."

Michel thought about Noah's plea and then shook his head. "The main room needs to have the birch paneling I picked out. Just tell your boss that I changed my mind after you arrived. If it helps, just have Thomas call me and I'll take the blame." Michel looked at his watch and then quickly shoved his hand into his pocket. "I don't have time to deal with this right now. I'm waiting for a friend to drop by. Just take it back and I'll deal with it later. For what I'm paying for the design and construction of this place, I should be able to change my mind a few times."

Michel turned around and rushed toward the steps of the dock. Noah watched as the heavy-set chef made his way up the steep steps and ran toward the cottage.

He untied the boat, jumped in, and pulled away from the dock.

The sun was directly over the cottage and the rays crawled through the thicket of trees near the stairs, shading the cottage and landing next to the steps. Noah remembered when the previous owners placed the island on the market. Most of the cottagers and residents from town rushed out to attend the one-day property showing.

It was rare for an agent to hold an open house event for an island cottage, however, the owner was near bankruptcy, and they were in a rush to sell the property. There was also a rumor that the owners offered the agent a bonus for a quick sale above the asking price. The dollar amount of the bonus varied depending on who told the story. In any event, the property was out of reach for most people who were looking to buy.

Most people, like Noah, dreamt about owning such a spectacular island. The dense forest, natural rugged cliffs, and private bay would ensure complete privacy. The only detractor, aside from the price, was Hugo Lawson.

Everyone who knew Hugo - diligently avoided him. His staunch involvement in anything that wasn't his business ramped up when he retired. His latest focus was on the preservation of the environment, and he aggressively argued against any new building permits and frequently submitted noise pollution complaints. Even if Noah could've afforded the island in Haven Bay, he wouldn't consider it until after Hugo Lawson left the area or died.

Noah glanced back at the bay, taking one final look at the scene that embodied the essence he associated with life on the lake. He wondered why someone would buy such a perfect island and then destroy the character cabin that captured the beautiful view while remaining hidden in the forest's shadows.

As he turned out of the bay, Noah wondered if the chef's quick departure had to do with his upset at the delivery, or the person standing in the shadows at the top of the stairs.

Either way, it didn't matter. What Noah needed to do was get back to Thomas and explain what had happened. And maybe then, he'd have a chance at keeping his job.

CHAPTER 13

Mary McLean watched the bay from the corner of her eye. It was a habit she found difficult to break after thirty-seven years as a teacher, and today it was a source of her afternoon entertainment. Her unathletic build, along with her ineffectual attempts to shed the extra weight she carried, lent itself perfectly to her days of gardening on the back side of her island and reading throughout the afternoons.

She was never one to swim laps around the bay or scale the rocks along the precipitous cliffs on Crescent Island or even spelunking in the underground caverns like the ones on Storm Island. Ever since she was a young girl growing up on a small farm just outside of Lake Pines, Mary preferred to be *with* nature as opposed to *in* nature.

Gentle strolls through cedar-lined forest paths, bird watching from the cover of her porch and even monitoring the nesting habits of the ducks that lived in the reeds next to her dock were how she preferred to spend her time.

Most of the students she taught at the Lake Pines High School fit into two distinct groups. The outdoorsy adventurer or the quiet recreationalist. Mary belonged to the second of the two groups. However, her unapproachable stare and husky voice gave people the impression she would rather spend her afternoons in a tavern as opposed to a canoe.

They couldn't have been more wrong.

As a teacher, the mannerisms she employed helped quiet the rambunctious teens in her class and weren't indicative of her genuine personality. Raised with a stern hand, and parents who worked from before sunrise to well beyond sunset, Mary didn't believe in coddling students. She knew she wasn't the most popular teacher in the small high school, but she believed she was the most respected.

After retirement, she realized the effect her sternness had on each student. Whenever she'd run into former students, she'd experience a combination of reactions. Some would dash around street corners or lean down below grocery store shelves as they aggressively avoided a conversation.

However, most greeted her with the warmth that you would approach a favorite aunt at a family gathering. Those were the positive interactions that reminded her she had done a good job teaching and caring for each student.

With the knowledge her class would never get out of hand and that everyone would be treated fairly, she created a safe space where teens could learn. Never once was a child bullied or intimidated inside her classroom.

Catching subtle movements or arm waves allowed her to keep her classes from getting out of hand. However, she couldn't control what happened outside.

When the age of retirement approached, she welcomed it with open arms. She longed to spend her days uninvolved in disputes or disagreements between people she could have no lasting effect over. As a teacher, it was her responsibility to become involved if there was a problem. But if she were being truthful, she enjoyed the fact that most things weren't any of her business. Outside of the entertainment factor in people-watching, she basically kept to herself.

Every afternoon she relaxed on her cottage porch enjoying an Irish coffee made in the same fashion as her grandmother taught her. A wee nip of whiskey warmed her cheeks as she coasted into the warmth of the approaching season. She would read as the afternoon sun drifted over the island and take pleasure in the fact the shifting shadows were her only sense of passing time.

Surrounded by books, and the peaceful quacking of the mallards that nested in the boggy shores along her bay, Mary eagerly awaited her regular afternoon routine.

Boat traffic had increased on the lake in the years since she retired, but Mary enjoyed the relative peacefulness in Haven Bay.

Looking onto the only island she could see from her cottage, Mary watched the comings and goings across the small stretch of water, ignoring the book on her lap.

Normally, she'd only catch the pudgy shadow of the angry chef as he moved around his island and dove off the end of his dock. Even that morning, in the early morning mist, a muffled splash carried across the water, and she knew he was enjoying his regular morning swim.

Nothing escaped Mary McLean's attention, and even though she avoided getting involved, she always knew what was going on.

Today there was an inordinate amount of traffic in Haven Bay and Mary wondered if Hugo was right about the proposed construction project.

A miniature set of binoculars rested on the table next to her chair, and Mary peered across the bay each time a boat approached the island. She wondered if she should alert Hugo. But then, realizing he would only intrude on her peaceful afternoon with his incoherent ramblings, she decided not to make the call.

No, Mary decided. It was best not to get involved.

If anyone had glanced at the shadowy image on her porch, they would have seen a stocky elderly woman, wrapped in a bright pink knit blanket, glaring over her cup. Unaware that she was watching everything that had happened in the private bay across the stretch of water.

Blowing over the hot liquid, steam coated her glasses, fogging them momentarily until the lenses cleared and restored her view.

That afternoon, she witnessed three people arrive at the docks at Storm Island. Except for Michel, who returned around ten from his early morning shopping trip, she didn't recognize a single boat.

A voice carried across the bay as indecipherable words spoken in anger made her reach for the binoculars resting on the table.

Two shadow figures jostled near the top of the stairs and the only thing Mary could make out was a blur of color through the lens.

She pushed her thin lips together, dry and wrinkled, and wondered if she should call the police. Then she recalled the day she drifted into Haven Bay years ago to welcome the new cottage owner to the area and decided against getting involved. He rebuffed the plate of homemade chocolate chip cookies, brushing them away with indifference, and turned up his nose at her invitation for an afternoon drink. Since then, Mary McLean avoided Chef Lalonde with as much vigor as her seventy-eight years could muster.

If there was a fight, it wasn't any of her concern. The chef had made it clear he wanted to be left alone, and she had no interest in forcing the matter.

Mary swallowed the final drops of her spiked coffee and gathered the bright pink blanket around her waist. Collecting her book, she pushed her body from the chair with the help of her cane and headed back inside the cottage. She moved slower these days and struggled with each step.

Until the trademark Lake Pines summer warmth returned to the evenings on the island, she spent the late afternoon indoors where a small fire and another wee nip would soothe her joints.

Just as she pulled the door open, the sound of an outboard motor reverberated through the bay. Mary impulsively twisted her head just as a blue and white boat drove around the tip of the island, catching sight of it in the corner of her eye.

A cry wailed from Storm Island, and it was the only time Mary understood what was said.

Reminding herself that the chef's life was none of her business, she turned away. But the scream piqued her curiosity when she heard the name that was shouted across the bay. She wondered who Paul was, and what had he said to bring such anger to the celebrity chef.

CHAPTER 14

The boat wobbled with the increased speed against the current, pushing the watercraft in the opposite direction. It was a short distance to the channel once the boat was on the north side of the island. From there, it would be easy to find a quiet place to stop and think.

The wind rushed past, and breaths came in short, ragged gasps.

How had this happened?

The only certainty was that there was no turning back.

The bloodied piece of wood shifted with the movement of the boat, rattling against the hull and echoing the words Michel yelled just before he tumbled from the top of the steps.

Splatters covered the front of the heavy raincoat, and except for the deep red of the darkening blood, they blended into the fabric. Someone would have to look closely to see that the smear went beyond the color of the material. Along with the coat, the piece of wood would have to be discarded as well.

The roar of the engine quieted as the boat slowed and drifted to a stop. Looking around the stolen boat, there was only a lifejacket, a safety kit, and an anchor stored below the floorboard.

Using the long rope, the jacket and wood were tied to the iron anchor and tossed over the side. With no boat traffic in the narrow stretch of water, there was time to sit back and think of what to do next.

It wasn't supposed to turn out like this, but Michel's anger started the argument. Hurting Michel was never part of the plan, but neither was opening secrets from the past, and that's what was going to happen.

Michel's words were unexpected and harsh. The wilful selfishness that Michel displayed made no sense.

He was a nobody until the contest thrust him into the spotlight and it was obvious by Michel's reaction that he had forgotten where he came from and who he really was. No matter how things played out, killing Michel wasn't how the day was supposed to end.

The sun dropped below the treeline and a cool shadow moved across the front of the boat. With the coat and blood-soaked wood at the bottom of the lake, there was nothing else to do but disappear.

Discarding the stolen boat on the Main Street dock was the best idea, wedging it between rows of protestors' boats.

As the boat pulled away from the shore, the engine churned, pulling weeds and debris from below to the surface of the water, and a thud knocked against the side of the boat. Among the pulverized plants and twigs was the bloodied piece of wood. It broke free from the rope and floated to the surface.

Removing it from the water meant another problem. With nothing else to weigh down the light wood, it would have to be disposed of on land. But it had to be where no one would find it.

If it hadn't been for the knock against the side of the boat, someone else would have discovered the wood floating near the shoreline. Splintered and soaked with blood, they would have taken it directly to the police. As bad as the situation was, there was at least time to find a place to conceal it before dark. But where?

As the boat moved away from the watery tomb that concealed the blood-soaked coat, another idea came to mind. With only a few hours until sunset and no other boat traffic in view, there was another place to hide the wood. Although the intention wasn't to hurt or kill Michel, the fact remained nothing would change what was important. Not even for a second chance.

CHAPTER 15

Lisa waited until the last customer paid their lunch bill before locking the door to her café, turning the open sign around, and lowering the blinds. At most, she'd miss a handful of customers, but the chance to meet Chef Michel Lalonde was worth the lost revenue.

She grabbed ten books and shoved them into a canvas tote bag, and then paused just before she left the café to add a few more. Lisa wasn't sure if she was more excited about meeting Lalonde or about Tanya delivering baked goods from her café. Then a worrying thought crossed her mind. What if he greeted her with disdain or thought her small café in the middle of Main Street in Lake Pines wasn't worthy of his attention?

Tanya had sworn Lisa to secrecy, and Lisa promised not to say anything to anyone about Michel Lalonde's arrival in Lake Pines. And she hadn't. However, the temptation to meet the world-renowned chef was too strong. Lisa considered the promise she made to her friend and thought she could explain her presence to Chef Lalonde as a lucky mistake and that she heard from a customer that he was in the area, leaving Tanya's name out of the conversation.

The dock where Lisa moored her boat was a ten-minute walk from her café, or a five-minute jog, depending on her schedule. The heavy load of cookbooks in her bag, however, put the trip closer to eight minutes as the strap dug into her shoulder as she ran.

She carefully placed the heavy bag of books on the front passenger seat of the boat, and then, after thinking about the rough water, placed them on the floor. Knowing that a bounce over a wave or a sharp turn around a buoy could send the bag of heavy books rolling off the seat.

Showing up with damaged books, creased and bent, was one way to leave Chef Lalonde with a negative impression.

Although the rain had stopped, Lisa knew that the humid morning signaled the start of a rainy week. She frequently planned her lunch menu depending on the weather forecast. Lisa learned that even in the summer, a rainy day always brought requests for chili or soup from her regulars.

She thought about the books in her bag and wondered if Chef Lalonde would allow Lisa to promote one of his recipes on her menu. Not that she needed his approval, but having his agreement would go a long way in promoting his books.

She imagined printing a little chef's hat next to each menu item from his book and wondered if she hadn't stumbled upon a unique feature to add to her café.

The renovations and expansion had forced her to dig into her savings when she hired additional workers to finish the painting before the summer. With several weeks to spare, Lisa opened her expanded café to less fanfare than she had hoped for. With the reduced number of people shopping along Main Street, Lisa's café was a casualty of the post-Covid economic downturn, along with the fear caused by the rise in crime.

Even the creation of a loyalty card and a free dessert with every dinner didn't drive extra traffic to her doorstep. She was running out of ideas to encourage customers to return to her café and ultimately entice them to spend money on books or gifts while they were there. Morning caffeine runs and students studying as they lingered over their single coffee purchase wouldn't cover her rent.

Lisa fronted the cost of the books to the tune of five-hundred dollars. Getting the book two months ahead of the expected release date prompted her to forego the purchase of new shelving, but with the attention that the autographed books could bring her café, it was worth the risk.

Each phrase and word played out in her head as she decided how she would introduce herself to Chef Lalonde. Would she greet him as a fellow chef or as a fan? From the little she knew about him, he would most likely welcome neither.

She could hardly feign her interest in his celebrity since she was arriving with a bag of books that she was hoping he'd autograph. She couldn't claim to be passing by, since Storm Island was out of the way of most destinations.

In the end, Lisa decided that she'd be honest about her arrival. That she was a huge admirer, and she was interested in having a selection of his books autographed for her café.

After all, he was making money from the sale of the books, so why shouldn't Lisa feel comfortable about the request? The closer she got to Storm Island, the more confident she felt about speaking to Chef Lalonde, and she pushed the throttle forward as she neared Haven Bay.

Lisa first saw the dark blue canvas shoes when she jumped out of her boat. His shorts and top blended into the hue of the dock boards, and from the level of the water, his body was barely visible from her boat.

Lisa quickly secured her boat and jumped onto the dock. Her sandals offered little traction on the damp boards, sending her skidding along the surface. Cursing the twist in her knee, Lisa called out Chef Lalonde's name as she rushed toward him.

He was lying on the dock, near the bottom of the stairs, and was unconscious from a fall.

He was facing the shore and his left arm rested at an unnatural angle, extended above his head.

As Lisa walked nearer, she realized his positioning was unusual, even for someone of his girth having taken a harsh fall. Lisa stopped abruptly, dropping the heavy bag of books she had so carefully guarded until that moment.

Lisa crouched next to his body, coaxing him awake with words and a gentle touch along his arm. She saw the blood on the dock and the vacant glare in the famous chef's eyes.

When she didn't get a response, she jostled Chef Lalonde's shoulder, pushing his body back and forth, hoping he would awaken at her touch.

His body swayed slightly before falling backward, and his dull, lifeless stare glared up at the gray sky.

Rust-colored darkness seeped into the golden tan of the dock's surface beneath his body. A pool of blood collected under his skull, blackening the damp boards and reflecting the clouds in the sky.

She carefully pressed her fingers along the side of his neck. He was warm to the touch, but she couldn't find a pulse. He was unresponsive and still.

She jumped back, stumbling over the discarded bag of books she had dropped on the dock.

Lisa fumbled to grab her phone from the bottom of her bag. It slipped out of her trembling hands and tumbled along the dock, lodging in the narrow space between two boards. She pried it free just as it was about to drop into the water.

Extending her arm above her head, Lisa turned her body as her phone searched for a connection. Her phone took a moment to locate a signal on the remote island, but finally, the bars flashed across the top left-hand corner of her screen.

Turning away from the chef, Lisa glanced out over the water and wondered what had happened on the quiet private island.

Across Haven Bay, a thin trail of smoke rose from the chimney at Mary McLean's cottage. Only a faint light illuminated the small cottage that was set back from the dock, shaded by the thick grove of trees surrounding it. Nestled in seclusion, Mary McLean made it clear to everyone that she was uninterested in resuming her perch as the local watchdog. Considering the distance, she wouldn't have had a clear view, anyway.

Finally, the phone began to ring and Sally's voice came through the line.

Lisa explained why she was calling and where she was, eventually bursting into uncontrollable sobs.

Glancing behind her, all she could think of was how much blood had accumulated from a simple fall. Lisa told Sally that she was alone on the island and that she believed the famous chef probably died not long before she arrived.

She ignored the bag of books she was eager to have autographed, and she forgot all about her old teacher who spent every day on her small island, just across the bay from where Michel Lalonde had fallen to his death.

What she would remember is the blank stare glaring back at her and the deep, guttural grunts of the cormorants on the shoreline.

Lisa dragged her eyes away, taking a deep breath before her head slumped to the side, and then, as the reality of the trauma sank in, she fell to the dock and wept.

CHAPTER 16

Kerry hated spending any amount of time in room 24B. It wasn't just that she lost the independence of coming and going from her own building, but having the additional space kept her organized and more streamlined when performing examinations, testing, and writing reports.

She spent two hours in the hospital's examination room that morning, performing an autopsy on Mr. Jason Rivers. She easily determined that he had died from a heart attack. His insurance company was anxiously awaiting the results of the autopsy, since Mr. Rivers held a sizeable policy that needed to be divided among three beneficiaries.

Simon's image flashed across Kerry's screen, and she lunged for her phone.

"Hi Simon," Kerry said, answering the call on the first ring and grateful for the interruption. "I hope you're calling me for a lunch break. I don't know how much more of this small room I can take."

"Sorry, no lunch invite, but I will need you to leave your office."

"Does it also involve a body?"

"Unfortunately," Simon said. "Can you meet me out on Storm Island?"

"Sure. Send me the coordinates and I'll plug them into my phone. How far away from town is it?"

"It'll probably be twenty minutes away from the hospital."

Kerry's phone buzzed as Simon's text came through with the exaction location of Storm Island.

"I got it," Kerry said as she focused on the location map on her phone.

"Go to the dock in Haven Bay," Simon instructed. "You'll see the police boat when you come around the island. And, Kerry, there's one more thing."

"What's that?"

"Lisa's the one who found the victim."

"Oh, geez," Kerry pictured her friend who was more accustomed to dusting sugar on croissants as opposed to finding dead bodies on islands. "Who was it?"

"A famous chef who has a cottage out here."

"Michel Lalonde?" Kerry glanced at the books that were on the small table in her tiny office and recalled how excited Lisa was that morning at the celebrity chef's impending arrival. "Lisa had a stack of his cookbooks in her café today."

"Lisa found him sprawled out on the dock when she came out here to get them autographed. It looks like he took a nasty tumble from the top of the stairs."

"Okay. I'll leave as soon as I reserve the examination room. His body will have to be sent to the hospital, but I want to make sure that Doctor Varanus won't be working on his research project."

After Kerry ended the call, she completed the final paperwork, filed it with the appropriate departments, and then turned off her computer. She glanced at the map once more before slipping her phone into her pocket. She was pretty sure she wouldn't have a problem locating the island.

Kerry opened the door, and her foot kicked a small box that was leaning against the frame. Despite frequently losing herself in deep concentration, she should have noticed the knock on the door.

Kerry picked up the box. She rested it on the table and examined each side, wondering who it was from or what it contained. It didn't have a label or postmark.

She was the only occupant in the small windowless room and found it impossible to imagine there was a previous employee that could've been expecting a delivery.

Kerry grabbed the scissors on her desk and ran one side of the blade down the middle strip of tape, and the lid popped open. Rolled-up newspaper filled the space in the box, and Kerry pulled out the balled-up inky sheets and tossed them in the blue recycling box next to her makeshift desk.

It wasn't a delivery from the lab. Those boxes were clearly labeled and filled with white biodegradable packaging peanuts.

There was something heavy inside which was haphazardly wrapped in paper. As Kerry tilted the box, the bulk of its contents shifted with each movement. She reached inside and lifted it out. The weightiness and the sharp uneven edges seemed odd as she wrapped her fingers around the strange package.

At the bottom was a rock resting on a mound of more crinkled paper. The newspaper, yellow and worn, caught her attention as she lifted the rock out of the box. She set the rock down on her desk and unfolded a piece of newsprint. The significance struck her as she glanced at the headline. In oversized bold lettering was the name of the paper.

Le Journal de Montréal.

Her eyes rolled to the date on the page and the air in her lungs went cold. Then she looked at the rock with much more interest and realized that it was more than just strange. It was a foreboding message from the past and involved the secret she thought she'd buried so many years ago.

And even scarier, she had to accept the knowledge that she and Jean weren't alone in the knowledge of what she had done.

CHAPTER 17

Pacing the small space in the windowless office, Kerry pulled out her phone and checked the time. Her pulse rocketed to a peak, and a dull throbbing resonated inside her head. Realizing the significance of the package, the cryptic note she received on the yellow paper became clear, and suddenly, the note and package seemed more haunting.

The first person who came to mind was Jean Lamont, her mentor, first boss, and the only person who knew what the rock and the note could represent. It had been months since she contacted him. Except for last August when she called to wish him a happy birthday, they only communicated through texts that they volleyed between their provincial zones.

Joyeux anniversaire, mon ami! Kerry had typed early in the morning. She wanted to be the first person to wish him well and was eager to show off her much-improved French. This call, however, would differ from the birthday wishes she offered last summer.

Jean's line rang several times before her call went to voice mail. Kerry paused, breathing into the phone, unsure of what to say.

How would she begin such a conversation?

Kerry disconnected the call. She'd call later when she would be undistracted and uninterrupted. This would be a conversation that would take longer than five minutes.

As she reached for the rock, her hand shook. The fear of the truth had subsided over the years. Her eventual move from Montreal, settling in Lake Pines, meeting Simon, and then adopting Dominique all did their part in erasing bits and pieces of the horrid image. But in the end, traces of what she had done were still there. Marked by a terrible decision and etched in time. No amount of good deeds or warm memories would erase what happened. Or more specifically, what she had done.

She locked the box, the rock, and the newsprint in her filing cabinet and left room 24B.

When Kerry emerged from the hospital basement, the morning rain had subsided, and a delicate dampness coated the pavement in the staff parking lot. She walked to the far end of the lot and took the stairs down to the dock, and jumped into the boat.

She pulled up the directions to Storm Island and followed the line on her phone. As she maneuvered through islands, around buoys, and avoided the rocky shorelines, she wondered who could've delivered the box and the note to her office.

The only person who was aware of the truth was Jean, and he helped cover up what she had done. Her rash actions, carried out in anger and propelled by pure emotions, would have resulted in her arrest if Jean hadn't stepped in when he did. She wasn't sure how to approach Jean, but she knew she needed to warn him.

Kerry pushed away the image of the box and focused on the islands as she neared Haven Bay.

Storm Island was the largest of the three islands in front of her. The island's forest was a mix of pine, birch, and spruce trees that softened the sharp edge of rocky cliffs. Several rocky outcrops surrounded Storm Island, acting like a barrier to the speedboats that toured the lake.

Large cabin cruiser boats couldn't maneuver through the shallow water near the island, and the orange and white buoys that warned of underwater lines deterred inexperienced boaters from entering the channel.

Kerry understood why this area of the lake would interest someone searching for privacy. She pulled her boat up alongside the dock, and Simon rushed over to tie it to a cleat.

"The rain stopped, but we pulled a tarp over the victim's body in case it started up again."

Kerry nodded, and with her chin down, she walked toward the stairs. She glanced over at Lisa who was off to the side, speaking with Josh. Lisa pulled her arms tightly around the waist of her red raincoat and nodded rapidly as Josh spoke. It was fear and not the weather that caused Lisa's shock, and Kerry instinctively wanted to rush to her friend and comfort her. Instead, she continued toward the blue tarp and the lifeless body of Chef Michel Lalonde at the base of the stairs.

"Hey, is everything alright?" Simon asked.

Kerry paused and turned to face him, "What do you mean?"

"You seem very distracted right now."

Suddenly, the image of the note, the rock, and the night so many years ago came rushing back to her, and she shook her head.

"There's something I need to tell you."

"About this case?"

"No, I contacted Peter earlier. I asked him to find a replacement for me. I'm taking a leave of absence."

CHAPTER 18

Simon pulled Kerry away from the prying ears of the officers standing next to them on the dock. "What do you mean, *you're taking a leave of absence*?" Simon asked. "You hate the idea of a replacement working in your office."

"I don't have an office anymore, in case you forgot."

"No, I didn't forget. But you know that's temporary. Peter will do his best to find you a better setup."

"You mean the basement of the hospital?"

Simon rested his hands on his hips, "If you need the break, I understand. Just make sure you're doing it for the right reasons."

"What do you mean by that?" Kerry asked defensively.

"It just seems like you're upset about being placed in the hospital basement."

"I am upset about being stashed away in an office that I'm pretty certain was a storage closet not too long ago, but that's not what my request was about. I just need a break."

"What are you going to do?"

"I think I'll go out to visit Jean and then join my dad and Elin and spend some time with Dominique on Vancouver Island."

"That sounds like a great idea," Simon said. "I wish I could join you."

"Why don't you," Kerry squeezed Simon's arm and leaned her body close to his. "You haven't had time off in a while. It'll be good for us as a family."

"You know that we're already short-staffed. Josh is busy with the string of robberies that have taken place over the last few months, and Grant is retiring in a week." Simon leaned forward, whispering into Kerry's ear. "I love you, Kerry, and if you need this break, take it. I'll do whatever I can to help your new replacement and make sure they don't screw anything up."

Kerry smiled, "Thanks."

"Until then," Simon nodded toward the blue tarp. "Let's get you to look at Mr. Lalonde."

Drops of rain dotted the tarp, collecting in the folds, and spilled to the side when Kerry lifted it off Michel Lalonde's body.

She crouched next to his body, examining the left side of his skull. Slowly turning the victim's head, Kerry examined the wound and then glanced up at the stairs and then down at his body. She looked around the dock, spotting two chairs, a portable sun umbrella on a stand, and a low table.

"Was there anything else on the dock when you arrived?"

"No," Simon said. "Lisa was standing on the end of the dock when I pulled up with Josh. She was pretty shaken up, but she knew enough not to touch anything once she realized he was dead. Why?"

"Because he didn't die from the fall. Someone hit him across the side of his head." Kerry pointed her gloved finger to the wound on the side of Michel Lalonde's head.

"With what?"

Kerry stood up and then walked up the stairs, glancing over the side of the railing, pausing at each step. "I'm not sure. A log or a flat board of some kind."

Simon searched the shoreline and near the bushes with the two officers. He filled Josh in on Kerry's hypothesis, and he joined them in their search.

"We may have to get a forensic team out to the island. If the murder weapon is on the island, then the killer probably didn't drop it near the body." Simon pulled out his phone and called Sally. "Hey, Sally. Can you send a couple of officers from the forensic team out to Storm Island? Tell them to be prepared to work in the dark. It's a fairly large island."

Kerry returned to the dock and walked over to Lisa.

"Did I hear you right?" Lisa asked. "You think someone murdered Chef Lalonde?"

"I think so."

"I can't believe it," Lisa muttered. "I know he has a reputation for being difficult, but all talented chefs are. I don't understand who would want to kill him."

Kerry wrapped her arms around Lisa. Comforting her friend as she burst into tears at the thought of someone attacking one of her culinary idols.

"He was more than just a great chef, Kerry," Lisa sobbed. "He gave hope to every average cook or baker. If a small-time cook from Canada could make it big on the global restaurant scene, then everyone had a chance."

Yes, Kerry thought. But obviously, someone wasn't happy with Chef Lalonde's success.

CHAPTER 19

Josh accompanied the body and Lisa back to town, leaving the other officers with Kerry to investigate the circumstances of Chef Lalonde's death. Sally had phoned Josh when he was searching along the shoreline, letting him know that there was another robbery. This time, there was some hope that the video security camera recorded them as they rushed away from the pharmacy. Josh had been investigating the string of robberies in Lake Pines and was worried that the criminal, or criminals, involved could become more violent as they became more comfortable in carrying out their crimes.

Along with prescription narcotics, the thief stole three hunting guns from the outdoor supply store this week. Ramping up evening police surveillance became more problematic with the reduced staff numbers.

It had been weeks since he and Thomas had dinner together, and although he missed his daughter, he was grateful that Elin stepped in and offered to take Lucia on a vacation with Oliver and Dominique to Vancouver Island.

Elin and Oliver's budding romance aside, it was a relief to not have to worry about leaving all the parenting to Thomas while he investigated the robberies.

Josh drove Lisa home and then headed directly to the pharmacy to see if there was anything he could glean from the security footage. When Josh arrived, Mr. Johnson was pacing the floor behind his counter and nervously glancing around his store.

"I just don't understand it, Josh," Mr. Johnson said. "I installed an up-to-date security system last year. Even if someone made it through the doors, they shouldn't have been able to get through the locks in the pharmacy. I thought I was lucky when the storm didn't damage my shop."

Josh felt sorry for the shop owners targeted in the robberies. Insurance covered most costs, but there were residual expenses that needed to be incurred, which cut deeply into their profits and savings.

Then there was the price of everyone's peace of mind. Store owners were becoming increasingly leery about keeping their shops open late, and with more stores closing before dark, Main Street would soon look like a scene from a ghost town.

"Unfortunately, Mr. Johnson, many of these criminals are quite sophisticated. They have high-tech electronic gear, frequency jammers, and apps on their phone that can disable your alarm system."

Mr. Johnson's eyes narrowed. "Then what's the point of having a security system?"

Josh was sure he could see tears edge the man's pale blue eyes. The pharmacy was one of the oldest businesses on Main Street, and Mr. Johnson was the man behind the shop's name. It was his baby and his pride and joy. Even though most business owners his age had retired, Mr. Johnson felt such a deep connection to the town and the people that he continued to work.

Josh rested his hand on Mr. Johnson's shoulder, "Believe it or not, security systems deter most criminals, but I'd definitely give some thought to having our technician, Jamie, examine your equipment." Josh handed a card with Jamie's direct phone number written on the back. "He'll give you some idea where you can improve your system."

Mr. Johnson took the card and waved it in the air, "I've already spent too much money securing this place. Any more tech gear and this won't be a pharmacy, it'll be an electronics store."

"Jamie will come out to check your system at no charge. It's a service we're offering to help combat the recent burglaries. Let the other store owners know about it, too."

Mr. Johnson nodded his head and then let out a sigh. "Do you still want to look at the tape? It's kinda fuzzy, but I still got an image of the little punk."

Josh watched as Mr. Johnson ran his fingers across his computer keyboard in the back office. He opened the file where he saved the digital security camera recordings and opened the one for the previous evening. He fast-forwarded to the time of the break-in, pausing just before the burglar came into view.

"There, he stops to look back." Mr. Johnson scrunched up his nose as his eyes narrowed on the image. "I can't tell if his hoodie is black or navy."

"I think it's black, but," Josh paused the image and zoomed in on the left sleeve. "I think that's a team logo. I'll have Jamie see if he can magnify the image so we can read it."

Mr. Johnson forwarded the digital recording to Josh's email and then promised to have his system reviewed for extra precaution.

The truth was, Josh wasn't sure the thieves were planning to stop anytime soon. However, what really worried him was that it would be just a matter of time before they hurt someone.

CHAPTER 20

Whether an argument precipitated the attack, or Chef Lalonde's assailant intended to kill him, Kerry couldn't be certain. However, the fact the police couldn't find the weapon that was used to strike the fatal blow probably meant the intent was fatal.

Simon focused his search on the exterior of the cottage, while Kerry searched the inside. Neat wouldn't be how she'd describe Chef Michel Lalonde's cottage. Compulsively organized austerity would be closer to the words that came to mind.

The interior resembled a modern villa that could be featured in an Architectural Digest article. The design stood at odds with the exterior of the cottage. However, a side benefit to such a sparsely designed cottage was that it was easy to search.

The kitchen was one that she'd expect to find in the home of a world-renowned chef. Top-of-the-line appliances, an oversized island, and antique copper pots hanging artistically from a wrought-iron gate that was suspended from the fifteen-foot ceiling.

Each of the five bedrooms was just as impressive, and none displayed any signs of a struggle or an argument.

The den and main living room were on the second floor, with half of the room extending out onto a second-floor balcony.

It was moments like this, when she was working with Simon, that Kerry enjoyed her job. She brought closure to families who needed to rebuild their lives after experiencing a painful loss. It was always the driving force behind helping every victim of a murder.

Her contribution was far greater than just stamping a cause of death on a certificate. Kerry's examinations and tests often helped the police secure an arrest in a case where they only had a gut instinct pushing them toward a suspect. Sometimes it was the only proof the police had to connect someone to a crime.

She moved around the room, pausing at Michel's desk, and examined the items that were neatly stacked on the surface. Except for a daily journal, there was a glass jar of pens, a set of keys, and a few photographs.

She moved to the opposite side of the room to search the last few tables and bookshelves before joining Simon upstairs.

The view from the second floor was breathtaking, and she could imagine the owner spending endless hours in this room looking out of this window.

Thick cushions invited a long afternoon of reading while enjoying the spectacular view of the private bay. A mug containing the remnants of black coffee and sporting a thin dark line around the rim rested atop a coaster on a side table. One pillow was askew and seemed out of alignment with the perfectly arranged furniture in the room.

A classic HBC striped blanket stylishly cascaded over the back of a chair and added to the interior design as much as the art on the wall. The Hudson's Bay Company sold the iconic Canadian symbol around the globe, but this blanket appeared to be more than one hundred years old. Unlike the one Kerry owned, which was bought last Christmas, and became one of Raven's favorite toys.

A bulky stack of white paper poked out from under a thick cushion and caught her attention. She carefully removed it.

There were more than four-hundred type-written pages, fashioned more like an essay or a book manuscript.

She wondered if it was a memoir. Many celebrities were publishing books, and even members of the royal family were churning out paperbacks and picture books, hoping to grab a slice of the literary market.

A three-inch thick black paperclip, more like a clamp, held the pages together. A folded piece of paper, tucked underneath, covered the title that was neatly typed across the top.

'The End'

What a strange title for a chef's memoir? Kerry thought.

She pulled the piece of paper from under the paperclip and unfolded it. On it was a name with a line drawn through it and a date. August 29th. It wasn't the name or the date that held Kerry's curiosity, but the paper itself. It was identical to the faded yellow parchment that was used for the note she received a few days ago. It was just like one that was slipped under her door, which referenced the secret from her past that she thought she buried long ago.

CHAPTER 21

The trip back to town was eerily serene as Kerry drifted in and out of islands, shifting her thoughts from the death of Chef Lalonde and the package that arrived at her office. The sun cast a warm glow across the tops of the pine forests that lined the shores of the islands near Second Channel, illuminating them in the early evening hours.

Cottagers that remained on their docks quietly enjoyed the sunset, slowly raising an arm as Kerry drove past. The head nod and arm raise were common on the lake and heralded back to an era when friends didn't rush through conversations. Kids existed unencumbered by the tethers of global social media, and everyone lived without crime. Or at least they believed they did.

It was the gentle oblivion that allowed everyone to accept the violence that existed around them. Often present in their neighborhoods or schools, and hidden deep within the darkened branches of family trees.

Innocent ignorance is what made the truth so difficult to carry for most people. She thought lies were usually easier to digest and ironically found a more accepting path in the search for justice.

Kerry had spent years burying the past as she hid the truth in her own justification that justice was served. She defended each lie with the reasoning that the victim couldn't speak for herself.

Suddenly, so many years after the fact, Kerry wished she had made a different choice. Time had taught her the patience that she needed in her career. If Jean hadn't stepped in when he did, she wouldn't even have that.

She knew the difference now. But back then? Could she have been so oblivious to the consequences of her own actions?

But if she was being honest, she'd have to admit she knew exactly what she was doing. It was a dark moment in her life that she couldn't ignore. She'd at least warn Jean, allowing him the respect he deserved as both her friend and mentor.

Kerry extended her head above the front window of the boat, enjoying the warm summer evening breeze that replaced the afternoon rain and mist.

She loved the lake and the unique, raw beauty of each island, especially as the sun was setting. No two land masses were alike, and each captured its own perspective of the water.

Enhanced environmental laws, appreciation for nature, and improved land and water stewardship by cottage owners resulted in the resurgence of wildlife on the lake.

Cormorants, pelicans, and bald eagles were just a few of the returning animals. Lily pads bloomed more regularly in bays where docks and motorized boats were banned. The soft yellow flowers were Kerry's favorite, and she enjoyed the peaceful canoe trips through the reeds at the opening of the hiking trail where water lilies would bloom in the summer heat.

Up ahead, an eagle drifted on the late-day breeze. Its peal call – soft, high-pitched, and prolonged, carried across the water. Flapping its wings until it hovered close to the water, at which point the majestic bird pulled back, extending its wingspan and its talons sliced the surface of the water.

Within seconds, the eagle splashed down before it soared into the air, returning to a nearby shore with its wiggling prey.

Life. It was particularly beautiful and extremely raw. Evil and goodness existed in the most basic realms around them every day, and her life mirrored what was happening in nature.

Kerry's thoughts drifted to Storm Island and the recent death on the lake. There was something odd about the timing of Michel Lalonde's death and the cryptic note she received under her door. No matter how much she wanted to take a break, there was no way she could ignore the secrets that seemed to connect her to the most recent murder in Lake Pines.

CHAPTER 22

Thomas yelled into the phone as he walked along the curved path, illuminated by low-lying solar-powered lights. He built the contemporary complex by the water's edge. Close to a public dock, primarily used by hikers, runners, and some of his clients who arrived by boat. Thomas' office was close to the controversial statue and he was growing tired of the heated debates that surrounded the rusty fish. Although he was firmly rooted on the anti-fish side of the argument, Josh's passion to see the sculpture renovated encouraged him to keep his opinions to himself. However, the frequent protestors stomping across his property were testing his patience, and he was considering shifting allegiance, just to make a point.

The incredible view was the only reason Thomas overlooked the fact he was in the direct path of the float planes that landed in the bay when he purchased the property. Most times he found the sound charming, but tonight he was growing frustrated as he pushed his phone against his ear and shouted into the receiver.

The reverberating thomp-thomp-thomp of the blades, as a float plane landed on the water in front of his office, was making it difficult to understand his mother's words. Since Elin took Lucia on vacation, Thomas was using the time to catch up on invoices. The investigation into the recent thefts kept Josh busy at work. Aside from his regular calls from his mother, Thomas spent most evenings alone.

The children's shouts on the other end of the line revealed a day filled with excitement and adventure. As Thomas looked forward to an evening filled with administrative duties, he wondered if he should've joined Oliver and Elin on their coastal journey.

"I said, are the girls enjoying the big ships in Burrard Inlet?" Thomas fumbled with his office keys in his right hand as he pushed the phone against his left ear.

"Oh, yes!" Elin said. "And Lucia especially loved the galleries. She said she's going to be an artist when she gets back to Lake Pines. She's going to paint all the islands you visit this summer."

"That sounds like a lot of fun, Mom."

"Are you and Josh at least taking advantage of not having a child to cook for and going out to dinner every night?"

"I wish," Thomas complained. "Josh has spent most nights working late because of these robberies. By the time he makes it home, he is so tired that he collapses on the sofa. To be honest, I miss your company most nights."

Elin's laugh burst through the phone. "That's not something I thought you'd admit."

"Trust me, I'm just as surprised as you are." Thomas dropped his keys and cursed as they bounced down the steps and into the pile of cedar chips in the garden. His mother immediately chided his use of bad language. "Sorry. But it's so dark in front of my office and I just dropped my keys."

Thomas moved his fingers over the ground and felt the sharp notches in the clump of keys attached to a brass ring, and wrapped his hand around them.

"What are you doing at the office this time of night?" Elin asked.

"Paperwork has been piling up because of the extra work I have this summer. I figured it would be better to get them out of the way and not sit at home thinking about how I'll be eating dinner by myself again."

Elin let out a sigh. "I'm sorry, dear. But, did you ever consider bringing some food over to the station and having a quick meal with Josh? Your father and I used to make time for quick breaks and short mini-dates while he was building his business. If Josh is busy with a case, at least you know he's not avoiding you."

Thomas felt the sting of guilt at not being more understanding about the pressure Josh was under. However, he also felt a glimmer of joy in his mother's support of his relationship.

"You've been sharing a lot of memories about you and Dad recently?"

"I guess I've been thinking about him more these days."

Thomas assumed it was the additional time she was spending with Oliver but chose not to mention it. There was no need to make his mother uncomfortable with the reminder that she was frightfully close to being an emotionally driven human.

"I'll pick up some takeout and swing by the station when I'm done here. Give Lucia a kiss for me and tell her I'll video call her tomorrow at breakfast."

Thomas slipped his phone into his pocket, turned the key in the lock, and pushed open the door. His foot landed on the smooth surface of the brochures that were supposed to be stacked on the entrance table as he walked into the dark room.

Something was very wrong.

He reached for the light switch and flicked it on before he heard the footsteps rushing toward him. The last thing Thomas remembered as the intruder raised his arm and struck him across the side of his head was the blur of the black hoodie and the red and gold patch that was sewn on the sleeve.

CHAPTER 23

Brutality from bullies, oppressors, or tyrants propelled her desire for justice, which ultimately led her to where she was now.

Insisting on the truth and eager to find justice, she made a decision that she should have regretted. But the look in the eyes of the family left behind was all she needed to soothe her guilty conscience.

She clutched her phone as she pressed the contact button connecting her number to Jean in Montreal. Patiently, she waited while Jean's line rang. He was the only person she could talk to about the questions she had right now. The note, as well as the box, posed a problem only if someone could prove what she did. But to establish if they were authentic would mean she'd have to admit that she broke the law and interfered in a murder investigation.

The court could overturn the original conviction. Kerry saw it happen often enough, however, it usually was because evidence had been overlooked or examined improperly.

Not because the coroner submitted a falsified key piece of evidence.

When Jean hadn't picked up after three rings, Kerry ended the call and placed the phone on the table.

She looked at the note, which was resting on the table next to the box. The sender didn't address them to her and outside of the old newsprint from Montreal, there was no indication of where they came from.

Kerry pressed her fingers to her forehead, squeezing her brow as a dull ache stabbed just behind her eyes.

Where would she begin?

It was a question that she wouldn't have to answer if she involved Simon in the search for who left the items or where they came from. But Kerry was working with reduced resources, especially since she didn't have any immediate plans to share what she had done.

The box was nondescript. It would be easy to find a box exactly like this at many offices or mailing supply stores, so she focused her attention on the yellow paper that was slipped under her door. Unlike the box that could have several prints on the surface, Kerry figured there should only be two people who touched the paper. Hers and the person who slid it under her door.

If the person who sent the cryptic note had used their bare hands, then Kerry knew she'd be able to get a sebaceous print from the paper.

There was only one other time she used magnetic powder to lift a print from a paper surface, but the magic of the science stuck in her memory. It was a long shot. But if the paper was porous enough, which it seemed to be, and the user had a natural oil film on their skin, then there may just be enough residue for her to lift an image from the page.

The fire damaged most of her lab supplies, however, there were a few cases of personal items she stored at home.

With the restricted space she had in the hospital basement, Kerry crammed her personal items on the shelving that Thomas had built above her desk.

She stood on the chair, cautiously rested one foot on the surface of her makeshift desk, and scanned the shelves for the small container that held her work mementos from Montreal.

The light gray box rested on a stack of medical textbooks. Kerry removed it from the shelf as she carefully stepped off the table and onto the floor. A long, thin wire twisted through the holes. It was a makeshift security lock, one she had no need for during the years she owned it.

Covered in a thin layer of dust, Kerry wiped the surface clean before twisting the thin wire and sliding it from the holes. With the surface of the small table clear, Kerry arranged the thin magnetic brush, the jar containing a mixture of iron and mineral particles, and a magnifying glass.

The magnetic powder wasn't something that would deteriorate, so there was no issue with using tainted particles to retrieve an image of a print. Her options for where she could test the paper were few. She couldn't use the examination lab without booking a time and registering the case file she was working on in the hospital log. Bringing the note to Simon would field an enormous list of questions that she neither had the inclination nor courage to explain. If she was going to find prints leading her to the person who sent the note, then she was going to have to do it in room 24B.

After scanning an image of the note, Kerry unscrewed the cap of the magnetic powder jar and shook the contents, leveling the powder in the container.

With light, steady hand movements, Kerry waved the brush over the shavings in the container and small slivers sprang up, attaching themselves to the magnetized base of the brush.

Gently, Kerry swiped the brush across the surface of the paper leaving behind a dark residue in the indentations of the paper. A second move over the page lifted the loose fragments of iron and Kerry saw the familiar curves and lines of a partial print.

When she was done, she found thirteen partial prints. Two were impossible to gain enough points of comparison. Seven were hers, which left four that belonged to the last person who touched the paper.

The architect of the cryptic note.

Even though she couldn't see it yet, she knew there was a connection between the note and the recent murder of Chef Lalonde. What it was, she couldn't be certain.

Kerry called the office of the Superintendent of the Provincial Police, and when Peter didn't answer his line, she pressed zero to be directed to his receptionist.

Lila Dubois worked for Peter since his first day as Superintendent of the Provincial Police. Their connection in the community, along with their focus on reducing the number of incarcerated minors, forged a bond that built an efficient office environment.

"Lila, it's Kerry. How are you?"

"Kerry!" Lila's cheery voice rang through the line. "I'm good. How are things for you in your new digs?"

An unintentional snicker escaped Kerry's pursed lips. "You mean room 24B that once was a closet?"

"Peter told me how disappointed you are. And for what it's worth, he's really upset about how the change in the budget has affected you." Lila sighed, "At least you got a room in a hospital. He consolidated two northern labs and reduced their schedules. As you can imagine, neither of them is happy about the forced arrangement. I think it's a good idea you're taking a break. Maybe the powers that be will realize how productive you were."

"That's what I'm calling about. I want to postpone my leave."

Kerry could hear Lila's fingers dance across her keyboard.

"Any idea when you'll want to take your leave?" Lila asked, still typing away on her computer.

Kerry glanced at the darkened prints on the surface of the paper. "It'll probably be when I'm finished with the latest murder investigation."

"Oh, is that the famous chef who was murdered at his cottage?"

"Yeah, and I can sense there'll be a lot of publicity attached to this one, so I'd prefer to stick around until the case is closed."

"Probably a good idea. I think the replacement was a fresh graduate."

Kerry squeezed her eyes closed. That's what she was when she made the worst decision of her life.

"Will you let Peter know that I've delayed my leave of absence?"

"I sure will," Lila said. She paused, slightly hesitating to continue, and then let out a huff. "Look, it's not my place to say anything, but I heard Commissioner Robertson arguing with the budget committee two days ago and he was really going to bat for several of the rural offices in the province. I don't know if he got through to any of the bean counters, but if he did, then it should be good news for you."

"Thanks, Lila. I won't let on that you said anything about it."

Kerry slipped the phone into her pocket when she ended the call and packed up the magnetic powder and forensic brush. She wiped the surface of the desk and then closed the lid to the gray box.

Slipping the wire through the lock holes, she twisted it shut and then pushed the box back on the shelf, returning it to where she found it atop a stack of medical books.

She needed to figure out how to search the fingerprint database. Hopefully, she'd be able to find a match to the prints she lifted from the paper.

As far as she knew, Simon kept a secret from her only a handful of times. None of the instances were as severe as the truth Kerry was concealing, nor did his secret threaten his career or put him in danger of being charged with interfering with a murder investigation.

Kerry based many of her decisions on what she thought was right and just. Her political views, how she treated friends and co-workers, and especially her career.

However, as she looked back on her decision, no matter how certain she was that she had done the right thing, the fact was, the right thing didn't resemble the law.

Not even slightly. And that was the problem.

CHAPTER 24

The time that Kerry had scheduled for Michel Lalonde's autopsy gave her use of the small examination room until ten o'clock and not a minute longer. If she had booked it for the next morning, Doctor Salvador Varanus would pace outside the large steel doors, watching the clock to ensure that Kerry was gone by the time her scheduled time elapsed. Before Kerry's arrival, he was the only one who used the room. Although their awkward working arrangement was probably to blame for his attitude, she knew his natural gruff demeanor played somewhat into his rude approach.

The exam and the autopsy for Michel Lalonde weren't complex, but she still didn't want to rush the autopsy. She didn't want to let her current distraction be the reason for a mistake. Every step of the examination needed to be carefully documented.

She placed the tape recorder on the end of the counter and dictated each step of her exam along with her interpretation of her findings that she would transcribe later.

Michel Lalonde was a large man, both in stature and girth. His broad shoulders masked his thick waistline, and a noticeable crease marked his skin where his belt had been cinched tight.

His attacker would've needed to exceed the chef's six-foot-two reach and be able to wield a piece of wood large and heavy enough to create the gash on the side of his skull.

Both the shape and the depth of the wound signified that there was a single, powerful blow to the side of the victim's head. There were no repeated swings at the victim or defensive wounds on his body. The attack was swift and powerful, killing him almost instantly. It didn't appear to be a murderous rage of an attack made during a crime of passion.

With careful deliberation, Kerry examined the victim's body for any signs of a struggle. His fingernails contained the residue of kitchen soap and disinfectant. There were no clothing fibers or skin tissues caused by someone grasping during a struggle or fighting for his life.

Kerry glanced at the report, indicating the areas on the victim's body where she noticed the bruising on his skin that was caused by his fall. Photos of the dock and the steep stairway were inside the file. Kerry pulled them out and spread them on the counter.

That's when she realized the murderer didn't have to be exceptionally tall or strong to cause the fatal blow that killed Michel Lalonde. If the murderer was standing at the top of the stairs, waiting for the chef to mount the steep climb, they would have the advantage of an elevated position to hit him with enough force to kill him. The attack against the side of his skull combined with his head striking the surface of the dock would have killed him immediately.

With less than an hour left to complete the examination, Kerry focused on the wound. Clearing the debris from his short hair, pulling wood slivers that were embedded in his skin, and measuring the width and depth of the gash.

The search team wasn't able to locate the murder weapon. Storm Island was large and densely treed, making an initial search difficult with the two officers that were at Simon's disposal that day.

In addition to budgetary constraints, Simon faced the prospect of dealing with an increased number of cases with fewer officers. Everyone was feeling the pinch of the province's budget woes.

Under a microscope, Kerry could tell the slivers of wood were from a softwood. She examined enough wood during previous autopsies and was confident of the classification. Determining the exact type of wood would take a little longer, but the absence of bark or tree mold was an indication that the murder weapon wasn't likely to be a thick branch as she initially thought when she briefly examined the chef on the dock.

Whatever was used to strike Michel Lalonde down didn't come from the dense forest on Storm Island.

Nearing the end of her examination, Kerry turned on the computer and entered her findings in the report. On the wall, behind the computer, Doctor Varanus had scribbled a number at the bottom of a staff memo regarding the updated computer system.

SV202RL.

It was Doctor Varanus' login information. Kerry hesitated for only a moment before she snapped a photo of the passcode and then slipped her phone back into her pocket. Once she cleared the examination room and returned to room 24B she could use his code to access the fingerprint database and possibly learn who sent the note.

She was calm in her plan to use Doctor Varanus' personal code to trace the fingerprints, and that terrified her more than the possibility of what she may find.

CHAPTER 25

Sixteen hours of videotaped surveillance from businesses on and around Main Street were going to cut into Josh's evening. However, getting the urgent call from Thomas after he was attacked, gave him the motivation he needed to struggle through an entire night of watching the fuzzy video feed.

Thomas was surprisingly lucky considering he walked into his office in the middle of a burglary. A painful bump and unsightly bruises were all the thief left behind.

"I just don't know why the thief would have targeted my construction site," Thomas rested a tray with a heaping plate of nachos, two beers, and salsa on the ottoman between his and Josh's chair.

Josh moved his laptop to the side and helped Thomas with the tray. "I should be doing that for you. You were the one who was attacked."

"And you're the one who is going to be up all night watching video feed trying to nail down who's been breaking into all the shops and businesses in town." Thomas lifted the frosty glass and raised it in the air. "Plus, I thought we both deserved a guilt meal after the last few days."

Josh glanced around the house, finding the quiet unsettling. Having Lucia and Elin around every day and every night filled the house with sounds and movements that he didn't realize he had grown accustomed to.

"Do you think we should get a dog?" Josh blurted out, causing Thomas to almost choke on the cheesy nachos he scooped into his mouth.

"A dog?" Thomas asked. "Where did that come from?"

Josh shrugged, "Lucia loves Raven, and it would be nice to have some company late at night."

"Let's talk about that another time. I'm so busy at work with the construction of two cottages that need to be finished by the end of the summer."

"I thought you had three on the go?"

"I did. But my client was killed."

Josh leaned forward, "You were building a new cottage for Chef Lalonde?"

"I know you think he was one of the best chefs around, but he was a huge pain to deal with."

"Anyone who could whip up a Coquilles Saint Jacques and make it look as easy as he did, deserves to be admired."

"Deserved. He's dead now."

"Ouch. That was harsh."

"You don't even speak the language or eat a lot of French cooking," Thomas joked. "And you didn't have to deal with him the way I did. He complained about every little thing. I have over fifty emails that he fired off last week alone. He was constantly changing the color of the siding, and the light fixtures, and this week he sent back an order of expensive lumber that he signed off on three days earlier."

"I didn't know. You didn't say a thing about how frustrated you were with him."

Thomas shoved his hand toward Josh's laptop. "You've been so busy with work and trying to solve the mystery of the break-ins around town that I didn't want to bother you."

"Are the other two customers easier to deal with?"

"Much," Thomas said. "One is a really nice family from Winnipeg. They own a business that is involved in agriculture and they're building a second cottage for their daughter and the other client is from Texas."

"Texas?"

"Yeah, I thought that was a bit of a stretch but apparently the wife spent her childhood summers in Lake Pines and wants to recreate the same memories for her kids."

"I can understand that." Josh was happy when Thomas agreed to their relocation to Lake Pines. Witnessing the positive change in their daughter and the relief Thomas was experiencing after leaving the stress of the businesses in the city, Josh knew it was the best decision for their family.

After the tense situation with Elin worked itself out, Thomas' mother moved to Lake Pines. She agreed to give it a year before she committed to a permanent move, but with her budding romance on the horizon, Josh thought the sale of Elin's condo in Toronto would be inevitable. "You must be pleased that Elin stopped trying to convince us to leave Lake Pines."

"Now that she has Oliver in her sightlines, I don't think she'll be complaining."

"Are you okay with them - dating?" Josh hesitated on the last word, sensing it was an odd way to refer to two grandparents falling in love. But that's exactly what they were doing.

"She's happy, he's happy, so who am I to interfere?" Thomas grabbed his book from the side table, balanced a plate of nachos on his knee, and smiled. "I'll dive into this book I've been meaning to finish while you comb through the video images from the security cameras from all the businesses in the shopping district."

"It could take all night."

Thomas opened the book, "I don't mind."

Josh shifted the laptop back around and pressed play, continuing with the footage outside of Lisa's café. He had honed his skill in speed-watching videos the same way several students learned how to speed-read.

However, searching for a dark hoodie with a patch sewn on the sleeve was more difficult than he imagined. Not because there were too many people rushing by on the videos, but because the rainy weather had distorted many of the images.

It was almost midnight and Thomas had nodded off in the chair, falling asleep on chapter twenty-seven. Josh was about to stop for the night when he paused the video. He pressed the rewind button and then stopped just as the figure came into view.

On the bottom right hand of the screen, a man wearing a black hoodie with a small patch on the sleeve quickly passed in front of the security camera positioned in front of the Lake Pines library.

He was jogging, and the video captured only a few seconds of his movements. But his hood was down and his face clearly visible, and Josh immediately recognized him.

Even with the black-and-white image, the artificially dyed blonde shoulder-length hair was easy to recognize. Displaying a few inches of dark roots that had unintentionally become his trademark style, his raggedy hair lent him a beach boy persona without any of the easygoing temperament.

His angular face and thin nose exaggerated the darkened inset eyes that darted from side to side.

Despite the narrow scope of the video, Josh saw enough to recognize the prowling movements as Casey Woodfield shifted from the window fronts of stores to the line of parked cars along the road.

He reached for his phone and called Simon. He wanted to question him as soon as possible and when he glanced up and saw the shadow of the deep bruise that was building on Thomas' face, he didn't want to wait until morning.

But unlike the time he had to let Casey walk after an altercation in the Lion's Head Pub, this time he would prove that Casey Woodfield was guilty.

CHAPTER 26

Kerry looked in the mirror and dragged her hands down her face, wiping the hardened sleep from her eyes. Dull patches rose under her eyes, and the lack of sleep was getting difficult to hide with makeup and caffeine.

Raven whimpered as he looked into the bathroom from where he lay blocking Kerry's exit from the room. Sprawled out in a superman pose, his eyes sluggishly shifted from Kerry to the floor. Kerry reached down and kissed the dog's head before she stepped over his body and rushed down the stairs and left for work.

The memory of that fateful day returned randomly, but thankfully not often. Until she found the note under her door, she never allowed herself to imagine what would happen if anyone found out what she did. But now everything had changed.

Kerry spent her morning organizing files and feeling guilty about leaving Raven alone. The image of her dog sitting by the door, his head drooping and his tail motionless, refused to leave her mind. Distracted by guilt and curiosity in the note paper she saw at Michel Lalonde's cottage propelled Kerry out of her office an hour after she arrived.

The first few drops of morning rain fell as Kerry pushed through the service door at the rear of the hospital. Emerging into an almost empty staff parking lot, Kerry was grateful for arriving early to work. It was getting more difficult to avoid questions from hospital staff about her lab's construction. Mostly because it reminded her that much of what she liked about her job in Lake Pines was drastically changing. Things were shifting from a predictable, comfortable pattern to an unsettling awkwardness where unwelcome surprises waited around each corner. Or at least that's how it seemed.

Simon had also left early that morning. After getting a frantic text from Josh in the middle of the night saying that he believed he located a viable suspect in the recent robberies, he knew the day would be busy.

After convincing Josh to wait until the morning to question Casey Woodfield, Simon promised he'd arrive at the station by six.

The entire morning, Kerry could only think about the prints she had lifted from the yellow paper. She was still deciding whether to use Doctor Varanus' login code to search the print database. That, along with recognizing the same paper at Chef Lalonde's cottage, had distracted her thoughts throughout the night.

A few times she was on the brink of blurting out her secret to Simon, but in each instance, she held back. What if the note was nothing more than someone who was upset with her investigation into a death of a friend or loved one? Not that she welcomed such an intrusion into her life, but it was preferable to the alternative that haunted her thoughts.

But each time she tried to brush away the coincidences, she couldn't ignore the item in the box along with the paper found at Michel Lalonde's cottage.

Kerry pulled the hood of her raincoat over her head and rushed toward the dock.

To the left of the hospital, workers draped the damaged iconic fish statue in orange tarps as the damp weather put a hold on the planned repairs. The recent storm severely damaged the hull, and along with a tight town budget, several residents had grown tired of the dated lake effigy and wanted it torn down.

Kerry was rooting for the old fish. Just as her own lab had suffered damage in a fire, the airborne branches and trees had smashed gaping holes in the structure, threatening its existence in the small town.

Kerry donated to the statue fundraising efforts and hoped that the renovations would put an end to the tension surrounding the controversy that had jokingly been referred to as Muskiegate.

She steered the boat out of Lake Pines Bay and drove west toward the channel that led to Storm Island.

A rhythmic pattering of rain drummed on the front windshield of the boat, increasing in tempo as thick clouds settled over the lake. Her mind drifted to the early morning message she left on Jean's voicemail.

After hesitating for several seconds, Kerry mentioned the cryptic note, and without referencing the specific case, she asked Jean to call her right away. Hopefully imparting the urgency to speak with him.

She was fearful of so many things relating to that case. Kerry worried for the family of the victims if they ever learned about the risk she took to ensure a conviction. Her concern for Jean's reputation only took a backseat to the thoughts she had of Simon struggling to come to terms with his own wife breaking the law in a murder investigation. But as she headed toward Storm Island to search Michel Lalonde's cottage, it was the similarity of the yellow paper that currently occupied her mind.

Unlike a crime scene in town, the island had no huge barriers preventing anyone from arriving. Thin yellow tape surrounded the base of the stairs and a wide swath of the dock where Lisa found the murdered chef.

After docking next to the boathouse, Kerry walked up the steep hill leading to the cottage, avoiding the main dock and stairwell altogether. She peeled back the police seal taped to the door and pulled it open.

Admittedly, the cottage wasn't off limits to Kerry or anyone else involved with the murder investigation, however, explaining to Simon why she was searching the cottage would have been difficult.

The morning, dulled by the band of thick clouds that shielded the island, flooded the rooms with a muted light, illuminating the open space inside Michel Lalonde's cottage. Everything appeared to be in the same place as it was the last time she was at the cottage. His daily journal, phone records, and a stack of mail rested on his desk near the front window.

Without the prying eyes of fellow forensic staff, Kerry methodically searched the cottage for the manuscript and the yellow paper that was attached to the front page.

The odd manuscript was irrelevant to the murder, and she hoped the forensic team hadn't removed it from the cottage. If it hadn't been for the yellow stationery clipped to the paper, she wouldn't have been thinking about it either.

She climbed the stairs to the second floor, where she had first seen the manuscript. Simon insisted that much of what they found in the cottage should remain there since it didn't seem relevant to the incident on the dock. Instead, he directed the officers to search for the murder weapon.

Kerry was a half hour into a search and she couldn't find the manuscript. She retraced her steps, positive she had left it on the table next to the chair where she had found it tucked under a pillow. Dropping to her knees, she crawled along the floor, searching below the tables and under the furniture.

Nothing.

She returned to the main floor and searched the living room of the cottage, opening desk drawers and searching inside cabinets. Although she couldn't find the exact manuscript, she found a package of the same yellow paper inside the bottom desk drawer. She reached in and slipped out a sheet.

A clattering of metal, followed by the slamming of a drawer, came from the kitchen, jolting Kerry's body.

She turned around and tiptoed toward the rear of the cottage where she was certain the noise had come from. Loud sounds of someone searching cupboards echoed through the cottage. A short dark hallway connected the front room with the kitchen at the back of the building.

Still clutching the yellow paper in her left hand, Kerry pushed her back against the wall. Her phone buzzed in her pocket, reverberating Jean's distinct ringtone, and the sound drifted through the cottage. The noise immediately stopped in the next room, replaced by the hurried footsteps of the intruder leaving the kitchen. She ran forward, turning the corner just as her phone stopped ringing, and she walked straight into Hugo Lawson as he was trying to get away.

CHAPTER 27

Offering a collection of poor excuses, Hugo Lawson stammered his reasons for being inside the locked cottage of a murder victim. With no other choice, Kerry phoned Simon informing him that she found the murder victim's disgruntled neighbor searching through the kitchen.

"You're where?" Simon asked the stabbing question as he collected his keys and rushed out the door.

Kerry held her finger up at Hugo as she spoke into the phone. "I'm at Michel Lalonde's cottage."

"Why?"

Quickly, Kerry grasped for what would be the most plausible scenario. "I came to see if I could find any wood that matched the murder weapon and that's when I heard Mr. Lawson fumbling around in the kitchen searching for God knows what."

Hugo slid down the wall, crouching on the floor as he held his head in the crux of his hands. After Kerry ensured Simon that she was safe, he told her to remain inside the cottage and he rushed out of the station.

Faster than Kerry had expected, Simon pushed through the front door of the cottage, tearing the police sticker from the frame. He found Kerry in a chair, facing a visibly agitated Hugo Lawson.

Trailing behind Simon was a second officer as they rushed into the cottage and placed Hugo Lawson under arrest.

"For what?" Hugo screamed. "I didn't take anything?"

"You were trespassing," Simon pointed to the large red crime scene sticker that was taped to the door. "That clearly explains that this cottage is a crime scene and only authorized personnel can enter."

"I didn't see it. I came in through the bedroom window." Somehow, Hugo Lawson believed that his admission of prying open a locked window was preferable to entering through the main door.

"That didn't seem like breaking and entering to you?" Simon asked. "Or did you miss the web of yellow police tape on the dock?"

Kerry thought back to how she peeled one side of the security tape off the door frame and then pulled it closed, causing it to adhere to the frame again.

"I beached my canoe on the back of the island," Hugo pointed to the side of the island where he arrived. "I didn't want anyone to see me."

Simon motioned for the officer to take Hugo down to the boat.

"Let's continue this conversation at the station."

Mumbling protests and claims of unfair treatment, an officer guided Hugo Lawson out of the cottage and down to the dock.

Simon turned around, now facing Kerry as she watched the officer and Hugo through the window.

"Why do you think he was here?"

"Him, I'll deal with at the station," Simon said. "Do you want to tell me why you came out here without letting me know?"

"I told you, I was looking for the wood that might match the slivers I found in the victim's wound."

"Then why did you sneak into the cottage?"

Kerry folded her brow and pressed her lips flat. "I didn't sneak in, I told you-"

Simon held up his hand, stopping Kerry mid-sentence. "The crime scene tape was on the door frame when I arrived. Hugo admitted he crawled through the bedroom window. But why would you sneak inside? Unless you were trying to hide the fact that you were here."

Kerry held her breath. A knot tightened in her gut as she looked into Simon's eyes. He stepped forward and rested his hand on her arm. "Kerry, I can tell something has been bothering you. First, out of nowhere, you want to take a leave of absence. Then, equally as fast, you change your mind and decide to stay until we close this case. Finding out that you snuck into the cottage concerns me."

The familiar sound of Jean's ringtone interrupted their conversation and Kerry reached into her pocket, pushing a button silencing the call. She turned away from Simon, hiding the tears that rose to her eyes and told him she had to get back to the hospital. She rushed down to the dock, avoiding eye contact with the officer leading Hugo Lawson to the police boat. She was halfway out of Haven Bay when uncontrollable sobs shook her entire body.

Pressure from the secret she'd kept for so long and the threat of it surfacing without her control was bearing down on the quiet life she had created for herself in Lake Pines, and she was about to explode.

CHAPTER 28

The unassuming bungalow where Casey Woodfield lived was even more unassuming on the inside.

A long plastic banquet table rested unevenly on a bent frame and seemed out of place in a room that was probably intended to be the main dining room. Casey had an outdated computer on one side of the table, and a pile of video games and random computer equipment scattered across the other.

A stale odor drifted from the kitchen into the adjoining rooms. Dampness from the lack of artificial heat in the small home during a cool rainy point in the season gave rise to the musty remnants in the carpet.

The heavy scent of smoke, wet dog, and mud filled the air, although none of those things were visible from Josh's initial inspection. It was probably a good guess that housecleaning wasn't high on Casey Woodfield's list of things to do.

Dishes, haphazardly piled next to the sink, bore the remnants of dried cheese sauce and hardened noodles that coated cutlery and glasses. A pot filled with greasy cold water rested on the counter, presumably left to soak several days ago.

It took a few moments for Casey to realize what was happening when two officers entered his room. The tipped over cans of empty beer next to his bed explained the blank stare in his eyes and the sour scent emanating from his breath. As well as the fact that Casey hadn't heard the repetitive banging on the door before Josh ordered an officer to force it open.

They searched the house as Casey pulled a wrinkled top over his head, shaking his fingers through his hair and then readjusting his belt. No longer full of swagger and vim, Casey moved slowly as an officer guided him out of his house and into the police cruiser.

Josh followed them outside, more frustrated than when they arrived.

He thought for sure that their search would turn up at least one stolen item from the list. If Casey was responsible for the recent thefts in town, then he wasn't stashing the items in his home or garage.

"What do you want us to do?" An officer asked.

"Bring him into the station," Josh said. "I still want to question him."

Josh left an officer at Casey's home and instructed him to search through every closet, corner, and cabinet for anything related to the strange collection of businesses that were robbed over the last couple of months.

"This town is terrified. Businesses are closing early during one of the busiest seasons and residents are afraid to go out after dark. And there's a good chance that if Casey is responsible he wasn't acting alone. Keep an eye out for anything that may connect him to any of the stores, no matter how unassuming it may seem."

The officer nodded, eager to find the robbers and put his own family at ease.

Josh returned to the station and guided Casey to an interrogation room. Leaving him in the locked room, Josh gathered the printout copies of the surveillance images and the paperwork he submitted for the search warrant and returned to question Casey. As far as Josh was concerned, Casey Woodfield was the perfect suspect for the robberies in Lake Pines.

Josh placed the printouts on the table.

Casey glanced down at the images and pushed the page back across the table. "So, you have me walking past the library. So what?"

"The security footage outside of Johnson's Pharmacy captured the thief with the same hoodie, and a man who walked in on a burglary in progress described the exact logo that's on your sleeve."

"I'm not the only one with that top." Casey snapped.

"But I'm going to take a guess that those other people don't have a record of complaints with the police department."

"That's all they are. Complaints." Casey said. "I was never charged, and isn't that kind of important?" Casey smirked, aware that Josh was still upset about not being able to charge him with disturbing the peace the last time he dragged him into the station.

"Where were you last night between the hours of seven and nine?" Josh asked, avoiding the obvious gaping hole in his case against Casey.

"I was out for a walk."

"Can anyone vouch for your whereabouts?"

"Do you look for alibies when you're out for a walk?" Casey folded his arms across his chest and laughed. "I want to see my lawyer now. That's my right, isn't it?"

Casey was more alert than when Josh shook him from his sleepy stupor just a few hours, ago and they both knew he couldn't deny the request.

Josh brushed the pages into a pile, slipped them into the folder, and left the room.

"Sally, can you get Casey Woodfield's lawyer on the phone?"

Sally glanced over Josh's shoulder and through the small window on the door of the interrogation room, and she froze.

"Is everything alright, Sally?"

She didn't answer Josh. Instead, she continued to stare at Casey Woodfield, as he fidgeted in his seat. Josh gently guided her away from the door and out of Casey's view.

"What's wrong?" Josh's gentle tone released Sally's focus on Casey, and she looked into his eyes.

"He's the kid who followed me home a few times last winter. I filed a complaint with the department." Sally shoved her hands into her folded arms, pulling them close to her body.

"There was no mention of that when I pulled up his file."

"That's because his crafty lawyer made sure the complaint didn't get any further than the first officer."

Josh looked back toward the room and then leaned forward and whispered, "Are you certain it was him?"

"Positive."

Josh rubbed the side of his clenched jaw. "We can't keep him from talking to his lawyer. I'll have someone else make the call. I don't want you to feel uncomfortable."

Sally shook her head, refusing to let Casey interfere with her job. He did enough to frighten her once, she wouldn't let him do it again. "No. I'll do it. I was just shocked to see him. Hopefully, you have enough evidence to charge him, because I don't care why he's arrested. I just want him gone."

CHAPTER 29

Vincent Haley strode into the station, and with no preamble or smile, walked past Sally and directly toward the interrogation room where his client, Casey Woodfield, was waiting. There was no need to introduce himself since Vincent had been a familiar face around the police station over the last few years.

As he rushed through the lobby and toward the back hall, Sally paged Josh and told him that Vincent Haley arrived and was on his way to speak with Casey.

Representing a collection of clients ranging from individuals arrested for DUIs, corporate malfeasance, and even murder, Vincent Haley made a name for himself as an intelligent, ruthless litigator. Holding designations from Osgoode Hall and Stanford, Vincent excelled on the international stage holding a seat with the International Labor Organization as a Canadian Employer Delegate. His business contacts encouraged him to shift to corporate litigation after he spent two years instructing the next generation of students on the art of negotiations at McGill Law School.

For fifteen years, Vincent practiced law in a fast-paced field enjoying every second of his time on the forty-second floor of a downtown Toronto skyscraper at the corner of King and York. However, Vincent's wife longed to return to her hometown, and his deep loyal affection for her left him with no other option but to walk away from his established career and move to Lake Pines.

Since moving to the small lakeside town, Vincent's client list had deflated to criminals much like Casey Woodfield. In fact, it was his second time representing the twenty-nine-year-old grifter.

His choice of clients was unlikely to change. Now, Vincent represented clients who, at one point, couldn't have afforded to spend twenty minutes in his lobby. Nonetheless, the law was his obsessive passion and even the simplest of cases fed his desire.

Retirement was still several years off, so until then, he did his best to make each case, arrest, or charge as entertaining as possible. Casey Woodfield being questioned regarding the rash of thefts in Lake Pines likely wouldn't result in a spine-tingling court case, but it would at least garner widespread local attention. Something he deeply missed.

His wife begged him not to take him on as a client. Even if the case went to trial, Vincent would be sure to win. He was simply that good. She knew that none of their friends or neighbors would understand that it was just his job.

The town had been shrouded in fear soon after the thefts began. They seemed random and haphazard. Everyone felt as if they could easily be the next target. The entire town prayed that the police would capture the people who were responsible, and everyone wanted to see the guilty parties arrested, charged, and put behind bars. No exception.

Vincent Haley being on Casey Woodfield's side of the table gave his wife every reason to be concerned. However, Vincent craved some excitement in what had become a boring legal career, and he agreed to defend the suspected thief.

The overly qualified lawyer dressed as if he was still representing corporate executives. As he moved through the station, he clutched his Saint Laurent leather satchel, avoiding eye contact with anyone in the lobby. The bag, his personal remnant of a bygone era, had become his trademark in every case he tried in Lake Pines.

Josh met Vincent in the hall. After a brief explanation of why Casey was brought in for questioning, he walked him to the interrogation room.

"Give me twenty minutes with my client, please," Vincent said as he sat down across from Casey. He carefully rested his oxblood-tinted bag next to his leg and then pulled out a yellow legal pad and his embossed Mont Blanc pen, resting them both on the table.

Josh closed the door and waited in his office until he was called back into the small room. The first thing Josh noticed was the smirk that shifted across Casey's face. The second was the Mount Blanc pen Vincent rolled between his fingers as he rested his arm on the overturned pad of paper.

"I don't see any reason for you to hold my client," Vincent said just before he launched into accusations of unlawful arrest, illegal profiling, and harassment.

"Harassment? How have we harassed your client?"

"You and your officers entered his home, waking him from a deep sleep and pulling him out of bed. He thought he was being robbed."

The irony of the accusation didn't amuse Josh.

"We received a proper search warrant, Mr. Haley. We have good reason to believe that your client is a reasonable person of interest."

"The sweatshirt?" Vincent shook his head. "You know that argument won't stand up in court. At best, you have my client walking by a library late at night. Which, I will remind you, is not illegal."

Josh clenched his jaw, knowing what was going to follow. He had hoped that they'd find at least one stolen item in Casey's home. Unfortunately, outside of Casey's bizarre collection of outdated video games, proof of his poor residential hygiene, and signs that he didn't know how to use a washing machine, they couldn't find one item that was reported stolen. Josh had missed his opportunity to find a valid reason to charge Casey Woodfield and had no choice but to let him go.

Within a half hour of Vincent Haley's arrival, Casey walked out of the station.

Josh slammed his office door and tossed the file on his desk. His gut told him that Casey was guilty and that he was the person responsible for the robberies in town, as well as the recent attack on Thomas.

The attack left Thomas dazed for almost half an hour, and by the time he called the police, the person who attacked him was long gone. Although Thomas escaped with minor scrapes and bruises and one nasty bump, they both knew it could have been much worse. Josh had never been so invested in an investigation since Wayne's death. No matter what it took, he would prove Casey's guilt.

CHAPTER 30

Diving back into the police reports only frustrated Josh even further. A brief conversation with Lucia when Elin called, was the only break he took during the day.

Josh needed to find the person who was guilty of the robberies and the violent attack on Thomas. Even though Thomas wasn't worried about returning to his office, Josh knew it was a matter of time before someone else was attacked, and they may not be so lucky.

Lake Pines was in a fragile state the last few months. Losing the feeling of safety that everyone took for granted along with the devastating storm that destroyed their iconic statue, blew a discontented mood through the streets and shops of the small town.

Solving the case of who was breaking into local businesses was more than just putting a stop to criminal activity. It would restore some hope that not everything from the past had been lost.

He was focused on the list of stolen items when the knock came at his office door.

"Knock, knock," Thomas said as he opened Josh's office door. "Is this a good time?"

Josh waved Thomas in, "Sure. What's up?"

He didn't want to tell Thomas that he released Casey Woodfield moments earlier.

"I think I remembered something that may help find the person who attacked me."

Thomas leaned on Josh's desk. "I remember a boat that was parked on the dock. I never complain about anyone parking on our dock since it's usually people out for a run or a hike and our property has easy access to the trails. But when I went into the office today, I remembered the boat was there on the day I was attacked."

"Why do you think it stands out?"

"There's a large orange sign at the entrance to the path, so outside of using the dock to come to my office, there would be no reason for anyone to dock there," Thomas explained. "It was late and I was on the phone with my mom, so I didn't think too much about what was going on around me. I dropped my keys at the base of the steps and was trying to find them while I was on the phone. It didn't even occur to me that the path to the trail had been closed for the last week."

"Closed? Why?"

"It's all part of the renovation of the fish statue."

"It's a muskie - but go on." Josh corrected Thomas, more out of habit since Josh was a huge fan of the iconic muskie statue and Thomas favored the idea of its complete removal from the waterfront bay.

Thomas rolled his eyes, "Anyway, the funds raised are also going toward upgrading the hiking trail that extends from the trail to the fish." Thomas held up his hand and raised his brow. "Don't tell me it's a muskie or I'll scream."

"Would there be any other reason for someone to park on the dock?"

Thomas shook his head, "Only to use the hiking trail or to come to my office."

"How much do you remember about the boat?"

Thomas' description of the white boat with the two pale blue stripes and a black engine matched several of the boats on the lake. But it was his memory of the mismatched rope attached to the dock that set it apart from other boats.

The yellow line replaced the normally stained and faded boat ropes and should be distinct enough to find the owner. Which would hopefully lead to an arrest and put an end to the fear that was spreading through the town. Then maybe things would return to normal.

CHAPTER 31

The crumpled yellow paper was slightly damp from the rain. Kerry had shoved it deep inside her pocket after she came face to face with Hugo Lawson and almost forgot about it.

Forced to call Simon, Kerry didn't know how to explain her presence in a murder victim's cottage other than to claim that she was searching for the wood that might match the description of what she believed was the murder weapon.

During her drive back to the hospital, Kerry had an unsettling feeling that Hugo Lawson's reasons for being inside Michel Lalonde's cottage weren't as innocent as he made them out to be.

In all the years Kerry knew Hugo, she never once witnessed any display of violence or aggression. His normal outlet when fighting a cause leaned toward filing complaints, petitions, or making incessant requests to the bylaw officials. Hugo Lawson's weapon of choice had always been his mouth. She always viewed him as someone who verbalized his upset, preferring to act out a role.

Then again, everyone had the potential to break the law. They just needed to be pushed far enough at the wrong time.

Kerry knew that firsthand. It was the reason she searched Michel Lalonde's cottage for the note paper. She believed it matched the one that was slipped under her door.

Until she closed the door to room 24B she had forgotten about the paper she found in the cabinet. When she returned to the hospital, she was focused on avoiding the hospital staff and ignoring the noise of the intercom echoing in the hall. Nothing more.

Simon's glare and probing questions made her feel guilty about the secret she was keeping from him, but until she spoke with Jean and truly figured out what the package and note represented, she needed to remain silent.

Kerry flattened the paper on her desk, rubbing out the edges with the edge of her hand. She retrieved the note from her locked cabinet and placed it on the table. Side by side, the two pieces of paper were identical. The distinct swirls of the thick specialty paper were uniquely artistic in design, and probably very expensive.

There would only be a few places where paper like this could be purchased. High-end stationery or card stores would carry them, but she wasn't certain any shop in Lake Pines would carry anything like this.

Most people used email or text, and very few people wrote notes or cards anymore. Gift bags with flimsy tags were the norm for birthdays or anniversaries. Kerry didn't have the resources at her disposal to test the paper, however, she didn't think it was necessary. They were definitely from the same stock, and most likely the same package.

She opened the image search on her phone and scanned the blank piece of paper on her desk. Within seconds, several internet results appeared for the same yellow note paper.

As she suspected, the paper was expensive, and the first three results listed one small package under a designer name that she associated with purses and scarves. Under the images, Kerry noticed a list of retailers outlining where someone could buy the same paper online or in-store. They were all located in Europe.

Jean had left two emails and a small red dot hovered over the email app on Kerry's phone. She pressed the button and heard Jean's concerned voice on the recording.

"Kerry, I think I know why you needed to reach me. I'm in the office all day today. Call me because-" A pounding on the door surprised Kerry and she pushed the button, ending the replay of Jean's message. She pulled open the door of her small office.

A young woman with dark black eyes and even darker hair pulled back in a ponytail, smiled back, "Dr. Dearborne?"

Kerry nodded. "How can I help you?"

"My name's Trisha Chen. I'm your replacement."

"I canceled that with Peter. I mean, Superintendent George."

An awkward blush rose to Trisha's face. "I know, he told me. But he said to come anyway because he thought you may need the help."

Kerry gripped the handle on the door, her knuckles bursting into a bright white. "I didn't need any help before I was shoved into this small basement closet. Why would he think I needed one now?"

Trisha shrugged, "I don't know. But,—"

"But what?" Kerry snapped.

"This is the third job I've been sent to in the last six months. It's getting harder to get some training with all the cutbacks. So many offices are reducing their staff across the country. I begged Superintendent George for this position. If I don't land something soon then I'm going to have to throw away my entire idea of what my career was supposed to be. Please, I begged Superintendent George for this job, don't make me beg you too."

Even at such a young age, the girl standing in front of Kerry looked more accustomed to a boardroom atmosphere and all the luxuries that accompanied such a position as opposed to a lab and the sometimes gruesome tasks associated with being a coroner.

As the thought rolled across Kerry's mind, another jumped to the forefront. Senior members of the Montreal office made the same comments about her when she first entered the profession, and if it hadn't been for Jean, her career would have stopped there.

Although the young girl's presence wasn't part of Kerry's plans for the next few days, she knew she couldn't turn her away. Reluctantly, she stood to the side and invited her into room 24B.

CHAPTER 32

The shocked look on Trisha's face was impossible to hide. Even the quick smile and gracious approach in her words of thanks, couldn't mask the disappointment in the size of Kerry's office.

"You work in here?" Trisha asked as she glanced around the space, wondering where a second chair could fit, and quickly determined that it wouldn't.

"Only for the last little while," Kerry explained. "There was a fire in my lab and until there's a decision made on where my new office will be, I'm working in the hospital."

Trisha caught the exasperation in Kerry's tone. "That must be very frustrating for you."

"It is," Kerry said. "But now there's the added issue of where to put you."

"I don't need a lot of space. I'll work wherever you can squeeze me in."

Kerry twisted her face in thought as they both looked around the room. "There isn't enough room in here, but there's a small room off the examination lab where I can set you up. Follow me." Kerry grabbed a brown file folder from the corner of her desk and walked into the hall.

Trisha followed Kerry out of room 24B, down the hall, and through a set of large steel doors.

"Doctor Dearborne, I have the room booked for the next few hours. You'll have to wait," Doctor Varanus shouted as she walked in the door.

"Doctor Varanus, this is Trisha Chen and she'll be assisting me with my caseloads," Kerry quickly introduced Trisha, ignoring his comment, and walked to the opposite side of the room. "Trisha is going to use this space since there's barely enough room to turn around in my office."

Trisha smiled and offered a shrug of apology as Doctor Varanus let out an impatient sigh.

Kerry turned on a light, revealing a ten-foot by ten-foot space with a dated but large metal desk, a computer, and an expansive window that faced the examination room where Doctor Varanus worked.

"I can see about getting you some blinds. Then you won't have anyone watching you while you work in here, but at least it's a room with some privacy."

"This is perfect, Doctor Dearborne," Trisha said as she glanced around the space, struggling to remain positive. "And the window won't be a problem."

Kerry admired Trisha's enthusiasm and she thought she should relax her harsh approach. "Sorry if I was terse with you earlier. I've been frustrated ever since the fire."

"That's okay," Trisha said. "Is there anything you would like me to work on?"

Kerry handed Trisha a file folder. "This is the report containing the findings from my autopsy examination on a recent murder victim. I want you to focus on his head wound. There were slivers of wood lodged in his skull and I would like you to narrow down the type of wood they're from as well as if there are any other clues in the wound itself that may indicate what type of weapon he was killed with."

Trisha read the file notes, scanning each entry as she ran her finger over the page. A method of speed reading Kerry used when she was in university. "The police didn't find a weapon?"

"No," Kerry said. "The victim was murdered on a large, heavily treed island. If we can give the police a more specific description of what he was hit with, then they can narrow down their search." Kerry stepped out of the room, pausing at the doorway to add, "The security code on the computer is 67893. You'll be able to access the reports on my cases from the main screen. If you need anything else, you know where to find me."

"Wouldn't it be more useful if I physically examined the body?" Trisha asked. "Maybe there's something I can gain from seeing the actual wound?"

Kerry's eyes narrowed and Doctor Varanus let a low, but audible, snicker escape his grin as he eavesdropped on their conversation from the opposite end of the lab.

"Let's start with the paperwork. I want you to get used to the documents we use during our examinations and the reports that need to be submitted. Depending on the cause of death, the final reports can differ greatly and there are different departments involved in each case. Once I'm comfortable with your knowledge of the procedures and reports, then we can move."

Without another word, Kerry turned around, ignoring Trisha's frustrated sigh, and left the lab.

Any other time Kerry would have welcomed the opportunity to work closely with a graduate and teach them the ropes. But the mysterious note arriving with the tinged threat in the two simple sentences shifted her focus greatly. She needed to figure out what the connection between her past and Michel Lalonde was. Specifically, if it had anything to do with the fifteen-year-old murder.

CHAPTER 33

It had occurred to Kerry that she was becoming obsessed with the small yellow piece of paper and the cryptic note. However, every time she tried to convince herself that it was just nothing more than an attempt by a disgruntled family member to intimidate her, the idea fell to the wayside.

The reference to her secret jumped out in the first line. No matter how veiled the threat was, someone was obviously threatening to reveal what happened. She had known other coroners that had received threats throughout their careers. Bribes intended to encourage coroners to alter toxicity reports weren't uncommon. Usually, however, it was a finely printed exclusion in a multi-million-dollar insurance claim that prompted the financial persuasion.

That didn't appear to be the case with the recent note.

There was no monetary benefit that Kerry could think of, which only left one other plausible explanation.

It was personal.

The last thing Kerry needed to do was go on a wild goose chase because someone shoved an anonymous letter under her door.

Kerry sat down at her computer and pulled up the web portal to access the fingerprint database. She entered Doctor Varanus' secure login code and rested her hand on the entry key just as her phone rang.

She answered Simon's call, leaving the secure login code up on her computer screen.

"Did you get my message, Kerry?"

Kerry pressed her hand against her forehead and squeezed her eyes closed. She had completely forgotten to forward Michel Lalonde's autopsy. "Sorry, Simon. I meant to send you the report first thing this morning."

"Before you went out to Storm Island?"

Kerry ignored Simon's remark and switched screens on her computer. "I'll send you the report now. I have my new assistant running a search on the type of wood that I found in the victim's wound."

"I thought you canceled your replacement?"

"I did, but Peter sent her anyway. I have a feeling that he thinks I need the help," Kerry said.

"Maybe he's right," Simon said. "He knows you just as well as anybody does. Remember, he's the one who hired you."

"Then he should know that I'm capable of doing my job," Kerry snapped.

"No one thinks that you're incompetent. We just think that you've been a little distracted lately."

"We?" Kerry asked. "Were you and Peter talking about me?"

"He reached out to me when you canceled your leave of absence. He's worried that you might be feeling a little overwhelmed."

"And what do you think?"

"I think it would be completely normal for you to feel stressed considering everything that's happened in the last year," Simon said. "It's only been a short while since Alex came back into our life and kidnapped you, and then there's the fire that destroyed your lab. Frankly, I don't know how you have been able to handle things as well as you have."

Kerry leaned back in her chair, realizing that her stress and distraction had been building up for a long time. The yellow paper on her desk added another element of stress that she hadn't yet shared with Simon, and she wasn't going to until she knew exactly what she was dealing with.

"Trisha will probably be a huge help with the latest murder investigation. I have her looking into the composition of the splinters of wood I found in the victim's wound. Once we have that, you should have a better idea of what your officers should search for."

"I have someone at Storm Island now continuing the search in the forest. Maybe he'll find something today. The weather is clearing up, which will be good."

"You only sent one officer out to search that island?"

"The cutbacks have hit us too."

Kerry hadn't realized that the tight budget constraints also affected the police station. Her reduced office space was just one casualty in the war against funding. She knew Josh was working alone as he investigated the string of robberies, and she was certain that Thomas being attacked only propelled his drive toward finding a suspect.

"How is Josh doing on the investigation into the recent burglaries?"

"He thought he had a suspect, but he had to let him go."

"Why?"

"Outside of the description of the hoodie, there were no witnesses that could identify Casey Woodfield."

"Maybe someone will come forward. I know a lot of people are concerned about break-ins. Especially the businesses that have been closing early to ensure their staff's safety."

"Well, sometimes it's just one small piece of missing evidence that stands between an assumption of guilt and having a solid suspect."

The box and the cryptic yellow note, which were locked in the filing cabinet, reminded Kerry that she thought the same thing once. And it was what drove her to make the worst decision of her career.

After a hasty end to their conversation, Kerry returned to the image of the fingerprints on the computer screen. It was the one link she could use to trace who sent the note and the box. If the person's prints were in the database, then she'd have a solid lead. Kerry promised herself she'd tell Simon everything once she had a lead, but not until then. He already had too much on his mind.

She uploaded the scanned image, entered the security code, and added a note requesting that the lab send the results to her instead of Doctor Varanus. She hesitated for just a moment, then let the faintest wisp of a sigh escape her lungs before she submitted the request.

CHAPTER 34

Hugo Lawson filed several grievances targeting many of his neighbors. Noise complaints were among the first violations that he filed with the town council. Powerboats, speeding through the Second Channel, passed in front of his island as boaters avoided the powerful undercurrents near the northern entrance.

Sport fisherman, angling inches from his dock and boathouse, disturbed his peaceful morning swims. On one occasion, Hugo threatened to damage their boat when he tried to get them to move. One particularly violent interaction landed Hugo in court when someone filmed him throwing rocks at an intrusive boater. The fisherman's defense was that he couldn't reach the fish concealed in the protected areas under the docks and in the bay's reeds. Hugo latched onto the idea of protected areas, and claimed he was defending the helpless marine creatures along with the endangered wetlands along his shore.

Luck was in Hugo's corner, as the presiding judge had experienced the continuous intrusions at her own cottage. Even though islanders didn't own the watery zone surrounding their property, many saw it as an aggressive move on behalf of the fisherman. The charges were dropped and since then, Hugo refrained from rock-throwing and verbal threats. However, he refused to back off on other matters of interest.

Using the town's regulations, Hugo focused on water frontage building restrictions, septic field regulations, and lake conservation management when he filed his complaints.

The file on Hugo Lawson was long and exhaustive. However, the file documented several complaints Hugo registered against his neighbors. Not the other way around.

However, it was his most recent complaint against Michel Lalonde that Simon focused on when he sat across from Hugo in the small interview room.

Simon placed the file folder on the table and tapped it with his finger. "There are five complaints that you filed with the town bylaw office in the last year. All of them are against Michel Lalonde."

"Those are legitimate grievances. He was skirting every rule concerning his building plans." Hugo listed the offenses, counting them off on his fingers. "The septic tank is not large enough, the dock extends too far out into the weed bay, he plans on removing most of the forest which has a nesting eagle in a tree and then there's the three-slip boathouse he wants to build."

"There weren't any signs of construction on Storm Island."

Hugo pointed his finger at Simon, regretting it instantly, and then folded his hands on his lap. "He's been planning it for over a year. I got wind of what he was doing when I overheard the contractor talking with him on the phone."

"That would just be hearsay. How could you file a complaint with so many specifics?" Simon asked. He was beginning to see the recalcitrant nature of Hugo Lawson's personality. "Each of your complaints contains specific measurements and numbers."

Hugo folded his arms and leaned back in his chair. "I saw the blueprints he had drawn up and took a picture of them."

"When did you see the blueprints?"

Hugo looked down at the floor and his right leg bounced under the table.

Simon leaned forward on the table, resting on his folded arms. "Look, Hugo, it already doesn't look good for you. You have a record of arguments with the deceased, and you were just caught inside his cottage."

Hugo bolted upright in his seat with the inference in Simon's statement. "Are you saying that I murdered Michel because I disagreed with how he was going about the construction of his cottage and boathouse?"

"Five complaints could be seen as harassment."

"If the town bylaw officer stepped in and stopped construction when I filed the first complaint, then there wouldn't be an issue."

"I read the file, Hugo. The bylaw officer found no proof that Michel Lalonde was building a cottage, or a boathouse or expanding his dock as you claimed."

"Then he's bribed the town bylaw officer, or he's paid the construction company under the table. But I know what I saw when I found those blueprints."

"Show me."

"I don't have the picture anymore."

Simon raised his brows and tilted his head. "That's convenient."

"I lost all my photos when I updated my phone, that's why I was there today. I was looking for the blueprints. I didn't want the new owners to carry on where he left off."

"You had a meeting with a bylaw officer just hours before Michel Lalonde was killed. That same bylaw officer added a note to your file that you were 'aggressively agitated' about her decision."

"Aggressively agitated? Those were the words she used?" Hugo seemed shocked at the bylaw officer's report.

Simon nodded. "Considering I found you in a murder victim's cottage, I need to ask you, where were you after the bylaw officer left your island? Let me be more specific. Where were you on the afternoon that Michel Lalonde was murdered?"

Hugo pulled his sunglass from his thick hair and folded them on the table. He fidgeted with them in his hands as he thought about how to respond.

"I decided it was probably time to speak with Michel about his construction project, so I drove over to his cottage."

"Did you two argue?"

"I never spoke with him. When I neared his island, I noticed he was speaking with a woman on his dock. I planned on going back later that night, but when I did, there were a bunch of police boats on the dock so I just went home. It wasn't until the next day that I heard he had been killed."

"What I don't understand is why go to Storm Island and break into a cottage of a man who was murdered when you have a history of disagreements with him?"

"I told you, I was looking for the blueprints?"

"And did you find them?"

Hugo shook his head. "But I remember the name that was stamped on the bottom corner of the plan. It was Graves Construction."

CHAPTER 35

Bringing up the issue of Michel Lalonde's construction project with Thomas was something that Simon couldn't avoid. He drove out to Thomas' office without telling Josh what Hugo Lawson had said, and since there was no physical evidence linking him to the murder, Simon had no choice but to release him. However, Simon warned Hugo not to leave town.

Graves Construction had grown three-fold since Thomas moved to Lake Pines. His expertise with environmentally friendly construction gave him an advantage when he bid on government projects, corporate building and renovations, and most recently, cottage construction.

The attack on Thomas left him with bruises, bumps, and scratches. All of which were still visible on his face. When Simon arrived, Thomas was reorganizing the keys for the updated locks as a set of bars was being added to the windows.

"How are you feeling?" Simon asked as he looked around the office. A box filled with broken glass was next to the door and Thomas tossed the torn brochures inside.

"I have a bit of a headache, but I don't know how much of that has to do with the attack or going through all this paperwork?"

"I still don't know why your business was targeted by the robber?"

"Outside of the fact that my office is out of view of the main road and most of the boat traffic, I don't either."

Simon cleared a stack of paper from a chair when Thomas invited him to sit.

"What was stolen?"

Thomas glanced around the small office, "Nothing that I can tell. I must've interrupted him. And if anyone was going to rob me, why not go for the tools in the shed? The only things in my office are paper, brochures, and my computer."

Simon noticed that Thomas' computer was still on his desk.

"Is that why you're here? Did Josh arrest Casey?" Thomas asked.

Simon shook his head, "He's figuring out how to work around his lawyer. I'm here to ask you about your dealings with Michel Lalonde."

"The chef that was murdered?"

"The one and only," Simon said. "I was just speaking with Hugo Lawson and he claimed that Michel Lalonde was about to begin construction of a new cottage on Storm Island."

"He was," Thomas confirmed. "He came to me about a year ago with the idea of a simple cottage and slight renovation to the boathouse and dock. But things changed each time I spoke with him."

"How so?"

"The first change was to the cottage. He went from wanting a small rustic cabin to an all-glass structure after he vacationed in Nice. He said he wanted an unobstructed view of Haven Bay. But then that didn't last long. After he worked a function in Holland, he sent me photographs of the lodge where he stayed and instructed me to replicate the feeling and warmth of the structure."

"Had you finalized the building plans? Hugo thought Michel Lalonde was violating several bylaws."

"He signed off on the final plans, but yes, there were several issues." Thomas reached his arm behind his neck and squeezed the base of his head.

"Are you feeling alright?"

"Yeah, the headaches come and go. But there should be fewer without Michel as a client." Thomas realized how harsh his final comment was and apologized. "Sorry, I know I shouldn't talk ill of the dead, but he caused me a lot of grief."

"Was he argumentative?"

"More demanding than anything, and he never admitted when he made a mistake. On the afternoon he died, one of my guys went out to his place to deliver some lumber. I thought if I delivered the lumber, then we could get him to move on the second payment and then we could start construction. But when he arrived, Michel claimed it was the wrong wood. When Noah showed him the signed invoice he claimed it was a mistake. Noah had to return the order, and now I'm stuck with a restocking bill. Plus I got charged for some boards that were missing."

"Missing?"

"Noah hit some rough water coming through the back tangle just past Second Channel and some thick trim fell out of the boat."

"Was there anything in the building permit that would substantiate Hugo's claims?"

"I always wait until the client makes the first payment before I apply for a building permit. The fees associated each time I file plans can dig into the budget, so I like to make sure the client is positive about what they want to do. Last summer, I had six cottagers approach me about renovations to their cottage and, after I give them a quote and rudimentary plans, they backed out. It's just part of the business."

"I should probably speak with Noah and find out if there's anything he can tell me about the afternoon he was out there. Maybe he saw something that could be useful."

Thomas grabbed a piece of paper and wrote Noah's name and phone number down, and gave it to Simon.

"Please go easy on him," Thomas said. "He's really trying to make a new start in his life."

"A new start? From what?"

"He had some problems with the police a couple of years ago. His probation officer had difficulty finding work for him because of his record." Thomas explained. "I hired him because I think he deserves a second chance. He's a good kid, Simon. He's a hard worker and never complains about the long hours."

Simon promised Thomas that he would keep his questions to the interaction on the dock and nothing more. However, Simon knew that if Thomas had trouble with Michel Lalonde that there would be many more people with an axe to grind with the celebrity chef.

CHAPTER 36

Noah Irwin arrived twenty minutes early. Simon was still on the phone with Kerry when Sally walked him to the interview room. By the time Simon had finished his conversation, Noah finished two sodas and had started on his third.

A thin layer of sweat glistened on Noah's brow and his fingers tapped the side of the can of soda. Simon stepped into the office, apologizing for keeping him waiting.

"That's alright. But I'm not sure how I can help you?" Noah said.

"You made a delivery to Storm Island on the same day that Michel Lalonde was murdered and I wondered if there was anything that stood out in your mind about that day."

"Other than the fact he was a headache to deal with?"

"Was that the only time you dealt with him?"

"It was the first time I was out at his island, but I was at the office when he came by last year. He gave Thomas a lot of grief over the design of the cottage he wanted to build."

"Thomas said that you were delivering a load of lumber to Storm Island and he made you take it back."

Noah shook his head, "I even showed him the signed invoice for the lumber, and he made it seem like it was my fault for loading it into the boat. How was I supposed to know what he was thinking? He signed off on ash, so I loaded ash into the boat."

Even though Kerry hadn't narrowed down the exact type of wood that the murder weapon was made from, she knew it wasn't a log or a branch that was used. The absence of bark at least told her that much.

"Did you unload any of the wood on the island?" Simon asked.

"No, I started to, but Mr. Lalonde rushed down to the dock and stopped me."

"I see by Thomas' records that not all the wood made it back to the construction site."

"I hit some rough water coming out of the channel and some boards must have fallen out. Thomas was awesome about not charging me the restocking fee." Noah clenched the can of soda and the crunch echoed in the small room. "Is there anything else? I need to get back to work."

"No. But if you do think of anything else, call me."

Noah pushed back his chair and rushed toward the door. He turned around, shaking his hand in the air, "There was one thing. I didn't think of it until now because at the time it didn't seem like a big deal. I just wanted to get away from the island before he complained about something else."

"What was it?"

"As I was driving out of the bay, I glanced back and saw him walking up the stairs and that's when I saw it." Noah paused, unsure how to describe the figure at the top of the steps. "I don't know if it was a man or a woman, but someone was standing in the shadows at the top of the hill, and it didn't seem like Mr. Lalonde knew they were there."

Simon thanked Noah as he walked down the hall toward the exit. He added the additional comment about the mysterious shadowy figure at the top of the stairs and then placed a question mark next to Noah's name before he returned to his office.

CHAPTER 37

The list of items that Josh compiled from the reported thefts was a mixture of prescription pills from the pharmacy, unspecific tools from the marina, and various pieces of clothing and giftware from stores along Main Street. Nothing stood out as a specific target.

Casey Woodfield had a hoodie with a logo that matched the description given by Thomas and appeared to be the same one captured on the security cameras. It wasn't something that Casey denied, nor did he need to. It was a common piece of clothing that every member of the Lake Pines Marina maintenance crew owned.

Erin Meloni, the manager at the Lake Pines Marina, agreed to meet Josh at the office near the dock when he called to ask about the records for the staff. By the time Josh arrived, Erin had printed a list of staff going back fifteen years and had them organized, stapled, and laying on her desk.

"I went back to when we first purchased the sweatshirt hoodies for our maintenance staff." Erin pointed to a pile in the middle of the desk. "That's the year that Casey worked for us."

Josh reached for the stapled package and flipped through the list of names which included the addresses and phone numbers of each staff member.

"This is great, Erin," Josh fanned through the pages and stopped when he found Casey Woodfield's name on the last page. "What was Casey like as an employee? Were there any issues?"

"Where do I start?" Erin answered with an added eye roll.

"How about with any instances of theft while he worked for you?"

"Nothing like that," Erin said. "He was frequently late for work and I caught him altering his timesheets."

That wasn't the best way to get recognized as a good employee, but it also was a far cry from being a criminal.

"How long did Casey work for you?"

"Just the one summer," Erin said. "I was glad when his contract ended in August. When it came time to offer the staff positions for the following year, I just told him that we were going to work with reduced staff. Even though I didn't want him back, I just didn't need the grief."

Josh stacked the stapled packages and tucked them in the envelope Erin handed him.

"Most of the phone numbers and addresses will be out of date, but you probably already know that," Erin said. "I hope this helps."

"Besides the employees on this list, was there anyone else who would've received one of the hoodies?"

Erin shook her head. "To be honest, Josh, they could be anywhere. Clothes get donated to thrift stores when people clean out their closets or move, girlfriends take them, they get left in the bottom of boats, you name it. We've purchased almost three hundred over the years. Casey is just one of the many people who received one."

Josh thanked Erin and left with the pile of names. As helpful as it was to have the information, Josh knew that it would only support Casey's claim that several people had the same hoodie. In fact, it was useless evidence.

Josh's gut instinct told him that Casey was guilty of the robberies as well as the attack on Thomas. But before Josh could arrest him, he'd have to find a piece of evidence that could connect Casey Woodfield to the thefts.

CHAPTER 38

Simon was deep in thought when Josh knocked on the window of his office door. Simon waved him in as he closed the file folder in the center of his desk.

"How's your investigation going?" Simon asked.

"If I'm going to use the black hoodie as evidence, then I've narrowed the suspect list down to ninety-two that still live in Lake Pines. Not counting anyone that may have ended up with a sweatshirt that didn't work for the Lake Pines Marina."

"So, you're worse off than before?"

"Not necessarily," Josh said. "Thomas remembered a boat being parked at his office dock."

"Correct me if I'm wrong, but isn't that dock used by several people in Lake Pines?"

"Normally, yes. But Thomas said since the repair began on the muskie statue, the trail has been closed."

"Was he able to give you a description of the boat?"

"White with two blue stripes and a black engine," Josh said, realizing it was a poor description. "In Thomas' defense, he didn't know he'd need to describe the boat."

"What time was Thomas attacked?"

"Around eight. Why?"

"The float planes land in that same bay. When the new flight regulations came into effect, the insurance companies insisted that each commercial flight in or out of Lake Pines is required to have an action cam mounted in the cabin. It's like a dash cam on a car." Simon reached for the journal on the corner of his desk and opened it to the page containing the main number for the Lake Pines flight control center and copied the number onto a piece of paper and handed it to Josh. "Give them a call and see if there were any flights that landed just before Thomas was attacked, and if so, which planes landed. If you're lucky, you'll be able to get an image of the boat that was docked on the shoreline."

Josh took the paper from Simon's outstretched hand, "Thanks. Have you had any luck in finding the murder weapon on Storm Island?"

"Kevin just got back, and he wasn't able to find anything. Not that I'm surprised. The killer could have thrown the weapon in the bay or driven away with it. The best we can do is hope that Kerry or her assistant can narrow down the type of wood that he was killed with."

"Did Kerry finally decide to take that leave of absence?"

"No, but Peter sent an assistant anyway," Simon said.

"I'm sure that'll be awkward the next time Kerry and Peter speak."

Simon let a momentary smile cross his face as he imagined Kerry going toe-to-toe with Peter, both on the issue of her assistant and her temporary office space.

"Is there anything I can do to help you with the Lalonde investigation after I check on the flight schedule?" Josh asked, knowing that everyone in the station was tight on time with the reduced staff and no reduction in workload.

"I'm hoping to track down anyone else who could've been on Storm Island the day Michel Lalonde was killed. Both Hugo Lawson and Noah Irwin recall seeing someone else nearby. Hugo said he saw the victim on his dock, speaking with a woman in a red coat when he drove past his island. Noah's description is a little vaguer. He only remembers seeing someone standing at the top of the stairs. He couldn't give me a description since whoever it was, was standing in the shadows."

"Sounds ominous." Josh stood and walked toward the door. He paused and then, after a few seconds he asked Simon, "Have you ever believed someone was guilty of a crime, even though there wasn't any solid evidence?"

"Many times. It's called gut instinct, and it's what makes us good cops and guides us toward the right suspects." Simon said. "You're talking about Casey Woodfield, aren't you?"

Josh nodded.

"Keep at it. Eventually, a piece of evidence will turn up."

Josh hoped so. He just wasn't sure how long he could wait for that to happen.

CHAPTER 39

With the grainy image of the suspect leaving the pharmacy on the night of the robbery, and Thomas' faint memory of the patch on the black hoodie, Josh needed to focus on the boat that was docked near the construction site.

Brendan Jacks was the information officer working at the Lake Pines flight control center and the only person responsible for scheduling flights in or out of Lake Pines.

Over two hundred flights a week landed in Lake Pines Bay during the summer, with a spike in traffic from the middle of July through to the end of August. International fishing camps and resorts drew tourists from around the world, but mostly from the United States.

In fact, eighty percent of the flight traffic in the area came from American tourists. Many visitors were now shuttled from the airport in Winnipeg or drove across Canada when they arrived for their summer vacation at the lake.

"We had three flights land between seven-thirty and eight-thirty on the day you asked about," Brendan handed Josh a sheet with the names and contact information for the pilots in question.

"And every plane would have cameras recording their flights?"

"They're supposed to," Brendan shrugged his shoulders. "Some pilots double up their load with passengers who pay cash to hitch a ride or they offer to make deliveries and they're carrying extra boxes."

"Doesn't the customs patrol catch them?"

"They're not doing anything illegal. Passengers still pass through the customs office and the boxes are mostly orders made by local shops that want to avoid the high price of shipping. The pilots document everything when they land. It's only a problem for the pilots when they make an insurance claim, or if there's an accident or a random screening of the operational gear."

Josh thanked Brendan and left with the names of the three pilots, calling the first one on the list when he reached his car. Reese Caine picked up the phone on the first ring and from the sound of lapping waves in the background, Josh figured he was standing on the edge of a dock.

Josh introduced himself and briefly explained how he received his name and what he was hoping to find.

"My camera is working every time I crank that engine up," Reese laughed. "The last thing I need is my premiums going up or my policy being canceled because I'm not recording my flight. It's a crazy policy but those insurance companies are always looking for a way to get out of paying a claim."

"How long do you hang onto those recordings Mr. Caine?"

"Call me Reese, everyone does," he joked. "And I have every recording backed up on my computer in my office. I'll have my wife email them to you right away. I'm just getting ready to take off for Maynard Lake so I won't be back in town for a few days."

Josh recited his email address and within five minutes, Reese's wife Ida had emailed the perfectly clear recording of his flight from Walleye Lake to Lake Pines. He fast-forwarded through the entire flight until the point where Reese Caine was making his final approach into Lake Pines Bay.

The quality of the video was perfect, and Josh quickly recognized several landmarks leading up to the bay. He paused when the Cessna 208 was above Thomas' construction site. There was a clear view of the finger dock that extended from the shoreline near Thomas' office and Josh let out a sigh when he noticed it was empty.

He dialed the next number on the list. His call went directly to a voicemail with no recorded greeting and following a long beep, the line went dead. The remaining name was that of a local pilot and someone who was one of Wayne's friends.

"Hello," Drew Gordon's voice was deep, steady, and sounded exactly like Josh remembered. Drew was one of Josh's brother's oldest friends, and after Wayne died, Drew helped organize his memorial.

If Josh had realized Drew's name was on the list, he would have called him first. "Drew, it's Josh. How are you doing?"

"Josh! How the heck are you? Are you finally going to take me up on my offer of a flight tour for you and Thomas?"

"Soon, I promise. But that's not why I'm calling today," Josh explained. "This is an official call."

"Is this about those parking tickets? That sign in front of the curling rink wasn't close to the road. There was no way for anyone to know that you couldn't park there."

"No, it's not about the parking tickets. I need a copy of the action cam video from your plane from a couple of nights ago. Thomas interrupted a robbery at his office and when the burglar tried to escape, he attacked Thomas."

"Oh, geez. Is he okay?"

"Bruised and angry, but physically he's okay."

"My camera is good, but you'd have a hard time picking out a clear image of a person from the height I was flying in at."

"Could you see a boat clearly if it was at the finger dock near his office?"

"That I would definitely be able to see," Drew put the phone on speaker and turned on his computer. "Let me pull up the video now. I have everything automatically backed up to the cloud. It was two days ago you said?"

"Yeah." Josh leaned his head back and watched the boats drift through the bay as the protective tarp on the muskie statue flapped in the breeze.

"There's definitely a boat at the dock. Do you want me to send you the file?"

"Please," Josh read out his email address for the station. "How clear is the image."

"Very clear. In fact, I can see the numbers on the engine casing and one yellow rope."

CHAPTER 40

Simon approached every murder investigation in the same manner. With caution and doubt. There is always the understanding that no one clue alone may point to the actual killer. Suspects could be many, and proof vague, but someone was always guilty. The skill was in finding the killer even when there was very little evidence.

Complicated outcomes usually arose when misinterpreted clues or patterns fell outside the expected norms. Although they had yet to find the murder weapon, the crime scene at Storm Island mirrored several cases, and it didn't appear difficult to solve. Someone struck out in anger and killed Michel Lalonde. He died from a blunt force trauma to his head. Simon needed to find the murder weapon, which would hopefully lead him to a viable suspect.

Sally was attempting to track down a family member or business associate so they could inform them of Michel Lalonde's death. However, the absence of personal documentation at his cottage was making the task more difficult.

With the few people Simon spoke with, he knew there would be no shortage of individuals who had heated disagreements with the celebrity chef. But would any of them be capable of murder?

Simon left the office and headed for Lisa's café. After he ordered a sandwich and a coffee, he asked Lisa to join him at a table. He wanted to ask her a bit more about Michel Lalonde and he knew his friend would provide an honest and realistic representation of his personality.

"I still can't believe I was the one who found him on the dock," Lisa said, recalling the fateful trip out to Storm Island. "I was just hoping to get him to autograph the cookbooks. I never imagined I'd find him dead."

"There was no way you could have prepared yourself for that, Lisa."

"There was so much blood." Lisa's tears rolled across her lips as she spoke. With her head tilted down, she folded her hands over her face.

"How long did you know him?" Simon asked.

Lisa lifted her head, "I didn't. Not personally anyway. I only knew him the way most people did. Through his cookbooks and the online videos of his preparation techniques.

"He didn't know you were coming out to his island that day?"

"He didn't even know I existed," Lisa said. "His book wasn't supposed to be released until the end of the summer. When I found out he was in Lake Pines, I thought it would be a perfect opportunity to ask him to sign the books."

"How did you know he was in Lake Pines?"

"Tanya told me. Chef Lalonde hired her for the last few summers. Before his arrival, he'd email Tanya a list of food items he wanted her to get for his cottage and she'd deliver them."

"Isn't that something that chefs usually like to do themselves?"

"He avoids the limelight, and he doesn't interact with the public. It's been that way since he became famous."

"Why is he so famous, then? Don't celebrities usually build their popularity by interacting with their fans?"

"He's more of the magical mystique persona, I guess."

"Is his food that much better than the other chef's recipes? Why is he so popular?"

"He won the first national cooking contest that took place in Canada. The judges traveled across the country visiting small towns, giving a lot of chefs and bakers a chance to compete against each other."

"Did he only work in France?"

"I think so," Lisa said. "The top prize from the contest was a year at a top restaurant in Paris. He worked at several top Michelin-rated restaurants and published three cookbooks. Each one made it to the bestsellers list, which is why I wanted signed copies. That sounds bad now that he's dead."

"It gives me some information about him I didn't have before."

"Well, then you'll want to speak with Tanya. She was going to quit this summer. Even though the money was good, she only agreed to do his grunt work because she was hoping to gain some insightful knowledge of his cooking methods. But Tanya said he refused to talk with her about food. He claimed his time in Lake Pines was his time away from the craziness."

Simon ordered a second sandwich to take back to his office and asked Lisa to write Tanya's number down for him. Aside from working late, Simon needed to speak with another person who may have been one of the last people to see him alive.

CHAPTER 41

Tanya pushed the large bag of flour to the far end of the counter and dragged her forearm across her face, leaving a white trail on her cheek. With two catering jobs and her cousin's wedding, Tanya needed to work late into each evening to prepare the meals and dessert items if she was going to make a good impression.

Her recent trip to Storm Island was the last time she'd set foot near or around Chef Lalonde ever again. No matter how much he begged or pleaded, she wouldn't go back to work for him. Her sister agreed to watch Sam so Tanya could work uninterrupted as she prepared for the upcoming events.

Even with all the stress and late hours working in the kitchen, Tanya preferred to be working for herself as opposed to being an errand girl for Chef Lalonde. No matter how good he was.

Simon walked into her small kitchen, catching Tanya off guard, and she almost dropped the tray of pastry cut-outs she was carrying across the room.

"You scared me, Simon!" Tanya lightly chastised her old friend.

"Sorry, Tanya. David let me in. He said you were working away back here getting ready for a few events."

Tanya glanced around the messy, but surprisingly organized kitchen. When it became clear Tanya was intent on running her own catering business, her husband renovated the detached garage, creating a commercial-grade kitchen using the magazine images she had pasted to the corkboard in her office.

David unveiled the bright, airy workspace as their young son held up a sign with the words Tanya's Bakery painted in block letters. That was the moment that she knew she had to succeed. With her husband and son's complete support, Tanya knew she couldn't fail.

"Hard to believe that so much good food can come from this mess," Tanya joked.

"Oliver is the only one in our house who can seem to create meals without the mess, so I'll be the last person to judge a chaotic kitchen."

"What can I do for you?"

"I'm here to talk with you about Michel Lalonde. Someone murdered him."

Tanya placed the tray on the table, wiped her hands on her apron, and invited Simon to sit next to the window. "Oh, geez. I had no idea."

"Lisa said Michel Lalonde hired you to do some shopping for him every year that he came to Lake Pines."

"Every year since he bought the cottage on Storm Island. He had some strange idea that there would be lines of people clamoring to see him. He was a very private man."

"How did he find you?"

"He didn't, his agent did. Her name is Camille Scott. She reached out to a few caterers in town, and I was the lucky one who said yes."

Simon wrote Camille's name down and would start searching for a next of kin by calling her.

"How much interaction did you have with him while he was in town?"

"Not much. In fact, he was pretty specific that I park inside the boathouse, stock the groceries in the fridge and on the shelves and then leave. I was planning on quitting at the end of this summer, but I guess that won't be necessary now."

"No, I guess it won't," Simon said. "Do you remember what time you delivered the food to the island?"

"I arrived sometime after twelve, but that's about as close as I can pinpoint it for you. I did a lot of running around before and after, and I didn't get home until close to five that night."

"Did you see him when you were on the island?"

"No. But as I was leaving, I ran into someone as I was getting ready to jump into my boat. I hate to admit it but I was trying to avoid him."

"Was he that difficult to deal with?"

"You have no idea."

"Who did you run into on the dock?"

"I don't know who it was, but when she realized I wasn't Chef Lalonde, she turned around, rushed back up the stairs, and ran toward the cottage."

"She?"

"Yeah, and she was mad about something. There was actually a small part of me that wanted to hang around and hear what she had to say to him. After so many years of being yelled at by him, it would have been a pleasant change to watch him be on the receiving end of some criticism."

"Can you describe her?"

"She was about my height, with long black hair pulled back in a ponytail. But the thing I remember most about her was that her eyes were almost black."

"Oh, and one more thing," Tanya added.

Simon lifted his head as he finished writing the description in his notebook.

"She was wearing a bright red raincoat."

CHAPTER 42

Murray Lowe had been housebound for most of the last six months. Barrelling down the black diamond run at Heavenly Mountain while trying to keep up with his younger brother wasn't the best decision Murray made in his life. Ken was an avid skier turned full-time instructor, spending the last three years at the Lake Tahoe resort. Murray, on the other hand, spent his days behind a desk and hadn't skied since he was sixteen.

The experience gave Ken bragging rights when he reached the bottom of the hill first and landed Murray in a hospital bed with two broken legs.

After returning home, Murray spent most evenings enjoying the sunset from the expansive back deck of his childhood home. Built on the top of a hill, Murray welcomed the sunrise from the kitchen and enjoyed the sunset's orange glow from his living room.

The warmer weather gave Murray the option to spend some of his time on the back deck that extended off the living room.

At the base of the hill and across the road, the wind rolled over the forest and the sound lulled him into a contented sleep. As the setting sun warmed his face, he slowly dozed off. The early morning clouds brought short bursts of rain, but when Murray rolled his wheelchair out onto the deck, the moisture had almost evaporated from the railings, and a large robin bounced along its perch.

It was difficult to judge how long he had been asleep when a loud crash echoed from his neighbor's house and jolted him awake.

With his heart pounding in his chest, he straightened up in his chair, trying to figure out what had caused the noise. For a moment, he sat there, listening intently, but there was only silence in the darkness.

Then, he heard it again - a scraping sound coming from somewhere near the back of Felicity's house. Murray's mind raced with possibilities, and he felt a sense of unease wash over him. She had been the target of protests in the past, but no one ever approached her house. He swung his chair around and rolled inside the house, bouncing over the metal step of the sliding door.

As he made his way to the table, his heart beat faster and faster. He reached for his phone and unlocked it with his fingerprint and pressed the phone icon.

He peered through the window, his eyes scanning the darkness in Felicity's yard. That's when he saw it - a shadowy figure moving furtively across the lawn. Murray's breath caught in his throat, and he felt a chill run down his spine. He knew he had to act fast. With shaking hands, he dialed 911, hoping that the police would arrive in time to catch whoever was outside before the thief could hurt anyone else.

CHAPTER 43

Felicity's eyes flew open, startled awake by a loud noise. For a moment, she lay there in confusion, her heart racing as she tried to figure out what had woken her up.

Miranda and Martin had refused to leave Felicity to deal with the press and protestors and had been following her every day since the committee agreed to the statue's repairs.

Most days, Felicity was more exhausted from dealing with the twins than she was with Benji Young and his marauding band of protestors. After an early dinner and a long hot bath, Felicity crawled into bed when the sun was just setting below the tops of the forest trees.

Disoriented by the dark, Felicity groped the surface of her nightstand, searching for her phone. Just as her fingers felt the cool glass screen, there was another sound, and she knocked it onto the floor.

Then, she heard it again - a sharp, sudden bang that seemed to come from somewhere in the yard. Her muscles tensed as a wave of fear washed over her.

She sat up slowly, her eyes scanning the room in the darkness. She strained to hear any other sounds, but there was only silence.

She shook her head, trying to clear the fog of sleep from her mind. That's when she heard footsteps outside her window. Her breath caught in her throat as the footsteps grew louder and the intruder moved closer.

Felicity wanted to scream, to call out for help, but she was too afraid to make a sound. The footsteps stopped, and for a moment, there was only silence. Then, slowly, the back door creaked open, and the figure disappeared.

Felicity rolled out of bed and crawled along the floor until she found her phone.

She listened as the intruder moved through the kitchen, opening and closing drawers in search of valuables.

Clutching her phone, Felicity dashed for the closet and pulled the door closed. She crouched below a pile of towels and dialed the emergency number as she whispered into the phone.

With an astonishingly quick response, a siren wailed as it neared her home. The flashing lights of the police car rolled along the crack under the closet door and Felicity felt a wave of relief wash over her. For what felt like an eternity, she crouched in her closet, listening to the intruder move through her house. His footsteps echoed through each room as he rooted through drawers and closets, getting nearer to where she hid.

She had been paralyzed with fear, unsure of what to do or where to go. But now, seeing the police car approaching, she felt a glimmer of hope. She heard Josh's voice calling out to the intruder to surrender, and then the sound of footsteps rushing across her lawn and then eventually bursting into her house.

It was like a weight had been lifted from her chest. She clung to the hope that the police would catch the intruder and that they could put an end to the nightmare that plagued Lake Pines.

CHAPTER 44

Felicity pulled the blanket around her shoulders as she spoke with Josh. Flanked by Miranda and Martin, Josh was unsure where to direct his questions. The twins arrived shortly after the patrol car rushed into the house. Following Felicity's 911 call, she called the two junior councilors, who Josh learned, were Felicity's primary source of support.

Red spray paint marked the walls in Felicity's kitchen and living room. Images of fish, with a large diagonal line over them, covered every wall. The pungent chemical smell was overpowering the enclosed space.

Drips of paint streaked the white walls and boot marks stained the carpet, marking the path from the back door, through the kitchen, and up the stairs.

"I still can't believe Benji did this," Felicity shook her head.

"Desperation can push people to break the law," Miranda said.

"If they think there's no other choice," Martin added.

Josh agreed.

"Benji is on his way to the station now. We'll be charging him for trespassing and destruction of property. But for what it's worth, I don't think he came here to hurt you."

Felicity pulled the blanket around her shoulders, "No. I don't think so either."

"So, Benji Young is not the robber?" Miranda asked.

"The crime still rages on?" Martin asked.

"I'm afraid so," Josh said and then turned to Felicity. "Do you have somewhere to stay tonight? The forensic team will want to spend some time here gathering evidence to use in court."

"Miranda and Martin invited me to stay with them," Felicity smiled.

Josh offered to follow them home if it made them feel safer. "I think we'll be fine. But, as odd as it sounds, can you go easy on Benji?"

Miranda and Martin snapped their heads in unison, turning in shock as they looked at Felicity.

"He's passionate about this town, just like I am. Maybe he can do some volunteer work instead of going to jail."

"We'll see what we can do. In the meantime, try to have a good sleep tonight."

Josh waited until Felicity packed a bag and left with Miranda and Martin, impressed with Felicity's compassion. Only moments after being frightened for her life, she forgave the man that threatened her safety. It was at times like this that Josh was proud to live in Lake Pines.

CHAPTER 45

Trisha arrived at the hospital before Kerry or Doctor Varanus. She finished reading the file for the fourth time, adding detailed notes on the side of the page. With each entry, she related her findings to a case study she practiced at school. Looking for patterns on the victim's skin that would normally go unnoticed, or slight abrasions that could point to a specific weapon.

Years spent studying, watching videos, and reading fiction and non-fiction books were all done so she could prepare herself for this job.

Michel Lalonde's bloodwork results showed no suspicious traces of poison. Not that Trisha expected to find any.

The wood slivers from his skin tissue didn't match the samples taken from the deck and the stairway. The wood was definitely a softwood species and the clean lines and sharp edge that was easily distinguishable under a microscope pointed to it having come from a manufactured piece of wood.

Her first thoughts were that it could be a piece of lumber or furniture. She made her notes on a separate piece of paper before she prepared a sample of the wood to view under a microscope.

Categorizing wood to a specific species was a skill learned over years, but Trisha had the benefit of internet search on her side. Once she had determined that it was a softwood sample, she searched images on the internet for softwood lumber and narrowed it down to either pine, fir, or spruce.

Pleased with her search, she typed up the final report, attached it to the front of the file, and headed toward Doctor Dearborne's office. Everything needed to be perfect if she was going to be taken seriously. She was top of her class and volunteered for extra practicum hours. Trisha even worked the overnight shift in the morgue to get over her fear of being around cadavers. She wanted to make a good impression because there was no way she was going to leave after everything she had been through in her life to get placed in Lake Pines. Specifically, to work with Kerry Dearborne.

Her current focus was to use her temporary position to solve an unexpected problem and Doctor Kerry Dearborne was at the root of that problem.

CHAPTER 46

Seven years ago, Michel Lalonde didn't exist. Simon double-checked the entries on the name and property search that he ran through the police database but each time the results were the same. Recalling Tanya's explanation about how the chef became popular, he searched the internet for the national cooking contest he won. As the winner, he received an internship in a Parisian restaurant working under the tutelage of a Michelin-rated chef.

He had entered the contest under the name Michel Lalonde, but before that, there was no record of anyone by that name.

Considering Michel Lalonde was a celebrity chef, there were few images of him online.

The latest online posting revealed that Michel Lalonde was opening a restaurant with Henri Badeau, a fellow Parisian chef.

Simon wrote Henri's name inside the file and searched for his social media profile. When he found Henri's page, he saw what he expected to see for Michel. With over six-thousand followers, and over nine-hundred posts, Henri Badeau was exceptionally active within the food community. His recent posts captured images of him in Italy, searching for specialty ingredients and artwork for the new restaurant.

Elusive as Michel Lalonde may be, there were no negative articles or posts surrounding his life.

Simon called Kerry, hoping to find out more specifics about the murder weapon, which his search team still couldn't locate on Storm Island. The next step was to drag the waters of Haven Bay, but the restriction on the wetlands would force him to have an officer dive into the bay.

Searching for a piece of wood on a densely treed island was about as close to a needle in a haystack as it could be.

He reached Kerry just as she was returning to her office. Kerry had asked Trisha to expand the search on the wood slivers found in the victim's wound, which, was the only lead the police had to follow in their search for a suspect.

"Trisha confirmed that the wood slivers are from a softwood species and she thinks that it's pine, fir, or spruce. We'll know more when we can have further testing done on it."

"Any guesses where it came from?"

"Our best guess is a piece of lumber or a small piece of furniture."

"There was a lumber delivery made to Storm Island, or at least one of Thomas' employees attempted to drop off some wood. Michel Lalonde insisted Noah return it all to Thomas claiming it was the wrong wood. Thomas said he took a hit on the bill because, in addition to a restocking fee, a few pieces were missing."

"Interesting."

"I'll find out what type of wood he was delivering, and in the meantime, I learned that Michel Lalonde wasn't who he said he was."

"What do you mean he wasn't who he said he was?" Kerry asked.

"There is no trace of him existing before winning that contest. And the name Michel Lalonde is extremely common in French communities. Hundreds of results pop up when you search for his name. Just no one matching his age."

Kerry recalled the oddly titled manuscript she found in his cottage.

"What evidence did the forensic team collect from his cottage?"

"Not much," Simon said. "Lisa found him on the dock and there wasn't any sign of a confrontation in his cottage so we just gathered his paperwork and his personal agenda."

"Was there something that looked like a manuscript collected?"

"Let me check the log," Simon pulled the record up on his computer screen and read out the list of items collected from Michel Lalonde's cottage. "There's an item that is described as a thick document secured with a large clip. There was also a yellow piece of paper attached to it."

"Was it titled 'The End'?"

"Yes. I thought that was a typo, but that's the comment that's typed under the entry. What do you think it means?"

"I don't know, but I think it's probably a good idea to call his agent."

CHAPTER 47

With surprising ease, Sally located the name and number of Michel Lalonde's agent from the company that published his cookbooks. It was early in the morning, and with the time difference between Lake Pines and London, he figured it was safe to call.

Camille Scott was a literary agent who, among other top clients, focused the last three years of her career promoting Chef Michel Lalonde's cookbooks. Completely invested in the chef, Camille dedicated her website's homepage to the launch of his most recent cookbook.

With the success of an early launch and topping the best-seller charts with a new restaurant on the horizon, Chef Michel Lalonde was Scott Agency's most profitable client.

All Simon could think of was how much the idea of cooking and the importance of chefs had changed since his mother worked in the lunchroom cafeteria at the local high school.

He opted for the phone number over the email. Telling someone that a friend has died is hard enough, but Simon had to explain that Michel Lalonde was murdered.

"Michel's dead?" Camille's voice quivered. Her tears sprang into loud sobs. Simon wasn't sure how much of it was for Michel's death or for losing her income.

"I'm sorry to have to tell you over the phone, but I thought you should know." Simon gave Camille a few moments to wipe her tears and blow her nose before he continued. "Normally we inform the next of kin, but there's been some difficulty with that. Do you know if there's anyone we should notify about Michel's death?"

"Only Henri. He was his business partner and friend," Camille blew her nose a second time, the sound blaring through the phone line. "Other than that, he has no family."

"No one?"

"He was an only child and his parents died when he was young," Camille said. "Didn't you read his bio?"

"No, I'm sorry," Simon mumbled. "We've been a little busy trying to figure out who murdered him."

"That was rude of me. I'm sorry, it's just such a shock to not only hear he's dead, but that someone killed him."

"When was the last time you spoke to him?"

"Just before he left France," Camille lied. "He was going to take a vacation before opening his restaurant this autumn with Henri. He recently published another cookbook, which meant he would be busy with interviews. He hated doing them, but it was part of the job if he wanted to be successful."

"Did Michel have any financial problems?" Simon asked.

"Do you know what a top chef earns?" Camille asked rhetorically. "Last year alone, he netted six figures. With the new restaurant on the horizon, he would have easily topped that. Money was the last concern for him."

"How well did you know him?"

"About as well as anyone, I guess," Camille said. "I took him on as a client soon after he won the national cooking contest. We spent a lot of hours together molding his career."

"I'm sorry to ask such a personal question, but were you romantically involved?"

"No, but I don't see how that would be relevant."

"I'm trying to form a picture of Michel's life. It'll help me narrow down who would've wanted to harm him," Simon explained. "Are you aware of anyone who would have been angry enough with him to want to kill him?"

"Most of the chefs who knew him would fit into that category, along with most of the people who worked for him."

"If he was so unlikeable, then how did he become so popular?"

"When was the last time you watched a show on the Chef Network?"

"Never."

"The most popular chefs are vile taskmasters. They're always yelling and throwing cookware in the kitchen. I think it's a persona they all strive to achieve. Strange, but it works in the ratings, and as Michel learned, it propelled his books to the top of the best-seller list."

"But is there anyone who stands out?"

"Michel had some legal trouble last year. He got too fancy with one of his recipes and instead of using the regular field mushrooms that were customary for the recipe, he used wild mushrooms he picked himself. A customer got quite ill and sued the restaurant. The owner fired him and then sued him. The legal system in France is very complex and his career would've been over if he went to prison."

"What happened?"

"Henri stepped in and made it all go away. Don't ask me how he did it, but he did. When I asked him why he risked his own career to help Michel, he claimed he saw something great in Michel's work."

"Can you reach out to Henri and let him know what happened to Michel?"

"Of course. It won't be an easy call, but he needs to know."

"One more thing. We found what looks like a manuscript in Michel's cottage. Do you know anything about it?"

"A manuscript? Like a book?" Camille asked. "The only book I'm aware of Michel writing was a cookbook, and that was just released."

"Alright, if you think of anything else, please give me a call."

"I will," Camille said and then lowered her voice to a whisper. "What will be done with Michel's body?"

"Since he had no immediate family to contact, were you aware of a Will he may have written?"

"I'll reach out to his lawyer and give him your number." Camille offered. "Could you keep me updated on your investigation? Even though Michel was a client, he was also my friend."

Simon promised to keep Camille informed of any updates on the investigation, and as he was about to ask her about Michel Lalonde's former name, Camille disconnected the call. She was gone.

CHAPTER 48

One faded lightbulb, hanging at each landing, illuminated the concrete stairs that descended three levels beyond the hospital basement. Trisha's steps echoed in the space as she rushed to reach the steel door leading to the main file storage area. She arrived early, hoping to avoid questions from administrative staff and Doctor Varanus, who was providing more attention than she was comfortable with. And so far, she moved through the hospital unnoticed.

In every eventuality of Trisha's plan, she never thought she'd be working in such tight confines and being monitored so closely. Yet, here she was, actively avoiding the one person she was trying to usurp. Kerry Dearborne.

Security in the file room was simple but highly effective. An electronic passcard unlocked the door leading to the storage room. Once inside, the guard had everyone sign a logbook.

Leaving was equally secure, and any documents or files that left the room had to be scanned and recorded.

Even if Trisha wanted to remove something from the evidence storage area, it would be impossible to do so. Luckily, her time in previous secure facilities gave her the knowledge she needed to devise an alternate plan.

Trisha walked up to the door and waved to the guard through the wire-framed glass, flashing him an excited smile and an exuberant wave.

Trisha flashed her badge too quickly for the guard to see her finger was covering Kerry's photo and then she tapped it on the security pad, releasing the lock on the thick steel door.

The guard slid the log book across the counter, "You're Doctor Dearborne's assistant, right?"

"Yeah," Trisha scribbled an illegible signature in the logbook. "Doctor Dearborne wants me to check something from one of her recent cases."

"Sure thing," the guard said. "If you need to take anything, just remember to register it with me before you leave."

"That won't be a problem," Trisha said. "She just wanted me to check a name in a file."

The guard directed Trisha to the shelves where they stored Doctor Dearborne's files and returned to his post.

Cody Jesper's file and the box she was searching for were in the same row. Working quickly, Trisha pulled the tainted sample out from under her sweater and slipped it into the box, removing the box of warfarin from the crime site and the original toxicology report. She tucked the report inside her shirt and left the security area, waving to the guard as she rushed out the door.

Several staff members were arriving just as Trisha emerged from the stairwell. She forced her breathing to a low, steady pace and greeted everyone she passed with a friendly nod and a pleasant smile. Just as she had done on her first day in the hospital.

Darkness filled the room leading to the small office that Trisha had used the day before. She suspected that Doctor Varanus would arrive shortly to view samples for his ongoing study. Had it not been for her current focus, Trisha would have found Doctor Varanus' coagulation studies intriguing.

Trisha closed the door and spread Cody Jesper's file across the desk. She took her time, ensuring that her notes were specific and carefully transcribed. When she was done, the copies were almost identical, except of course for the toxicology findings which Trisha carefully altered.

When it was time, she gathered the paperwork, and left her office, heading straight for room 24B.

Trisha hesitated for only a moment before knocking on Doctor Dearborne's door. She knew if she waited, she wouldn't have the nerve to follow through with her plan.

The door flung open and Doctor Dearborne looked surprised to see Trisha standing in the hall, clutching a file in her arms.

"I have something I wanted to run past you," Trisha held the file in her hand, lifting it slightly.

Kerry glanced down and noticed the name on the front.

"Why do you have Cody Jesper's file?"

"It was in the pile you gave me yesterday to go through. I thought you wanted me to go over it so I could learn how you conduct your autopsy reports." Trisha fidgeted with the file before stretching her arm out toward Kerry. "I found something that looks a bit odd."

Kerry took the file from Trisha's outstretched arm and opened it to the note she clipped to the inside flap. "What is it?"

"The test that was done on the box of warfarin in the victim's home."

"I know. The police found it, along with the bottle of painkillers in the couple's bathroom."

"I thought it was odd that they stored the poison in the bathroom so I looked at the report a little closer and I saw this," Trisha pointed to the page where she had placed a yellow sticky. "The contents of the box weren't warfarin. It was just baking soda."

Kerry fanned through the pages of the file, searching for the toxicology report that confirmed the poisonous contents and she couldn't find it. She had just worked on this file a few days ago and she was certain it was there.

"I don't understand," Kerry muttered and then turned away from Trisha as she read the report once more.

Trisha pulled the security pass from her pocket and dropped it into Kerry's purse when her back was turned. Returning it to the pocket she extracted it from the night before.

"Leave this with me," Kerry said, still distracted, and turned away from Trisha.

Trisha opened the door, "I'll see if Doctor Varanus needs any help with his samples."

Kerry waved her hand in the air and muttered something resembling an acknowledgment as Trisha stepped into the hall. She felt uneasy as she read the report. Sodium bicarbonate. How could she have missed it?

An unfamiliar chill ran through her. It was different from the expected self-blame about missing a fact or clue in a case. This was more visceral. She tried to ignore it but it instantly pushed her back to the case that had been at the forefront of her mind since receiving the cryptic note.

She had been putting off submitting the requisition for the case files for the fifteen-year-old murder investigation hoping that the necessity to reach back into her past would fade. Instead, the need was stronger. She had to revisit the old file.

Kerry filled out the required fields, along with the address of the hospital where she wanted the box delivered, and pressed send.

She grabbed the Jesper file, pulled her security pass from her purse, and headed for the file storage one floor below. Hoping her mistake hadn't caused an innocent woman's arrest.

CHAPTER 49

Simon stared at the wall, his eyes fixed on the chart, wondering how so many visitors could arrive at Storm Island without anyone seeing the killer leave.

Sally walked into his office and left a file on his desk, and then paused when she realized he was staring at the wall.

"Are you feeling stuck with this investigation?"

"I just don't see how no one saw anything in the middle of the afternoon."

"Did you speak with Mrs. McLean? She lives directly across the bay."

"Eagle Eye McLean?"

"The one and only."

"No, but I'll head over there right now."

With one hand clutching his keys and the other reaching for his phone, Simon rushed out the door. If his former teacher was on her dock or porch the day Michel Lalonde was murdered, she definitely would have something to share.

Simon pulled his boat up to the dock just as Mary McLean peered out her window. After he secured his boat, he walked up the steps and greeted her with a smile.

Mary stood at the door for a moment and once she recognized Simon, she invited him inside. She sat down in a large chair and flashed Simon a warm smile. Simon had always been one of her favorite students, and she was one of his favorite teachers.

Once she learned about the chef's murder, she assumed that someone from the police station would be out to speak with her. It surprised her they hadn't arrived sooner.

After a few introductory pleasantries, Simon asked Mary what, if anything, she remembered about the afternoon Michel Lalonde was murdered.

As she spoke, Simon wondered why someone hadn't thought to question the person living across the bay from the murder victim earlier.

Mary gave a detailed statement of what she saw when she was reading on her porch. She remembered seeing a blur of red and beige as Michel struggled with someone at the top of the stairs and then there was the boat speeding away from the island. She also told Simon that she heard one word clearly from across the bay.

"I heard him yell the name Paul."

Simon wrote the name in his notebook, knowing better than to ask his former teacher if she was sure about what she heard. It was one word, tucked away in Mary McLean's memory, but it was probably the name of the killer. Simon knew it was the biggest break they had in their murder investigation.

After a brief visit and a warm chat, Simon left the island and returned to the station with the name of a suspect. Now, he had to figure out how to find him.

Mary waved as she watched as Simon's boat pulled away from the dock. His two hundred and twenty-five horsepower engine sent a cascade of waves over the reeds along the shoreline.

Three ducks sprang into the air, their wings flapping frantically. With a harshness of quacks and honks, they lifted off the surface of the water and soared into the air, shattering the peaceful bay.

Mary McLean didn't like the chef, in fact, she hated him. Yet, the questions surrounding his murder gave her a feeling that a sense of death was taking over the tranquil bay.

CHAPTER 50

Except for some mild fading, the fifteen-year-old box was exactly as Kerry remembered. A red and white security label, affixed to the lid, displayed her signature next to three other staff members who worked on Vivienne Strong's murder investigation.

The murder of the young mother shook the rural town just north of Montreal. They were the unprovoked actions of an unstable man. Paul Buchanan was Vivienne's co-worker and fit every stereotype for an aggressive abuser. His own wife fled in the middle of the night, escaping to the protection of her parent's home shortly before Vivienne's murder.

Vivienne, a quiet woman, and a recent immigrant to Canada, was an assistant at the small engineering firm. The company worked on the structural upgrades for the province's hydro dams but had entertained overseas corporate ventures where their expertise with water power plants could prove extremely profitable. Paul led the global expansion venture, and he promoted Vivienne to his team.

Excited at the opportunity to work in the field she spent several years studying for, Vivienne jumped at the opportunity. Excitement quickly turned to fear when Paul became obsessed with her. Human Resources eventually transferred her to a different department. She refused to file an official harassment complaint against Paul, not wanting to risk the job she worked so hard to get.

Instead, she silently endured the late-night calls, confrontations in the lunchrooms, and glares from his desk. However, on one fateful night, she fought against Paul's advances during a corporate holiday party. Fueled by rage, Paul followed Vivienne out to her car and when he couldn't convince her to return to his room, he killed her. Hitting her with a nearby rock.

Police found the killer's DNA on the victim's body. Skin samples were collected, labeled, and filed by the young intern, Kerry Dearborne.

The forensic team collected DNA samples from every staff member at the company party. Skin samples collected from under Vivienne's nails matched the samples the police had collected from Paul Buchanan.

Everyone thought the case was airtight. Paul Buchanan was arrested and charged with first-degree murder. However, his lawyer questioned the chain of custody concerning the DNA samples. Paul's lawyer argued that there was a moment when the samples were left unattended and someone could have placed his client's skin tissue in the tube. The judge had no choice but to dismiss the key piece of evidence in Vivienne Strong's murder investigation.

Because of Kerry's clerical error, a killer was going to walk free.

Images of Vivienne's family clouded Kerry's judgment, and she brushed a sample of Paul Buchanan's DNA residue across the base of the rock. When the prosecution admitted the secondary piece of evidence into court, they convicted Paul Buchanan of the lesser charge of second-degree murder.

Kerry revisited the painful memories of the investigation and recalled Jean's upset when she admitted what she had done. There was no mistaking Paul Buchanan's guilt. However, the legalities surrounding the chain of custody meant he would walk away from any charges.

Jean agreed to conceal Kerry's illegal actions under one condition. That she would continue to work as his assistant so he could ensure she'd learn how to temper her drive for justice within the confines of the legal system.

And with her agreement, they both put their jobs and freedoms on the line when they submitted the rock with Paul Buchanan's DNA residue into evidence.

She removed the crime scene photos, the witness statements, and the final report describing the cause of death. Reading each one with the same caution that she viewed a new case file. They were all as Kerry had remembered them. Everything was the same, except for one thing. The rock was missing.

Her hand clamped over her mouth, stifling the cry that came from deep within her gut. The pain grew quickly, clawing deep within her as she imagined her entire world collapsing around her. A blinding pain seared through her skull, and she replayed the events from fifteen years earlier at a dizzying pace.

Steadying her hand, she pushed the key into the lock, releasing the cabinet drawer. She lifted the box out, placed it on her desk, and folded open the flaps. The gray slate rock rested in the center of the crumpled newsprint. Both were from fifteen years ago and one should have been inside the evidence box on her desk.

There was no mistaking the intention of the note and the delivery of the rock. Someone was aware of what she did.

Kerry clutched her phone so tightly that her hand grew numb. She could no longer give in to the hesitation she felt over the last few days when dialing Jean's number. Ignoring what happened wouldn't change anything. She needed to tell Simon, he was her partner in everything important in life, and keeping this information from him wasn't fair. Especially since it would directly affect the lives of their entire family.

But there was one call she needed to make before she could speak with Simon. It was a call she was putting off and avoiding. This time, the call couldn't wait. She needed to speak with Jean and figure out what they should do next.

CHAPTER 51

Noah sat in the lobby, avoiding eye contact with the police officers at their desks, as he waited for Simon to arrive. Fighting for recognition as an honest, hard worker in Lake Pines was an uphill battle whenever anyone learned about his past. He performed each job with a focus that exceeded his co-workers. He never complained or argued with a client. One thing Noah learned was that the assumption of guilt was never far away and he always needed to be on his best behavior.

Although Michel Lalonde hadn't been aware of his record, the man's status and wealth put Noah on edge. Even Thomas agreed the cottage was becoming more work than it was worth. Primarily because of the man they had to deal with.

The latest accusation of arriving with the wrong lumber delivery was one of his many complaints. Noah was confident that Thomas wouldn't hold him responsible. However, after the police questioned Noah about the day the chef died, he became concerned about their past interaction.

After a fitful night's sleep, Noah drove to the station. He wanted to tell Constable Phillips the one piece of information he left out of his statement. Mostly, the comment made by Michel Lalonde was irrelevant. But the police may view the comment made by a man who was murdered as relevant in hindsight.

Several officers arrived at the station, offering only a minor glance in Noah's direction. Although he wasn't guilty of a crime, Noah still had difficulty relaxing in a police station.

"Relax, Noah," Sally whispered. He was sitting directly across from the receptionist's desk which was next to the front door. Noah wanted to speak with Constable Phillips the moment he arrived. "Your bouncing leg is shaking the entire floor," Sally joked.

Noah nodded and offered his best version of a relaxed smile just as Simon walked through the door.

Simon walked over to Noah as soon as he saw him. "Is everything alright?"

Noah jumped up, pushing his chair against the wall with a noise that reverberated through the station. Several officers looked in their direction, but when they realized it was just Noah's chair and not an argument, they returned their focus to what they were doing. Sally tried, but failed to suppress a smile and then offered to get them both a coffee as Simon guided Noah to his office.

"No, I'm good. I need to get to work," Noah said. "I wanted to let you know I remembered something Mr. Lalonde said just before I left the island."

Simon folded his arms and listened patiently as Noah calmed his nerves, speaking slowly as he explained his visit to Storm Island on the fateful afternoon when Michel Lalonde was murdered.

"What did you remember, Noah?"

"After Mr. Lalonde stopped me from unloading the lumber, he rushed me back into my boat. Almost like he was trying to get rid of me, and not just because he thought there was a screw-up with the lumber order. He said he was waiting for a friend to arrive."

"Are you sure he said a friend was arriving?" Simon asked.

Noah nodded. "I didn't think anything of it at the time, because to be honest with you, I just wanted to get out of there. I didn't want to give him any reason to call Thomas and complain about me."

"I understand," Simon said. "I'm just curious because you said you think you saw someone standing in the shadows at the top of the stairs. Which would mean there was someone else he was expecting."

"I guess," Noah shrugged. "That's for you guys to figure out, but I wanted to make sure that you had all the information. I don't want you to think I was holding anything back."

"Why would I have thought that?" Simon asked.

"I guess I'm just gun-shy when it comes to the police."

"Don't worry, Noah," Simon said. "Thomas explained your situation. If you're honest with us about everything that happened that day, then there won't be a problem."

Noah nodded his head, offered an awkward smile to Sally, and left the station, hoping to never step foot inside again.

CHAPTER 52

The young assistant had done nothing to raise his suspicion, yet Doctor Varanus watched every move she made from the far end of the room. The expansive window in the small room that Kerry stashed her in was visible from where he worked. Occasionally, he glanced up to find Trisha looking back at him as if to monitor what he was doing and when he'd be leaving. It was the same way his teenagers looked at him when he walked through the living room when they were on their phones.

He honed his subversive glares and a unique watching-but-not-watching stare. Several times he noticed Trisha pulling extra files and paper from the lower drawer in the desk. It was an anomaly for someone with Kerry's workload to have an assistant at all, but for her to be granted one when she barely had enough room for herself made Doctor Varanus wonder if Kerry's position was being reviewed.

A large pharmaceutical company provided the funding for his research. However, that was due to run out in a year. At that point, he would be in the same position that many of the hospital staff were in and the tight budget could signal an end to his tenure in Lake Pines.

Everyone in the hospital felt the pressure of the tight provincial budget, and he knew he wasn't too far away from being cut. Which is why it was odd that Kerry received an assistant.

Shortly before Trisha's arrival, a rare but congenial conversation between him and Kerry revealed that her workload had lightened enough that she could focus on figuring out a plan for her new office. The hospital basement, they both agreed, wasn't an ideal work environment for two highly scheduled individuals to share.

Trisha was friendly and keen to learn everything she could about Kerry's role as coroner. Sal thought maybe a little too keen.

Whenever he glanced over at Trisha, she was feverishly reading documents or sorting through files. But it was the moment Kerry entered the main room and Trisha swiped the documents from the top of her desk into a drawer that he became suspicious.

He wasn't enthusiastic about sharing a workspace or lab area with Kerry, but he was less pleased about the province having potentially sent someone to spy on her.

What, or who, would be next? It occurred to Sal that his grant funding would end soon and the hospital would be eager to relieve themselves of his six-figure salary. He desperately wanted to know what Trisha was concealing inside the desk in case she was compiling information on both him and Kerry.

Sal walked toward Trisha, smiling as he neared the small room. She closed the folder containing the pages she was reading and rested her folded hands on the pile.

"Trisha, I wonder if you could do me a favor?" Without waiting for her response, Sal continued as he asked her to collect a completed test result and the container of samples from the third-floor office. "The lab delivered them to the administration office in error, and I can't leave what I'm working on now."

"I can watch your lab," Trisha offered.

Sal glanced back to the microscope he had been standing near all morning and then shook his head. "Until I'm comfortable with your work, I'd rather not. I'm sure you understand."

The look on Trisha's face revealed anything but understanding. She pushed back her chair and through her clenched jaw, she muttered, "Of course. I'll be right back."

Sal returned to the microscope and waited until Trisha left the room and her loud measured steps faded, and then completely silenced as she entered the staircase.

He rushed to her office and yanked the desk drawers, finding each one locked. He dragged his hand along the edge of the desk as he searched for a spare key just as her phone rang from inside a locked drawer. Flinching at the sound, Sal's arm flew sideways as he jumped back, sending the file folder and the pages inside, flying to the floor.

For someone of Sal's poor athletic status, the jolt quickened his breathing, and a rising heat wrapped around his neck, coating his forehead with perspiration.

Without ensuring which pages he was grabbing, Sal scooped up the errant sheets of paper and shoved them into the folder.

The hollow tapping of Trisha's heeled shoes echoed in the hall as she neared the doors to the main room. Sal tapped the edges of the pages sticking out from the folder and placed them on the table, hoping Trisha hadn't put them in any specific order. And then before she pushed through the doors, he rushed out of the small room and was leaning over his examination table when she burst through the doors.

She handed him the container and the printed results she retrieved from the third-floor administration office. He spun around and leaned his face on the eyepiece of the microscope, shielding his flushed face and forcing his rapid breathing to a halt.

"Is there anything else you need help with?" Trisha asked.

Sal raised his arm and brushed the air with his hand, signaling that he wanted to be left alone. Trisha rolled her eyes and returned to her desk, suddenly understanding why Kerry was often short and abrupt when she spoke with Doctor Varanus. After all, she wasn't here to make friends. She came to Lake Pines with a specific goal in mind and she couldn't lose sight of what that was.

Sal adjusted the dial on the microscope just as an alert signaled a new email on his computer. As he read the message, Sal furrowed his brow, trying to make sense of the unfamiliar report. The reference to the fingerprint database results confused him, but only momentarily. His fists clenched around the edge of his keyboard as he read the added note at the bottom of the submission.

Why would Kerry have submitted prints under his personal security code and not her own?

He wondered how he could've been so blind to trust her, and even more, he wondered what Kerry was hiding.

CHAPTER 53

With the printout clutched in his hand, Sal stormed out of the examination room and down the hall to Kerry's office. He didn't wait for a response to his knock and burst into the room, dropping the printout on Kerry's desk.

"Do you want to tell me what this is about?" Sal asked.

Kerry lifted the crinkled sheet and her confusion turned to shame when she realized it was the report on the fingerprint search. "I can explain."

"Good, because I have to justify why I submitted a fingerprint search. They returned the request because there was no file number added to the form."

Kerry realized the lab didn't run the prints through the database, and she was still clueless about the identity of the person who sent the note. Kerry closed the door to her office and tried her best to explain the bizarre situation she found herself in the last few days. The truth would be out soon. She may as well tell Sal at least about the furtive note that was slipped under her door.

Sal listened patiently, and as he did, Kerry saw him in a new light. He leaned forward, nodding attentively as Kerry explained. Patiently, he listened, without interrupting or judging, offering comfort and support with a sympathetic ear.

When Kerry finished her explanation, Sal closed his eyes, took a deep breath, and without prompting or coaxing, he asked, "What can I do to help?"

CHAPTER 54

After Sal left her office, Kerry found it impossible not to think about the note or the box that she locked inside the cabinet next to her desk.

Knowing her rash decision was coming back to haunt her, made it impossible to focus. Trisha discovering an error in the Jesper examination made Kerry doubt herself and question her competence.

Why did she always act so rashly?

When Sal offered his help, Kerry thanked him and told him she'd keep his offer in mind. Realistically, she wasn't sure what he could do. He suggested she take some time before speaking with anyone else. Reflective time, he called it, and Kerry took his advice.

Her father's birthday was fast approaching, so Kerry thought she'd use the afternoon to distract herself with a shopping trip to his favorite outdoor store. His recent fishing trip with Simon renewed his love of camping, and Oliver promised to take Dominique on an overnight camping trip this summer.

Rutger's Outerwear was a small independently owned outfitter that specialized in outdoor gear. From skiing to canoeing, their specialty brands had become a favorite in town.

Janus Rutger opened his store in a small refurbished bank that stood apart from the stores on Main Street. Built in 1890, the rough-hewn bricks and long angular windows lent a historical charm to the town's oldest street.

Kerry opened the thick oak door and stepped inside. Towers of electrical scanners flanked the entrance, and they emitted a beeping sound when Kerry walked between them.

"Sorry, Kerry," Janus apologized as he watched the store floor from behind the counter. "I had the security company adjust those to the most sensitive setting because of all the thefts. Now it beeps whenever anyone walks near them."

"That's alright, Janus," Kerry smiled. "You need to protect yourself."

It was a feeling Janus shared with many of the shop owners and residents of the small town. An overwhelming sensation of violation had washed over the town. Neighbors and friends experienced an unsettling sense of danger. As if it lurked around every corner. Ever since the thief attacked Thomas, the worry shifted from just being robbed to being attacked.

"I sure hope that the police find whoever is responsible," Janus walked around the counter and shook Kerry's hand. Something Janus did with every customer who walked into his store. "I've been closing early because I don't want to take any chances and I've ramped up my security system. As you found out." Janus pointed to the gray plastic towers flanking the front entrance. He shook his head and then changed the subject. "What can I help you find?"

"A birthday gift for my dad. Do you have any ideas?"

Janus raised his hand and smiled, "Oliver was in here last week looking at a fleece and some hiking shorts. Do you want to see them?"

"No need," Kerry said. "Ring them up. If he liked them, then they'll be perfect." Kerry selected a pair of socks, a pale blue cotton shirt, and a lightweight hat, and added them to the pile.

"Do you want me to wrap these for you?" Janus asked as he carefully folded them on the glass countertop next to the register.

"No, Dominique and I will wrap them." Kerry slipped her credit card out of her wallet and handed it to Janus. "How has business been this summer?"

"Pretty good," Janus smiled as he scanned each item and slipped them into a large paper bag. "That famous chef came in here and bought almost a thousand dollars of outdoor gear. He said he was going to come back and get a kayak for his cottage, but I guess that won't be happening. Sad about what happened to him."

"You're one of the few people who saw him then," Kerry said, recalling Lisa's claim that he avoided everyone when he came to Lake Pines. "It sounds like he was quite the recluse when he came to his cottage."

"He was very friendly to me, but I got the feeling that he was less than pleased to be speaking with the woman who followed him into the store."

Kerry perked up, "Who was that?"

Janus shrugged, "I don't know. I had never seen her before. After she rushed out of the store, he tried to act as if nothing happened, but I could tell their conversation upset him."

"Would you be able to describe her to a sketch artist at the station?" Kerry asked. "Simon has been trying to find anyone who may have seen him on the day he died."

"Yeah, I probably could. She was quite pretty. Tall, long black hair pulled back in a messy ponytail and she was wearing a bright red raincoat."

"Sounds like she really stuck out in your mind."

"I think it was her eyes," Janus explained. "They were almost black. Something like that is kind of hard to forget." Janus handed the bag to Kerry and walked her to the door. "I'll give Simon a call and go by the station on my way home tonight."

Kerry thanked Janus and left his store feeling like she helped move the investigation along a little for Simon.

As Kerry walked back to her office, she played out the scenarios in her mind. She knew the most difficult sentence would be the first one. But no matter how many ways she imagined telling Simon what she had done, they all brought a knot to her stomach.

With one hand in her pocket and the other holding her phone, Kerry walked briskly down the street, her eyes darting between the screen and path as she fumbled to dial Simon's number.

Before she was finished dialing, her phone rang and she quickly answered it with a casual greeting, before realizing it was Michel Lalonde's agent.

Kerry spoke, while skillfully dodging pedestrians on the path. She offered her condolences and filled Camille in on the latest breakthrough in the investigation.

"Good," Camille said. "I'll be glad to put this entire mess behind us. That's why I was calling. I received Michel's Will from his lawyer. He placed me as executrix and he left instructions on what I needed to do with his remains. Can I arrange for you to help me with that? I'm at a bit of a loss."

Grateful that she could delay the awkward conversation she needed to have with Simon, Kerry spoke with Camille while she walked back to the station. Offering to help her arrange the cremation of Michel Lalonde's body.

CHAPTER 55

The orange tarp waved in the light breeze. Its surface, streaked and spattered with lines of dried dirt stained the cracked seams. The metal crampons clinked against the metal base of the statue as the workers tried in vain to hold it straight. Driven by the gusts, the loud pattering sound echoed inside the damaged structure, hurling an unnerving noise into the bay.

From a distance, the tarp looked like it was dancing in the wind, but in reality, the work crew struggled to secure its grip on the rusty frame. They were tired of fighting the weather along with the protestors as they repaired the damaged structure between bursts of rain.

The work crew completed most of the structural repair on the large fish statue. Welding and support enhancements were done, and now the exterior patches and paintwork were underway.

A hum of the backhoe droned in the dense cover of the surrounding forest, as the landscape architects widened the path. Adding benches and information plaques that pointed out landmarks in the distance and local flora and fauna that edged the trail.

Landscapers and environmentalists carefully chose each plant. Enhancing the area with native grasses and perennial flowers.

As the committee assembled the team to work on the statue, they hired a young artist to repaint the exterior of the structure. The crew arrived early that morning and was eager to work while the weather was warm and dry.

Except for a light breeze, there were only clear skies forecasted for the rest of the week.

The lead artist, Will, submitted his proposal to the committee the morning after they voted to raise funds for the project. He had been visiting his parents and the opportunity to bid on a project and earn some money before his move out west was too good to pass up. Along with his portfolio, Will had an extensive list of references from local businesses that had hired him to complete unique projects over the years.

As soon as the committee hired him, he contacted five artists who he worked with in the past, assembling a team who were eager to add the iconic statue to their resume.

The work was difficult, the elements harsh and the protestors problematic. But no one had suggested they quit work on the statue since they all saw the renovation as a rare challenge.

Will cursed as the rough plastic hit the side of his hand, tearing the scabs from the edge of his knuckles. He couldn't wait until the renovation project was over and then he could return to the west coast. He had accepted the renovation job for the forty-foot statue mostly for the pay.

Initially, he believed the tempestuous weather on Lake of the Woods would be his biggest obstacle when patching the damaged hull of the oversized trout, muskie, or whatever it was supposed to be. Instead, the protestors and proponents of the extensive renovation to both the statue and the trail leading up from the shoreline proved to be more of an issue.

Small children cried at the sight of the fish when the gapping hole along its tail revealed the rusted metal support. Up close the peeling paint held dried pine needles, dust, and muddy debris. The twisted fish faced the brunt of the lake storms and icy onslaughts in the colder months which only hastened the fading exterior and crumbling base.

On the opposite end of the spectrum, representatives from the Office for the Taxpayers' Ombudsman rallied to put a stop to the renovation, believing that the expenditure was unnecessary and that funds should go toward public projects that serviced the residents of Lake Pines.

Everyone lost sight of what the statue represented. It should have been a point of local pride. Bringing together the people of the town as they joined forces to repair the statue and upgrade the trail that would benefit locals and tourists alike.

He wondered if the completed project would bridge the gap of discontent that surfaced in the small community. He witnessed neighbors fighting and arguing in stores and on the docks. The controversy split the people in the small town into two distinct camps. Pro-fish and anti-fish. His parents were in the pro-fish camp and supported the work he was doing, proud that they could claim their son would be leaving his indelible mark on the well-known statue.

Will climbed the ladder to the platform, holding the paint scrapper and sanding tools. He smoothed out the sharp edges of the metal opening, chipping away the loose paint and sanding down the bent shards that would make applying the patch difficult. It was the final day of prep work before the welder attached the precut piece, at which point they could prime and paint the exterior.

He'd be finished the project in less than a week and he let his thoughts drift to the rolling surf in Tofino and the low melodic song of the gray whales as they migrated north. He had been planning the move for the last year and with the money he'd earn from working on the renovation, he could finally realize his dream of opening a small studio on Vancouver Island.

As his mind drifted to the plans for his studio, the sanding block sprang out of his hand and bounced into the hull of the statue.

He cursed his negligence. His tight budget couldn't afford any more supplies. Especially after needing to replace the brushes and cans of spray paint that were stolen after their first day of work. As much as he hated tight spaces, he needed to climb into the dark cavity and retrieve the sanding block.

He flashed his light into the hollow space and leaned over the side before he hoisted his body over the opening. The yellow stream of light cascaded inside the statue and each move echoed Will's steps as he walked along the angled side.

The brown sanding block rolled to the small inner cove at the base of the statue, and it would've missed it if not for the bright beam of the flashlight. He reached down toward the block just as his hand brushed across a broken piece of wood.

Probably a branch, he thought. Having blown in with the storm that created the damage in the first place. On his first day, he spent three hours clearing leaves and branches from the interior of the damaged structure.

He recoiled as a bright white glow of light illuminated the object, casting long shadows across the side of the rusted hull and revealing intricate details that hid in the darkness. The flashlight cast a harsh, unflinching light on the object, illuminating the secret that someone intended the interior of the statue to conceal.

As he slowly moved the light from the base of the oar to the shattered paddle, he realized that his day had just become a lot more complicated.

Will reached out, paused, and then stepped back. The implications of what he found were obvious. Even with the poor lighting, he could see the splintered edges were stained with dried blood. Moving slowly but carefully, Will climbed out of the hull and disappeared into the light, wondering how he'd explain what he had found to the police.

CHAPTER 56

Once Janus locked the storage room and the back door, he placed all the receipts in the safe. He lowered the window shutters before locking the front door and left, feeling more like a prison warden than a shopkeeper.

He stood on the sidewalk and glanced up at the green and gold hand-painted sign that hung from a decorative wrought iron arm extending out over the sidewalk. His store had become a beacon, welcoming visitors into the town every season.

Everyone came to his shop at one point. Summer cottagers stocking up on sports equipment such as kayaks, diving gear, and tents to the fashion-forward outdoors enthusiasts who wanted the latest in trend-setting clothing. It was a business that thrived outfitting customers' recreational activities. Every season there was marketing potential, which included everything from clothing and equipment to guidebooks. Janus ensured he was up-to-date on the latest trends and needs of his customers.

However, Janus wasn't sure how much longer he could continue under the mounting pressure of the weakening economy. And now, with the reduced hours and fear of the robberies, his age was even becoming a factor. Staying open late and needing to spend more money on security features was digging into his profits and his energy. For the first time since he opened the store, he looked forward to the end of each day.

The evening was warm, and the sky was clear and Janus enjoyed the walk to the station. He called Simon after Kerry left his store and agreed to give a description of the woman he recalled seeing with Michel Lalonde. Simon warned Janus that the artist would work off an electronic tablet and that the image could appear more lifelike than he might be expecting. Simon knew Janus preferred a pen and paper to a computer, and it was a running joke that the most profitable store on Main Street was one that didn't specialize in electronics. Janus claimed his success had been because people not only wanted to get away from their everyday lives but that they also needed an escape.

The darkened storefronts saddened him as he strolled down Main Street. He offered solemn waves as he passed friends and neighbors who felt the financial sting to their businesses. Two days ago, his own accountant highlighted the reality that he could only weather the current financial storm until the end of October. At that point, Janus would have to dip into his hard-earned savings if he wanted to keep the store afloat. But the longer he thought about the stress and extra work, the more difficult it was to remain hopeful.

He pushed his hands into his pockets and glanced down the hill. His mind wandered to the peacefulness of an evening boat trip and thought a weekend trip with his wife was overdue. They could talk about the future of the store and his early retirement. He recalled the years when neighbors and cottagers comfortably strolled in and out of stores.

As he walked toward the bay he realized the boat traffic had diminished immensely too. The shifting atmosphere affected everyone in town, and a dull throb radiated through his body as his eyes filled with tears.

Janus slowed his pace, taking in the town he lived in most of his life. Their family relocated from the west coast when his father accepted a job at the pulp and paper mill. Janus was in his mid-teens and angry about having to move away from his friends, but a summer spent canoeing on the lake and hiking uninhabited islands sprouted a love for the outdoors that lasted his entire life.

It was how he spent his spare time, where he created memories with his children and was the main focus of his livelihood.

Giving up the business would be like walking away from a part of himself. But he knew that if he was going to retire to his cabin in Big Moon Bay, he'd have to consider making the difficult choice.

The one thing that always surprised Janus was the scent of the lake and how it changed with the seasons. Carrying the powerful aroma of the evergreens across the open bay or the soft musty wisps of rain that hovered over the water as a storm approached.

Tonight, however, his mood reflected the light calmness in the air. As he looked out onto the rising moon's reflection across the bay, Janus felt a slight tinge of hope.

Yes, maybe if he could help the police identify the mysterious woman who he saw with Michel Lalonde on the day he died, it would bring some luck in the police department's efforts to solve the murder. Then maybe they could pour all of their energy into capturing the thief.

Good deeds begot good luck. It was an adage his wife, Ida, was fond of repeating and it had sprung to his mind. He quickened his steps as he crossed the road and headed to the station.

"Mr. Rutger," the woman's shrill voice strangled the calmness of the night air as she blocked Janus from his path.

Janus pulled back. His instinct to step away from the woman was strong. Although she hadn't threatened him, the mere fact he was on his way to the station to describe her to the police sketch artist when she jumped out from the parked cars had cautioned him. "You?" His voice was low but not warm or welcoming the way it had been when he greeted the same woman days earlier when she walked into his store with Michel Lalonde. "What do you want?"

CHAPTER 57

Simon glanced at the sketch artists rendering and contorted his face. "I don't know why, but I feel like I recognize this woman from somewhere."

Sally, Josh, and Kevin looked at the electronic sketch tablet. Twisting their heads as they took in the intricate lines and angles of the computer-generated image.

"It's really spooky how lifelike the picture is," Sally said and then faced Kevin and Josh. "Don't you think?"

"I don't know. Her stare looks kind of vacant to me," Kevin said.

"You both know it's just a drawing, right?" Josh joked.

"Do you want me to send it out to the officers?" Sally asked.

Simon handed Sally the tablet, "That would be great, and remind them we just want to talk to her. We don't know if she's done anything wrong."

Sally uploaded the image and pushed it out to every mobile device, along with a reminder that they only wanted to ask her a few questions.

Josh followed Simon into his office and handed him the file he printed just before Janus arrived to speak with the sketch artist.

Simon leaned close to Josh and whispered, "Did you think Janus acted differently when he came in today?"

"I don't blame him," Josh said. "All the shop owners are on edge. I have an officer dropping in daily to let the store owners and shoppers know we are around and still searching for the thief. I hope it's made a difference."

Simon hesitated and then rubbed his hands together, "That must be it. Hopefully, this woman has information that can lead us to Michel Lalonde's killer. Then we can focus our entire effort on helping you identify the person responsible for the break-ins."

"That's what I wanted to talk to you about," Josh held out the file folder he had been clutching for the last forty minutes. "I really think that Casey Woodfield is the person we're looking for."

Simon opened the folder and read Josh's notes. "You found more security images of the night of the pharmacy robbery."

Josh pointed to the photograph stapled to the top of the page. "If we can enhance that corner of the image, I'm certain we'll be able to see the birthmark above Casey's eyebrow."

"Your gut instinct and identifying him on a security camera won't be enough to make charges stick against him." Simon flipped through the list of complaints filed against Casey over the last few years. "He fits the profile of the person we're looking for."

"It's him. I just know it." Josh said. "If I could just find one stolen item in his possession then I could close this case."

Simon closed the file and handed it to Josh, "That's the thing with what we do, Josh. Our instinct and experience guide us, but it's the hard evidence that we need."

Josh returned to his office and slammed the door, barely able to mask his upset. He knew Simon was right but the look of fear that still resided in Sally's eyes when she recounted her experience with Casey, the attack on Thomas, and the forced caution that residents continued to live out their days rushed to the forefront of his mind.

He read the list of items that were reported stolen and marked the items he knew would be the easiest to sell. Reaching out to pawn shops may be the best place to start. But he knew the ideal situation was to find the stolen items in Casey's possession. He needed to return to Casey Woodfield's home, this time, however, he'd turn in upside down looking for whatever evidence that he could use to justify an arrest.

CHAPTER 58

Simon stood at the base of the statue as a member of the forensic team carefully removed the broken and bloodied oar from the hull. Protected from the elements, the oar most likely contained enough trace evidence to link it to their murder victim and, hopefully, the murderer.

The foreman who discovered the oar was standing next to Simon, seeming more frustrated at being delayed than uncovering a murder weapon. "How much longer until we can get back to work?"

"Not until I have the interior examined."

"Do you know how many people have been touching that thing?"

"Which is why that lady in the white jumpsuit is getting everyone's fingerprints," Simon explained. "The faster we can rule out who was working and who may have been responsible for stashing the oar inside the statue, the faster we'll leave you to your repairs."

Will let out a frustrated groan, "I was supposed to be out of here by the end of the week." He stormed off toward the line that extended from the officer who was taking everyone's fingerprints, recording every worker's name, and documenting their identification.

Eventually, the news would spread that the work crew found a murder weapon inside the iconic Lake Pines statue. Simon knew the discovery of the oar would create a frenzied passion between the pro-fish-statue and the anti-fish-statue crowds and he'd suppress the information for as long as he could.

"Simon, look at this before I bring it back to the lab," Kerry pointed to the curved handgrip and the owner's name etched in the wood.

"Looks like I need to have another conversation with Hugo Lawson," Simon said, frustrated and confused. Since he didn't see Hugo as the type of person who would lash out in anger.

Kerry turned around and walked toward the path when Simon called her back, "What was it you wanted to talk to me about?"

"Don't worry about it. Let's clear up the matter with this oar, and then we can sit down." Kerry left before Simon could prompt her for more information. She headed back to the lab in the hospital basement, where she could test the blood on the oar, hoping to give Simon an answer before the end of the day.

After texting Josh to meet him at the police boat, Simon let Sally know that he was driving out to Hugo Lawson's cottage to speak with him.

"There are still no reports of anyone recognizing the woman in Janus' sketch," Sally updated Simon on the canvasing of the stores in town.

"Well, with any luck, Kerry will pull traces of the killer's DNA from the murder weapon, and who the woman is may be irrelevant."

CHAPTER 59

Hugo Lawson was sitting on his porch when Simon and Josh arrived. He was dressed in a thick polar fleece, knee-length cargo shorts, and thick black socks and sandals. What Kerry lovingly referred to as dad footwear.

He lowered the book he was reading and pulled his glasses to the top of his head as he greeted the two police officers.

"Can I get you fellas a drink?" Hugo offered. "I just brewed a pot of coffee." Hugo wiggled his body out of the low-riding Adirondack chair and stood.

His porch held a collection of furniture that represented every decade that Hugo owned the cottage. There was a small iron patio table, with rust that accumulated in the crevices and swirls of the cutout design that was paired with folding chairs with blue and green fabric webbing. Antique butter churns, stuffed with plants, flanked the top steps, and an 80s retro lawn gnome with a fading smile was being used as a doorstop.

"This isn't a social visit, Hugo," Simon said. "We have a few more questions for you about Michel Lalonde."

"I thought you guys looked a little too serious."

Simon turned his phone around and showed Hugo the image of the paddle, which was zoomed into the handle. "Is this your paddle?"

Hugo reached for his glasses and slid them to his nose. "Yeah, that's mine. That's how I mark most of my stuff. You'd be surprised how many people help themselves to items in my boathouse. Just last week somebody even stole one of my boats!"

Simon then retracted the image, revealing the full photograph of the damaged oar, and he watched as Hugo's face shifted.

"Is that what I think it is on the paddle?"

"Doctor Dearborne is testing it now, but I suspect it'll test positive for Michel Lalonde's blood and hopefully we'll have prints from the person who attacked him with it."

Hugo raised his hands, "Woah! You don't think I whacked him? Do you?"

"You had a long-running disagreement with the victim over his construction plans, and sometimes things can get very heated between neighbors."

"I was upset at the fact he was harming the environment," Hugo said. "Why would I have killed him?"

"Well-intentioned conservationists have broken laws and hurt people in the past."

Hugo looked down at the image on the phone and muttered, "Yeah, I guess that's a good point, but I didn't kill him."

"You also admitted to breaking into his cottage after he was killed."

Hugo looked into Simon's face, a man he had known for many years, and suddenly felt at odds with him.

Simon's phone buzzed as the expected text came in from Kerry. He had asked her to let him know the moment she completed the DNA analysis of the blood residue on the oar.

She confirmed that Michel Lalonde's blood and skin tissue were lodged in the splintered end of the oar. Simon turned to Josh and, with a slight nod to his head, they knew what he needed to do.

"Am I going to need a lawyer?" Hugo asked.

"It probably would be a good idea," Simon said.

After Josh placed Hugo under arrest, he escorted him to the station while Simon instructed the forensic team to search Hugo's property. He was looking for the matching oar, along with any evidence that may link his obsession and anger toward Michel Lalonde.

There was a reason the celebrity chef was murdered, and with all his years of experience, he knew that anger over a new cottage would be just as good a motive as any.

CHAPTER 60

The last test returned a positive match for the victim's blood, hair, and skin tissue. The broken oar that was discovered in the hull of the fish statue was definitely the murder weapon.

Trisha had been having difficulty distinguishing the exact type of wood. However, with the murder weapon in their possession, Kerry confirmed the match.

She drew on her experience with Jean to walk Trisha through the points of identification as she explained each slide and test with her. After an exhaustive afternoon, Kerry filed the reports after Trisha left for the day.

Sal walked into the examination room as Kerry was filing the last of her reports.

"I'm almost finished, Sal. Give me a few minutes."

He raised his hand, "Take your time. I was hoping to catch you before you left for the day."

Kerry looked up from the counter and lowered her laptop screen, "You sound serious."

He pointed to the anti-room, "Is Trisha gone for the day?"

"Yeah, I sent her home early." Kerry pointed toward the oar, which was wrapped and lying on the table. "We found the murder weapon, so I'll probably take my planned leave soon. I can move Trisha into room 24B so you'll have your privacy back again."

Kerry was eager to take the time to focus on the case from fifteen years ago and to do that she needed to be away from the hospital and, most importantly, she needed to speak with Jean.

"That's not why I asked," Sal pulled a chair up next to Kerry. "How much do you trust your new assistant?"

Kerry leaned back in her chair, "That's an odd question?"

"I overheard you explaining what should have been rudimentary tests. If she's as keen as you think she is, she could've identified the wood splinters in one afternoon."

"What are you saying, Sal?"

"The entire time I've been working in here, she's been acting odd. Plus, she's constantly locking her desk as if she's trying to hide something."

"You've checked her drawers?"

"Have you given her a lot of work? Any work that she would need to lock up?"

Kerry thought about the case files she had Trisha work on. She made a point of collecting them at the end of each day and storing them in her office. There would be no need for Trisha to keep any of the files.

"I think she's collecting information for the province."

Kerry laughed, "You mean like a spy?"

"Laugh all you want," Sal pulled a folded sheet out of his pocket and handed it to Kerry.

As she read the memo, she realized that Sal's preoccupation with budgeting constraints was not because of his paranoia. The inter-provincial memo included a list of the departments they wanted to merge, which ones required a reduction in staff, and, more frighteningly, the ones that would be closed altogether.

Her name was in the last column.

CHAPTER 61

Kerry returned to her office after she brought the oar into the evidence room and made the phone call she had been putting off for days. She left her unfinished coffee and turned her attention to the phone call she had been avoiding.

"Kerry, you are a hard person to reach," Jean let out an exasperated moan. "There's something I need to tell you."

"Wait, Jean, there's something that I need to tell you first. And it's far more urgent, I can assure you."

Jean listened as Kerry explained the cryptic note, the box with the rock, and then the official evidence box from the Vivienne Strong murder investigation.

"Someone knows what happened and they're coming after me. I'm worried that we're both being targeted. What's even worse is I didn't see it coming and I don't know who would have any motive to revisit Vivienne's case?"

"Maybe I can answer that for you," Jean said. "The reason I called was to let you know the parole board granted Paul Buchanan early release. Vivienne Strong's killer is out of prison."

CHAPTER 62

Josh respected Hugo Lawson. Over the years, Hugo was a fixture at town hall meetings where he supported bylaws that benefited the environment and worked tirelessly with the water stewardship board as a volunteer.

Outside of some raised voices at community meetings, Josh never knew Hugo to strike out in anger or threaten anyone. And there were several people who Hugo disagreed with throughout the years.

Hugo was a big supporter of Thomas' work and was excited when he discovered that Thomas' designs were based on environmentally friendly construction. However, if Josh learned anything as a police officer, it was that everyone is capable of breaking the law. If pushed, even lawmakers could cross the line.

After a quick phone call to his lawyer, Hugo let Josh place him in a holding cell without argument. His lawyer wouldn't arrive until after four-thirty as he was in the neighboring community of Minaki for the day dealing with an insurance fraud case.

Sadness and shock swept across Hugo's face, and several of the officers struggled to know how to act around him.

Like Josh, many of the staff knew and liked him. Sally brought Hugo a green tea and sat with him for ten minutes while the daily routines in the station buzzed around them.

Josh returned to his office and resumed the paper trail of Casey Woodfield's life and troubles with the law. Josh stood with his arms folded, examining the notes on the board, trying to connect the strands of information.

Josh primarily focused on the list of evidence and clues that he had amassed from all the robberies and the attack on Thomas at his construction site.

The only business that made any sense for the thief to target was the pharmacy. Opioids, painkillers, sleeping pills, and diabetes medication were commonplace on the black market.

Restrictions on cross-border prescriptions and increased pricing outside the country made Canada a target for such thefts.

What Josh couldn't understand was the connection between Thomas' office, fleeces from Rutger's, and books from Kathryn's Book Nook.

Josh ripped the page off the pad of paper and started with a blank sheet.

He needed to approach the thefts from a different angle. The attack Thomas suffered didn't fit the pattern of the thief. In fact, that was the only instance of violence associated with the robberies and Josh needed to put Thomas aside and treat him like any other business owner and not as his husband. Emotion couldn't factor into his investigation. If it did, Josh would plant evidence in Casey Woodfield's home, and that was a line he was terrifyingly close to crossing.

Josh divided the page into three columns. In the first category, Josh wrote the names of every business that was robbed. The second contained the items that were stolen. The third column took longer for Josh to fill. In it, he listed several bullet points outlining any comparison between the businesses.

He outlined the type of customers and average sale price for common transactions and even made a list of any renovation work that may have been done.

When he was finished he leaned back in his chair and tried to make sense of the random facts and points on the list, then he lurched forward and reached for the detailed list of damage inside each business and it hit Josh.

The link between each business was clear when he compared the list of items found in Casey's home. They weren't on the list of stolen goods, but their existence allowed Josh to connect each business and, more importantly, why they were targets of a robbery.

Simon was walking down the hall speaking into his phone, and Josh rushed out of his office and followed him. Simon ended the call when he saw the urgent look on Josh's face.

"I think I've figured out why our thief targeted certain businesses." Josh showed Simon the piece of paper itemizing the items found during the search of Casey's home. He circled the item that caught his attention in red.

"Do you really think it was that simple?" Simon asked.

"I do. And if we can get one of the shop owners to agree, I think we can set a trap and catch the robber in the act."

CHAPTER 63

Lisa stared at Josh for a long time, unsure if she had heard him correctly. "You want me to be the bait for the robber?"

"Not you, your café," Josh clarified. "I would never put you in danger, Lisa."

Lisa shifted in her seat, crossed her arms, and looked out the window. They were sitting with Kathryn, her friend and the owner of the local bookstore, as Josh explained the connection between the businesses that were robbed.

"If Thomas' construction site hadn't been robbed, I'm not sure when I would've made the connection," Josh explained.

Kathryn leaned forward, "You're saying the thieves targeted every business that applied for funding to run email marketing campaigns?"

"Not funding for emails, but the local business grant program that was put in place to assist businesses with expanding their e-commerce program."

"I don't understand how names and contact information could be valuable to a thief," Kathryn said.

"Identity theft was on the rise before Covid, but after the lockdowns, it increased exponentially. Businesses were expanding or establishing their online presence and, to do that, they collected a lot of personal data. Information that's used to create bank accounts, apply for credit cards, you name it."

"Identity theft?" Lisa asked. "Are you sure?"

"No," Josh replied honestly. "But it's the only connection that makes sense. I found a computer scanning stick in the suspect's home, along with equipment that appeared to be used to play games online. I couldn't examine Casey's computer because his lawyer had him released and the search warrant expired before we finished going through his house. But if we can catch him in the act, then we can finally put an end to the robberies."

"And an end to the fear that's been keeping my shoppers and employees away," Kathryn added. "I paid upfront for the books and products in my shop. If I don't get my customers back in my store, I'm going to go out of business."

Lisa knew the businesses in Lake Pines couldn't survive the summer with the reduced shopping hours they were currently experiencing. At the continuing rate, most of the shops along Main Street would be out of business by the end of the year.

"Okay," Lisa leaned forward. "But if we are going to do this, I have some guidelines."

Josh smiled and rested his hand on Lisa's arm, "I expected you would."

CHAPTER 64

Jean's words reverberated in her mind, and he repeated them when Kerry didn't respond.

"Did you hear me, Kerry? The Parole Board released Paul Buchanan from prison."

"Why? They convicted him of second-degree murder," Kerry said.

"After ten years, anyone convicted of second-degree murder can apply for parole," Jean explained. "This was his second time up in front of the parole board and his behavior in prison was exemplary. His therapist testified he made huge strides during his time in prison. She said he worked hard to rehabilitate, and that he's not a threat to society."

"Tell that to the child and husband that were left without a mother or wife."

"I know how you feel about this, Kerry, but it's the way our justice system works," Jean said. "Do you really think that Paul Buchanan was beyond rehabilitation?"

Kerry rubbed the side of her temple with her left hand, "I don't know, Jean. Do you?"

"I think, in many instances, people can leave prison and lead a productive life in society. Every case depends on several factors. The biggest one is the prisoner. If they're willing to change, I think they can. Fifteen years is a long time, and if Paul was determined, then maybe he has made some lasting changes."

Kerry glanced at the calendar, "When was he released?"

"Two weeks ago."

"That fits the timeline for when I received the note and the rock," Kerry said. "Paul's the only person who would benefit from revealing what I did. And if his plan for revenge has been brewing for fifteen years then he is far from being rehabilitated."

"The note I can understand, but the rock?" Jean's sigh stretched out over the phone line.

"Does Vivienne's husband know?" Kerry asked.

"The court had to inform the victim's family each time Paul applied for parole. The family was at the hearing and read a witness statement pleading for Paul to remain behind bars."

If Paul Buchanan spent the last fifteen years combing over his case, then there's a chance that he realized the record showed it took two tests to prove his DNA was on the rock. Everyone who worked on Vivienne Strong's murder investigation was aware of Kerry's frustration when the court ruled the skin tissues found under the victim's nails inadmissible. All because of her error in establishing the chain of custody with the evidence sample.

She had come to terms with her decision and although she never repeated the same mistake, she still believed that her actions resulted in a killer going to prison.

However, the pressing matter was the cryptic note and the rock. Their timing and meaning were precise. It would be the perfect revenge for Paul Buchanan.

"One more question," Kerry asked. "Have you ever heard of a man named Michel Lalonde?"

CHAPTER 65

Posts were popping up on social media. News of the chef's death was spreading. However, Simon kept the mention of finding the murder weapon out of the news.

Simon carried the box of evidence into the conference room and unloaded the contents. There weren't many items that the forensic team removed from Storm Island since the murder took place on the dock, and removing the contents of Michel Lalonde's cottage was both unrealistic and unnecessary.

If there was a further connection between Hugo Lawson and Michel Lalonde, then maybe Simon could find it among some of the victim's private papers and journals.

For the next hour, Simon carefully read each piece of paper and every note. The box even included the shopping list he sent to Tanya.

He located information on the original cottage design along with Thomas' responses to the environmental impact and the bylaw restrictions that made many of Michel Lalonde's requests impossible.

There were no physical threats made toward or by Michel Lalonde, and Simon could find no evidence that the victim had been concerned about his safety.

Simon left the conference room and headed directly for Jamie's office. "I still haven't received the call log for Michel Lalonde's phone. Were you able to bypass the security code?"

Jamie slapped his palm against his forehead, "Sorry. I've been so busy scanning all the local security footage that I forgot to bring it to you when I was done." Jamie rolled his chair along the length of his computer desk and grabbed the printout he placed in his outbox and handed it to Simon.

"Thanks," Simon said and then glanced at Jamie's screen. "How many hours do you have left to go through?"

"About sixty combined from all the businesses," Jamie wheeled his chair back in front of his computer. "Let me know if that's all the information you need."

Simon returned to the conference room, frustrated at the extra work his staff was taking on because of the cutbacks. No one was complaining, but Simon could tell that everyone was feeling stretched to their limits. He was worried his staff was going to become burned out soon.

Before he read the phone log, Simon called Peter's office and requested an urgent meeting to discuss the budget. He booked a date and time with Peter's assistant and ended the call. He missed the days when each call would go through directly to Peter and when his assistant wasn't running interference for him. The irony didn't sit well with Simon. As he, Kerry, and other government offices in Lake Pines were feeling the sting of the budget cuts, Peter still had an assistant.

Simon rested the phone log on the desk and compared the numbers that Michel Lalonde telephoned with the numbers on his contact list. Absent was Hugo Lawson's number, which to some degree, Simon was grateful to see.

Calls made before the victim arrived in Lake Pines were to numbers in France and several to his agent. Camille had mentioned that they spoke before he left France to vacation in Lake Pines. They were outlining the processes for his book launch and the upcoming promotional interviews that they were coordinating.

What Camille hadn't mentioned was that Michel called her on the day he died. The time stamped on the call was two-minutes-twenty-four seconds. It was long enough for her to either have a short phone call or leave a message. Simon phoned Camille, hoping she could explain the call, but after four rings, he got her voicemail instead.

Simon rolled his eyes, frustrated at the number of times his calls went to voicemail in the last couple of days. He left a brief message and asked her to get back to him as soon as possible.

He had examined every item in the evidence box and compared the phone log. There was nothing else to examine. Except for the manuscript which was found under a pillow on Michel's second-floor porch.

Simon pulled out the thick stack of paper and read the title.

'The End'

He had to agree with Kerry. It was an odd title for a book written by a young celebrity chef who was at the pinnacle of his career. Simon brushed it off to artistic leanings, and he turned to the first page and took in the first line of the dedication.

"For my mother, Eloise, who bravely fought to give me a better life."

Simon didn't expect to become engrossed in the manuscript, but he was. He didn't find a boring account of a self-absorbed celebrity chef. Instead, he found the story of a young boy who suffered a painful childhood with an abusive father that culminated in him and his mother fleeing for their safety and living with his grandparents.

It was the story of a young boy who fought against the guilt and shame of what his father did and of the crimes he committed. And most importantly, it revealed that it was his drive to live a better life that prompted him to change his name on his eighteenth birthday.

He assumed his maternal grandmother's maiden surname along with the French given name his mother chose for him, but that his father forbade him to be given.

A knock on the door pulled Simon from the pages and Kerry walked in holding two drinks and a bag that smelled of Lisa's pizza melts.

"I thought I'd bring you dinner," Kerry raised her arms. "Want to have an impromptu dinner date? I need to talk to you about something anyway, and I'm going to need some strength to get through the conversation."

"I have news too," Simon slapped his hand on the manuscript as his eyes lit up. "I figured out who Michel Lalonde really is? Or was. He legally changed his name when he was eighteen. What's interesting is why he changed it."

Kerry placed the drink tray and bag of food on the table and listened while Simon excitedly revealed what he learned in the first half of the manuscript.

"His name was Paul Buchanan Jr. He applied for a name change when he reached the age of eighteen because he no longer wanted to bear the same name as his father who was a convicted murderer."

Kerry drew back her hand, covering her mouth as Simon continued to explain.

"His father was convicted of second-degree murder," Simon said. "That might give us a bit more insight into who else may have wanted to hurt him, and it probably wasn't Hugo Lawson."

"Oh, no." Kerry let out a deep breath and slumped into the chair.

Simon leaned forward, reaching out and grabbing Kerry's arm. "What is it?"

“There’s something that I’ve been meaning to tell you and now I wonder if I’ve waited too long.”

The look on Kerry’s face frightened him.

Simon realized that whatever it was, it was probably the source of Kerry’s anxiety. He lowered the manuscript and nervously waited for Kerry to speak.

“You’re probably right about Hugo not being guilty, and I think I know who might be responsible for Michel Lalonde’s death.”

CHAPTER 66

Simon held his gaze. He remained motionless and without a hint of what he was feeling. Betrayed? Confused? Angry? Kerry couldn't tell what thoughts were rolling through Simon's mind.

"Please say something," Kerry whispered.

"Is Jean the only person who knows about this?"

Kerry nodded.

Simon leaned back in his chair, letting his hands fall to his lap. "I won't say I don't understand, because I do. I know firsthand how difficult it is to let someone walk free when you know in your heart that they're guilty. Josh is going through that now with Casey Woodfield."

Tears came to Kerry's eyes, "I'm scared, Simon."

Simon nodded his head, calmly and slowly. "What do you want to do about it?"

"I never thought I'd have to do anything," Kerry shamefully admitted. "Once Paul Buchanan went to prison, I thought everything was behind me. I thought I could forget about what I'd done."

"The past never goes away, Kerry. You know that."

"Jean protected my secret for two reasons. The first was because he was terrified that the police would charge me with tampering with evidence. The second was because we knew that Paul

Buchanan was guilty of murdering Vivienne Strong and if we couldn't prove it, then he was going to be released."

"But you proved nothing. You just gave a convicted murderer the upper hand. If he ever finds out about it, he could drag you, Jean, and the police force into court. Not to mention that every single investigation you worked on will need to be re-examined."

"I should've told you sooner."

"You never should've done it."

If Simon had responded in a rage, it would have been easier to accept. But when she looked across the table, it was a sense of disappointment that Kerry saw reflected in his eyes. That was more painful that the thought of being charged with tampering with crime scene evidence.

How was she going to explain everything to her father? And down the road, would she ever be able to look Dominique in the eye? She didn't think she'd be able to do either.

"I need to tell Peter," Kerry said. Excusing Simon from needing to say the words himself. "I'll call him today."

Simon nodded, "That's a good idea. Do you want me to be there with you?"

"No," Kerry shook her head. "You need to solve a murder. I'll have Trisha retest the paddle, so she can register the results in her name."

Kerry reached out and squeezed Simon's hand, and he surprised her by pulling her toward him and wrapping his arms around her body. He held onto her, and she felt the rise and fall of his chest as he cried.

Failing Simon was the worst thing Kerry could've done, and she was more determined than before to do what was right.

Kerry pulled back and wiped the tears from Simon's face. "I'll do my best to fix this."

Simon brushed a strand of Kerry's hair behind her ear and leaned forward and kissed her. It was his silent promise that he wouldn't leave her, no matter what she had done, or how hard the road ahead was going to be. He disagreed with her actions, but because he knew Kerry better than anyone else, he understood the drive behind why she did it.

It was the same passion and focus that made her exceptionally good at what she did and why they were a good team.

Kerry opened the door and stepped into the hall.

"Kerry," Simon called out. "You said that you knew who may have murdered Michel Lalonde."

Kerry nodded, "The one person who was most affected by Vivienne's murder. Her husband, Curtis Strong."

CHAPTER 67

Simon received the case file on Vivienne Strong's murder investigation within twenty minutes of his request. Everything was as Kerry had explained. He read the eyewitness statements from co-workers who supported claims that Paul Buchanan was obsessed with Vivienne, and no matter how hard she tried to brush off his advances, he refused to believe she wasn't interested in him.

Several female employees filed complaints about his unwelcome advances. But each time, the human resources department ignored the complaints. The women were either transferred to another department or quit their jobs.

It was the same discrimination that Simon saw at the beginning of his career and although instances of harassment still existed, he knew there were also more resources in place for victims of these assaults.

When he finished reading the file, Simon was confident that no one would easily figure out what Kerry had done. If she hadn't told him, he wouldn't have been the wiser.

He wrote Curtis Strong's address and number, searched the database, and found a number listed under the same name in the same small town just outside of Montreal.

Simon dialed the number, but before he could press send, Josh knocked on his door.

"Hugo's lawyer is in with him now, and they'll want to speak with us in a few minutes."

Simon returned his phone to his pocket and closed the file on his desk.

"I also decided how to move forward with the investigation into the recent robberies," Josh said. "With Lisa's help, I'm hoping to set a trap for the thief."

"Do you still think it's Casey Woodfield?"

"I do. But I think he's targeting the shops to steal their customers' information."

"That, I didn't see coming," Simon said, impressed with Josh's investigation. "Good work, Josh."

"Do you think Hugo's lawyer will get him released?" Josh asked.

"I do, and I'm not sure he's the only person who has a valid motive to want to harm Michel Lalonde. Or I should say, Paul Buchanan Jr."

"You figured out who he was?"

Simon explained why Michel changed his name from the one that aligned him with his father, who was a convicted killer. However, Simon refrained from adding the information regarding Kerry's involvement in Paul Buchanan's conviction.

"His father was granted parole a couple of weeks ago. The parole hearing report included a letter from Vivienne Strong's husband. Let's just say he wasn't supportive of Paul being granted parole, nor doesn't believe he's a changed man. He said that if they released him, they'd be putting a murderer on the street and that he'd kill again."

"Were those his exact words?"

"Pretty much."

"So, Vivienne's husband—"

"Curtis Strong."

"You think Curtis Strong would search out Paul's son and murder him?"

"We all agreed that it was a quick attack. Noah recalled seeing someone at the top of the stairs when he drove away from the island. Maybe he wanted to track down his father and the discussion got heated."

"That would explain Mary McLean hearing someone yell out the name Paul," Josh said. "Except it wasn't Michel that was yelling it out as she thought. It was probably the killer yelling Michel's birth name."

"That's why we were confused. We didn't need to search for someone named Paul, because Michel was Paul all along."

"From the little bit that you told me about the victim's manuscript, he didn't like his father. Why would he have argued with Curtis Strong? It sounds like they would be on the same side."

"There was a note in the file from a member of the parole board. They said that a statement from Paul Buchanan's family in support of Curtis' motion would have helped keep Paul behind bars. But when the hearing was over, and no one from Paul Buchanan's family argued against him being paroled, the board went with the report filed by the court-appointed psychologist."

"That would've made Vivienne's family furious."

"Maybe even furious enough to lash out at Paul Jr."

CHAPTER 68

Peter spent most of the last year putting out administrative fires throughout his jurisdiction. The political pressure that every province was facing to reduce spending only complicated his days. Filling his calendar with secretive meetings as he reworked budgets.

What Peter wanted to do was to shift his budget, not cut it back. It was difficult to place Kerry in a small room at the Lake Pines hospital, but what she didn't realize is that the alternative suggestion from the Commissioner was to close her posting and merge her lab with the larger operation in Thunder Bay.

He avoided her calls for the last week while he figured out how to rework the numbers and keep Kerry and give her a new lab in Lake Pines.

Lila walked into his office and placed the sorted files on the edge of his desk. "I categorized them according to case numbers, just as you requested."

Peter reached for the stack of files. "Thanks, Lila."

He opened the top file and read the stats for the first lab on his list to reassess. Realizing that Lila was looking down at him, Peter raised his head. "Is everything alright?"

"It's the third time that Kerry's called today. Don't you think you should call her back?"

Peter glanced out the window and dragged his hands across his face, "I don't know what to tell her."

"Tell her the truth, Peter. That you're doing your best to figure out how to not fire her."

"It's not as simple as that, Lila, and you know it."

"Think of how she must see it? Her lab gets destroyed in a fire and she gets stuffed into an old closet in the hospital's basement where she has to share a lab with an overbearing researcher."

"That's what she called Doctor Varanus?"

"And even though you got her message that she wasn't taking a leave, you still sent Trisha Chen to Lake Pines!" Lila exclaimed, recalling the argument she and Peter had regarding the decision.

"You know why I did that," Peter reminded her. "My hands were tied. Plus, on paper, it'll look like she needed the extra help. It may benefit her if I need to defend keeping her position."

Lila nodded. "She knows you're avoiding her."

Peter glanced down at the pile in front of him. "Let me read through these files and then I'll call Kerry. I want to give her the respect of my full attention."

Lila smiled, pleased with her words of persuasion, and then headed toward the door. Before she stepped into the hall, she turned around, "I've already blocked off the rest of your afternoon. That way, no one will interrupt you."

Lila closed the door, leaving Peter with the stack of files and the prospect of telling one of his closest friends that he was going to have to let her go.

CHAPTER 69

Trisha left after spending six hours sorting through files. Kerry gave her the exhausting task of compiling a list of every case she worked on in Lake Pines. Under the guise of wanting to categorize her results in each case so she could develop a cheat sheet of sorts for future cases, she asked Trisha to sort through hundreds of cases.

Kerry held back the Jesper file and brought it to the lab where Sal was working.

"Kerry, your extra work project tired your assistant out today," Sal joked. "She barely made it to the door without yawning."

Although it hadn't been her intention, Kerry was grateful to not have to deal with training or working with Trisha. However, after she spoke with Peter, she'd have to hand over her caseload and small office to the young intern. At least until Peter decided the fate of the Lake Pines coroner posting.

"I need a favor, Sal," Kerry handed him the Jesper file, unsure of how much to reveal to him. "Trisha found some inconsistencies with my tests of the contents of the warfarin box, and I'd like you to review the file."

Sal took the file and opened it. "Inconsistencies? That's not a word I'd associate with your cases."

Kerry strained at the comment, forcing down the emotion that unexpectedly came to her.

As Sal read the file, a confused look coated his face. "Baking Soda?"

He looked up at Kerry, "There's no way you mistook baking soda for poison."

"That's why I'd like to you look the file over and see if I missed anything. Retest the box if you need to, I don't care. But I need to have you complete the tests alone."

"Do you believe me now that Trisha is a plant from the people pulling the budget strings?" Sal jabbed his finger at the ceiling and raised one brow.

"It is a little convenient, but if you could just do this for me, I'd really appreciate it," Kerry said. "Oh, and Sal, can we keep this between us?"

"Don't worry, my lips are sealed."

Kerry left the lab and hoped that Sal would find what she had missed and hopefully her error hadn't caused an innocent woman's arrest. Her phone rang just as she reached her office and she answered it as she stepped inside. Because of the poor reception on his end, Kerry could barely hear what Peter was saying.

"Hi Kerry," Peter shouted into the line. "Lila said you called a few times today."

"Peter, do you have time to talk?" Kerry asked as she closed her door behind her.

"Unfortunately not. There's been a train derailment just west of Thunder Bay. I'm on my way there now. It's going to be a mess because the company transporting fuel had their license revoked after an accident last year." Peter explained. "I wanted to speak with you this afternoon, but then this call came in."

"Can you call me tomorrow morning?"

"Why don't I drive in and we can talk in person," Peter suggested. "I think that may be better."

Kerry agreed. "Call me when you get into town tomorrow. We can go somewhere private and talk. There's not much room or privacy in the hospital."

Muffled shouts of emergency personnel came from the distance, sounding not too far from where Peter was standing. "I have to go Kerry. I'll see you tomorrow."

Perhaps the truth will be more difficult to share as she was looking into Peter's face. Kerry wondered if she should warn Peter that what she had to talk with him about involved her work on an old case, but as she was about to speak, the line was dead.

CHAPTER 70

Lisa stood nervously at the counter of the administrator's office as she filled out the application for the business grant. Using numbers and key metric terms that Josh prepared for her, Lisa fumbled her way through the e-commerce marketing terms that were foreign to her in her line of work.

The entire process took forty minutes, and by the time they neared the end of the application form, Lisa was ready to bolt from the office.

Josh was waiting for her in her café, and as Lisa walked through the doors, with her thick black curly hair askew, he knew not to ask how it went.

She pointed her slim index finger in his direction and wagged it back and forth, "This better work because I'm not going back in there."

"Did you remember the figures I gave you?"

Lisa tossed her purse on the shelf behind the counter, "Yes. I was very clear when I said that the release of the cookbook brought a flood of online orders and that I received hundreds of requests in the first week and that I was unsure what to do with all the names and credit card information that was being sent to me."

"It's weak, but let's see if the robber is smug enough by now to fall for it," Josh said. "Did you mention you would wait until tomorrow to move the data on your computer to a secure server?"

"Yes. You'll be happy to know that I sounded like a complete computer neophyte. And I was speaking loudly enough that I'm sure the staff in the second-floor office heard me." Lisa handed Josh the keys, "And I said that I'd be closing early so I could go out to a movie."

Josh took Lisa's keys and slipped them into his pocket. "Now, let's hope we can catch a thief."

CHAPTER 71

Simon sat with Josh in the far corner of the café while two officers were positioned in the back alley and another in an unmarked car that was parked directly across the street.

Josh grabbed another cookie from the tray of food that Lisa left for them. "I noticed Hugo wasn't at the station when I left today."

"We released him on the promise that he wouldn't leave town and that he'd remain under his lawyer's supervision."

Josh smiled, "I heard his lawyer is staying with him at his cottage."

Simon shrugged his shoulders, "His lawyer argued he could find several items of Hugo's at other people's cottages. And he's right. It would be difficult to prove that Hugo was the one who swung the paddle, and no one saw him near Storm Island around the time that Michel was murdered. We checked the police records and he was telling the truth about his boat having been stolen."

"Really?"

"He came into town to get groceries and when he returned his boat was gone. It also matched the description that Thomas gave of the boat that was docked at his office. Right down to the yellow rope."

"And then there's the case of the mysterious woman who keeps popping up," Josh added. "First it was Janus who saw the victim with a woman at his store, then Tanya ran into her before she left Storm Island."

"I'm surprised that no one recognized the woman in the image. Those drawings are so lifelike."

"Hopefully, something will turn up," Josh said as he grabbed a slice of pizza from a plate. "How's Kerry? She seemed distracted when she was at the station."

Simon hadn't mentioned Kerry's confession of tampering with evidence from an old murder investigation or the cryptic note she received suggesting that someone else knew what she had done. And until Kerry spoke with Peter, he wasn't going to.

"She just misses Dominique," Simon explained. "She's been calling her twice a day. I'm sure Oliver is fine, but she feels better when she can hear her voice and see her smile."

"I know what she means," Josh said. "I love the break and I think Thomas and I needed it, but I miss the noise and the messy fun."

Simon laughed, "I think Raven misses the extra food Dominique tosses him."

For the next twenty minutes, they sat in the darkened café, laughing about old stories and sharing plans for the summer. All the while, Simon was thinking about the problems Kerry had caused because of one rash decision fifteen years ago, as Josh watched the door, waiting for Casey Woodfield to break into the café.

CHAPTER 72

It was two-fifteen and Josh had just received a warning text from the officer stationed in the back alley on their group chat. They named their stakeout operation The Stinger Crew. None of them had been on an overnight stakeout for years, and all four officers reveled in the rush. Feeling like kids at a sleepover, Kevin coined the fun moniker when they set up their group chat and no one tried to change his mind.

Josh nudged Simon's arm and jolted him awake.

"Someone's approaching the back door," Josh whispered as he stood. He pulled out his weapon, and positioned himself behind the partition, blocking his view from the back door.

Simon moved to the opposite side of the room, pressing his back against the wall.

The hollow creak of the hinges followed the familiar clicking sound of a lock pick on the heavy steel door.

As the door opened, a stream of artificial light crawled along the length of the hall, creating a yellow line along the floor.

They had agreed to wait until the thief searched for Lisa's computer and attempted to retrieve the data information from her files before they revealed their positions.

"Hold steady," Josh whispered into the microphone that connected them.

He knew that the officers outside were getting into position near the doors and were waiting for Josh's signal before they burst through the door.

Although Josh assumed the thief was working alone, they couldn't be sure if accomplices were waiting outside. And they wanted to be ready.

The shadowy figure moved stealthily, their footsteps nearly silent as they creep inside the café. The intruder slipped past the dark windows, their silhouette shrouded in shadows until they reached the door leading to Lisa's office. With a few swift movements, the intruder disappeared into the darkness.

The sound of the USB drive clicking into Lisa's computer broke the silence in the café.

The shadowy figure leaned forward and pushed an electronic scanner into the back of Lisa's computer and then typed in a sequence of keys before pressing a red button on the side of the box.

Josh jumped out first, followed by Simon, who alerted the officers outside that they were approaching the suspect. Their moves out of the shadows took the thief by surprise and Josh landed his hands on the intruder's shoulders.

He pushed him toward the wall, reached for his right arm, and bent it back. As he uttered the warning that he was under arrest, the thief spun around, unexpectedly landing a punch on Josh's jaw and giving him just enough time to push away from the wall and run toward the door.

Josh recovered his stance just as Simon stretched out his arm, pointing his gun at the face of the hooded assailant, preventing him from taking another step.

He tugged the black hood from the intruder's head and a thick mane bounced out from underneath. A grin spread across Josh's face when he looked into Casey Woodfield's face.

"Casey Woodfield, you're under arrest," Josh pulled Casey's arms back and pressed the metal handcuffs onto his wrists. "Would you like to call your lawyer now or when you get to the station?"

CHAPTER 73

Morning came a little harder for Simon than it did for Josh since he had the added stress of knowing that Kerry was going to speak with Peter and confess to tampering with evidence from a murder investigation.

The husband in him wanted Kerry to remain quiet. After all, the evidence pointed to Paul Buchanan being Vivienne's killer. He knew Kerry, and he believed that was the only instance that she knowingly interfered in a police investigation.

She was driven by the desire to bring justice to victims of crime. It was that same passion that guided her to make a huge mistake in her judgment fifteen years ago when she feared that Paul Buchanan was about to walk away a free man. However, it was that same passion that helped the police pinpoint suspects in several cases where they otherwise would've had difficulty proving a case for an arrest.

Although he was a husband, friend, and father first, Kerry reminded him he was also a police officer. Several people looked up to him and whether or not Simon liked it, the entire town depended upon him making the tough decisions. Even when it affected people he cared about. Residents of the small town counted on him to guide them with honesty and to be above reproach.

If he was to align himself with Kerry's lie and deception, she wouldn't just be ruining her life, but she would ruin his.

This was a point that Kerry refused to argue about.

In the end, neither of them slept nor did they speak at breakfast.

Simon held Kerry in his arms for what seemed a terrifyingly long time before she walked out the door and left for work.

He headed to the station and kept busy tracking down Curtis Strong and figuring out once and for all if Hugo landed the deadly strike against Michel Lalonde or not.

It could either be revenge or passion, depending upon who was guilty.

Sally was always the first person in the office and was reading a magazine at her desk when Simon walked through the doors. "You're early."

"Thought I would get a jump on the day before everyone showed up."

"You mean before people start bothering you," Sally joked as she lowered her magazine. "Do you want a coffee? I was about to get one for myself."

Simon paused at the edge of Sally's desk and lifted the magazine, and stared closely at the image on the cover.

He turned it around and stabbed the image on the cover, "Who does this woman look like?"

"You don't know who that is?" Sally asked. "Even my uncle knows who she is. She's the British actress who played Stormeye in the latest superhero movie that came out."

Simon pulled out his phone and retrieved the image from the sketch artist's digital rendition of the woman Janus Rutger claimed was in his store with Michel Lalonde on the day he was murdered.

"Now, let me ask you again. Does the actress remind you of someone?"

CHAPTER 74

Simon was waiting outside Janus' store, waiting for him to arrive. He jumped out of his car and called out his name when he saw Janus walk around the corner.

He had calmed down since he first realized that the description Janus gave to the police sketch artist was of an actress and not the actual person they had been searching for.

If it had been anyone else, Simon would have thought that he did it to mock the police officers or simply cause trouble. But Janus was an upstanding citizen. He loved Lake Pines and worked and volunteered in the community year-round.

Janus was one of the final holdouts against closing early under fear of the thefts, and Simon knew him as far back as he could recall.

Simon wondered if Janus intentionally gave a false description to protect someone he knew or if he feared for his safety.

Janus turned around when he heard his name, "Good morning. I just heard the good news. I was grabbing my morning coffee at Lisa's and she told me you guys caught the thief. Great work. And a little heads-up, I think Lisa is pumped about the fact she was part of a sting operation."

Janus laughed and then noticing the seriousness of Simon's stare he quieted his tone. "Is everything alright?"

Simon held up Sally's magazine, making sure that Janus could see the image of the actress.

Janus glanced down at the sidewalk, his eyes filled with guilt and shame. A faint blush tinged his cheeks, and he opened his mouth and then, after a slight hesitation, he pushed his lips together. Janus struggled to find the words to explain and then simply invited Simon inside the shop, where they could speak privately.

"Maybe we should talk inside," Janus unlocked the door. He rushed to press his code on the alarm pad and then placed his coffee cup on the counter. "I can explain."

"I sure hope so," Simon snapped. "Do you know how many hours my officers spent traipsing around from store to store asking if anyone recognized this woman? We're already on a tight budget, and let's not forget that I have a murder investigation underway."

Janus dropped his gaze and then turned away from Simon.

Simon leaned on the counter, lowered his voice, and spoke to Janus as a friend and not a cop. "Tell me why you did it, Janus. Because I know you too well to believe you intentionally wanted to steer us away from finding this woman."

Janus turned around, "She threatened to send someone to hurt me if I gave a description to the police. I don't know how she found out that I was going to the station to give you a description, but she did. I didn't know what else to do."

"You could have told me."

"If this woman has something to do with the guy who was murdered, then she's dangerous enough to take seriously."

"Would you be willing to give us an appropriate description?"

"What about Ida? I don't want my wife hurt."

"I'll have a car drive by your house every hour to check on her."

Janus nodded and then followed Simon to his car and they drove to the police station where Janus would give an accurate description of the mysterious woman who was seen in his store arguing with Michel Lalonde on the day he was killed.

Simon understood the urge to protect people you love and care about, and how sometimes that forced you to make decisions you wouldn't otherwise make.

He'd be a hypocrite if he didn't admit that sometimes he preferred the darker side of a lie to the bold truth.

CHAPTER 75

Excited couldn't describe Josh's emotion. Relieved at the prospect of putting the minds of the residents and tourists at ease was top of his mind. Lake Pines had made the list in Cottage Travel magazine for the wrong reasons. They were warning tourists of the rise in thefts and encouraging vacationers to find other places to visit.

Hotels in the area had a decrease in bookings and several of the annual guests that resorts, hotels, and fishing camps could normally rely upon were canceling because of the reports.

Hopefully, Casey's arrest would translate into increased tourism.

Although he was ashamed to admit it, Josh found it difficult to not smile when he informed Casey's lawyer that not only was his client not being released, but if there was any proof that he sold the stolen information to criminal organizations outside of the country, he'd possibly be facing charges there are well.

The legalities sunk in faster for Vincent Haley than they did for Casey, prompting a request for a meeting first thing in the morning. After Casey and his lawyer had a short meeting, Josh joined them in one of the interrogation rooms.

Josh dropped a thick file on the table, strategically opening it as he revealed the typed sheet on the top of the pile. A pro at police tactics in interrogation rooms, Vincent didn't flinch. He held his eyes directly on Josh's face, refusing to glance down at the document Josh obviously wanted them to see. Whereas Casey turned to face his lawyer, giving him a gawking stare as he looked at the numerous charges that were listed on the sheet on the top of the stack.

"If you asked for this meeting to push to be released until your trial, you can forget it. Besides catching Casey red-handed at the café, we found some of the stolen items he sold to a pawn shop outside of town," Josh said. "And before you ask, I received the Commissioner's agreement to alert the authorities across the country that some of these thefts may be related to cases in their districts."

Vincent leaned forward, still avoiding his client's stare. He folded his hands and placed them on the table and in a calm, steady voice he asked for the one thing that Josh was prepared for but had already refused.

"Sending my client to prison for all of those charges won't change anything," Vincent wiggled his hand toward the open file without looking down, revealing a flash of gold from his watch as his sleeve shifted above his wrist.

"I think it's going to send the exact message we want it to send," Josh said. "And the message is that crime doesn't pay."

He knew it was corny, but it was also something he truly believed. He tried to ignore the image of Thomas' green and yellow bruises that discolored his face where Casey Woodfield had hit him with his tiny fists. Fists, that if he was in a real fight with a dangerous criminal wouldn't offer him the defense, he might expect them to.

Thomas made Josh promise that no matter how upset he was that he would focus on the robberies and not make Casey's arrest and the ensuing charges about his attack. They both knew that Thomas was in the wrong place at the wrong time and if he hadn't startled Casey then he wouldn't have been on the young thief's radar.

"What if my client could give you the names of the individuals who are buying all the data and the person who gave him information from the town files?" Vincent asked.

"What kind of information?"

"Let's talk deal first." Now it was the lawyer's turn to open a file folder, however, this one was tucked inside an expensive leather billfold.

I guess crime does pay, Josh thought to himself.

"I'm not sure what kind of deal you expect to leave here with today, but the best you can maybe hope for is a lighter sentence since this is the first time your client has been charged."

"What if my client could give you the names of the individuals who are buying all the data?" Vincent let the question hang before adding, "My client is just one small speck in this operation but he's in the perfect position to give you the people at the top."

"We aren't even near being done searching your client's computers. I'm sure we can charge Casey and retrieve the names you're talking about."

Vincent shook his head, "What if he kept the information and records separated?"

Josh held his gaze, trying but failing, to hide his frustration.

"Why don't you run that scenario by the Commissioner and see how intent he is on sticking with charges against my client? I think he'll be open to discussing a deal."

The idea of granting leniency toward Casey's crimes didn't sit well with Josh. He terrorized the residents of the town by instilling a deep fear that no one could put a name to. They couldn't put a face to the robber which meant that everyone was blindly avoiding the enemy and had no way to fight back. Everyone from the police, business owners, residents, and even tourists. Once known as a calm, relaxing, safe place to spend quality time, Lake Pines was almost unrecognizable. Instead, it moved from one of the most recommended vacation spots in Canada to one of the most criticized. Josh closed the file folder on the table and left the room. No matter which way he approached the situation, he knew he had to run the idea by Commissioner Robertson. It's just that the idea left an uneasy pit in his gut.

CHAPTER 76

Commissioner Gris Robertson closed his office door, walked to the far side of his office, and leaned against the window. Josh begged him not to extend the plea bargain. He needed to proceed with the charges against Casey Woodfield to give the people in Lake Pines some closure and relief. However, he also recalled the recent internal police report on the rapid increase in identity thefts.

An increase in online transactions and people refusing or being unable to leave their homes left the digital sphere filled with more people figuring out how to transverse the unfamiliar new economy.

Steeped in darkness, it granted the criminals further immunity from the reach of local police officers because they were physically unreachable. Lockdowns added to society's stress, which was compounded by the financial and emotional pinch of the economy. Within months, they became worried that criminals would reach into their lives and steal the little security they had left.

It was, as Gris' wife said, a complete and utter shit show. And now he was able to help quash a huge part of the operation. Essentially stepping on the neck of the beast and all they had to sacrifice was a little pride at a local level. In his estimation, it was a price he was willing to pay.

"Did Casey or his lawyer indicate how high up he can take us?" Gris asked. He was already pretty certain of the answer since his past dealing with Vincent Haley proved the lawyer was as prepared as he was strategic. He wouldn't have presented the option of a plea bargain if he didn't have the names of the people in the criminal organization. Instead, he would've argued for reduced time or probation for the relatively young offender.

"He said they would be names that we could also use internationally. Not just in Canada."

Gris glanced out the window and across the crumbling parking lot and over the ridge that opened into the expanse of the Nor'Wester Mountains. Everyone was affected by this type of crime. It wasn't about avoiding dangerous areas in town or adding security features to your home or business.

"I think you know what my answer is going to be."

They both drifted through the weighted silence, feeling uneasy about the decision but understanding that there were few choices available.

Together, they came up with the wording of the offer that Josh would return to Vincent Haley and his client. Along with dropping the robbery charges Casey would enter into voluntary probation outside of the Lake Pines district.

Gris was eager to tackle one of many issues he oversaw daily, and Josh was uncomfortable offering Casey Woodfield a deal. But neither of them could change the outcome of what needed to be done.

CHAPTER 77

Doctor Varanus read the file twice, making his own notes on a separate piece of paper. When he reviewed the comments that Trisha had added to the file, nothing stood out as a glaring mistake. But no matter how many times he reviewed the file, he came to the same conclusion that Kerry had. He followed each step of her process, reviewed the toxicology report and the final submission, and always came to the same conclusion.

Cody Jesper died of poisoning and all the evidence pointed the finger of guilt at his wife.

Their initial differences aside, he would be the first person to defend Kerry's aptitude and her attention to detail. His mind hadn't changed, even after considering what Trisha had found. If anything, it made him more suspicious of Trisha's sudden appearance as Kerry's assistant.

Sal was grateful that Kerry came to him with the Jesper file and asked for his opinion. Especially since he was already suspicious of Trisha's sudden presence. He had seen worse when departments struggled over tight budges.

Extra caseloads were piled on already overworked senior staff members, hoping the pressure would encourage them to quit and take early retirement, and minor infractions or mistakes at work were suddenly documented. All to avoid large severance payments and encourage staff to quit.

He wouldn't put it past their superiors to have placed Trisha as a mole, hoping to find a reason to cut large swaths of funding across their district.

Along with most of the town, Sal was surprised to learn that the work crew found a murder weapon inside the lakeside fish statue. In fact, he thought it was quite ingenious and wondered if the rise in crime had anything to do with the popular chef's murder or if it was just a coincidence.

Kerry thought it would be the perfect opportunity to get Trisha out of the small office so she wouldn't disturb Sal. As Kerry explained crime scene procedures and evidence collection to Trisha, Sal would dive into the Jesper file and try to find out what went wrong.

He cleared his schedule for the rest of the afternoon and planned to examine the contents of the evidence box while Kerry distracted Trisha outside the hospital.

He turned off his computer, grabbed his security pass, and left the lab. As Sal walked, he couldn't help but wince as his sore knee throbbed with every step. He slowed his pace, taking smaller steps, hoping to minimize the pressure and impact on his joint.

He avoided stairs and inclines, opting for flat, even surfaces, and stayed out of view from other staff in the hospital. His funding depended upon his ability to work the long, sometimes draining hours in the lab. Which is why he ignored his physiotherapist's advice to use a cane. Opting for the illusion of vitality and efficiency over the concern for his own health.

Despite the discomfort, he kept his head up and shoulders relaxed, maintaining a good posture. As he continued to walk toward the empty elevator bay, he breathed deeply, focusing on each step and taking it one at a time. He welcomed the wait as the elevator returned from the sixth floor. Even if he wanted to, he wasn't sure he could tackle the cold, dim stairwell.

As the doors slid open on the lower level, Sal waved to the record attendant as he tapped his security pass on the safety pad.

"Doctor Varanus, what brings you down to my level?" Jordi, the long-serving security guard joked with him as he approached the front desk.

"I'd like to sign out a box," Sal reached for the logbook and scribbled his name and hospital staff identification number on the first available line. "And call me Sal. We've known each other long enough."

"Sure thing, Doctor Varanus," Jordi laughed. "What file are you looking for?"

Sal gave Jordi the file name and the corresponding case number.

"That's one of Doctor Dearborne's files, isn't it?"

"Yes. I'm helping her get some files organized. She's been reorganizing everything since the fire in her lab."

Jordi typed the case file number into his computer and pointed Sal toward the aisle and shelf where the box was stored. "It's nice to see you both getting along finally. I always said you'd work well together. And you're almost as friendly as Doctor Dearborne's assistant." Jordi added with a wink.

Sal paused as he stepped through the doors and turned around, "Trisha's been down here? When?"

Jordi rested his fingers on his chin and closed his eyes, "There are so many people down here, but I think it was three days ago."

Sal reached for the logbook and flipped the pages until he saw the day that Jordi was referring to. But it wasn't Trisha's name and signature on the line. It was Kerry's name, but the signature was nothing like the one in the case file that he was holding in his hand.

CHAPTER 78

Using the extensive database and the police department's ability to search names and contact information as far back as fifty years, Simon located the registered address for Curtis Strong. If the information was correct, he had been living in the same home, in the same small town just north of Montreal where he and Vivienne lived fifteen years ago.

Simon phoned the local police department and asked the officer on duty if he had any information about the Strong family. The officer was familiar with the Vivienne Strong murder case, but not her family.

"However, that only means that he's not in trouble with the law," Officer Joubert explained. "Is there a problem with Monsieur Strong?"

"No, nothing like that," Simon said, not wanting to relay the specifics concerning Michel Lalonde's murder and his connection to Curtis Strong. "I just want to speak with him. I have some questions concerning his wife's murder."

"Mon dieu," Officer Joubert exclaimed. "You want to call him fifteen years after his wife's death and ask him some questions? No wonder the residents are having a difficult time trusting the police."

"It really is important that I speak with him. I've tried the phone number that's registered to his name, but I can't even seem to leave a voicemail. Is there any way you could have someone check in on him?"

After some reluctance, Officer Joubert agreed to send an officer who was out on patrol to the address registered as Curtis Strong's primary residence.

Later that day, Officer Joubert called back, catching Simon just as he was about to leave the office.

"I think I know why you couldn't reach Curtis Strong," the young officer said, in a thick French accent that reminded Simon of Jean Lamont. "He doesn't live at that address any longer. In fact, his neighbor said he moved away a couple of years ago."

Simon grabbed a pen, "Did the neighbor have any idea where he moved to?"

"Chêne Doré. In English, it's what you would call a retirement home. They're about twenty minutes from here. If you would like, I can send an officer tomorrow?"

"No, that's alright. You've done a lot already. I really appreciate it." Simon said. "But if you have a phone number for them, I'll take that."

The officer recited the number just as a crash echoed behind him, "Merde!" Officer Joubert yelled into the phone. "Darn dog. If there's nothing else, I have to go. My dog has just knocked over my lunch."

Simon thanked the officer again and heard him scold the dog just as he ended the call. He knew that if the dog was anything like Raven, a perfectly timed twist of the head with his ears pulled back would save him from any punishment.

A friendly receptionist answered the phone at Chêne Doré. She greeted him in English as well as French, which made his odd explanation for why he needed to speak with Curtis Strong easier.

"Yes. Mr. Strong is a resident here," the woman confirmed.

"Great, may I please speak with him?"

She cleared her throat, paused, and then spoke softly into the phone, "Chêne Doré is a care facility. Mr. Strong came to live with us after he suffered a hemorrhagic stroke. He can't walk or speak."

"I'm sorry, I had no idea. There's a report in my file that he was represented at a recent parole hearing that was being held for his wife's murderer so I just assumed I'd be able to speak with him."

"He probably was represented, but not by going there himself. Mr. Strong and his wife had a child. That's who probably represented him at the hearing. They're in charge of all of his affairs."

Simon sat up, "Is there any way you could give me their name?"

"I can do one better. I have a phone number too."

CHAPTER 79

Simon pulled the list of names and the corresponding phone numbers and added Vivienne Strong's child to the list. He was about to call the number when his phone rang. Without looking to see who it was, he answered the call. It was Camille Scott.

"I got your message, and I was about to just send you an email but thought it would be better to call," Camille's words were hard to hear under the sound of a passing train. "Sorry, my office is next to the tracks."

They waited for the train to pass and then Camille explained why she called. "After we spoke, I thought more about who Michel could have upset. I knew about the one lawsuit, but there were two others. Would you like the names?"

"Sure." Simon wrote the names of the two people that had filed a claim against Michel and asked Camille to forward an email with the details of each case. "You didn't know about those?"

"They happened before I became his agent. When I called Michel's lawyer to inform him of his death, he told me about the two cases." She explained. "I was so excited about landing a top client, that I never imagined that he'd have these skeletons in his closet."

"Then there's something else you probably weren't aware of?" Simon said. "His real name isn't Michel Lalonde."

"What? I don't understand," Camille stammered. "Oh, geez. This is going to destroy my reputation with promoters in the industry. I was just getting on my feet again."

"Is that why you pushed his cookbook out a few months early?"

Camille cleared her throat, surprised to learn that Simon was aware of what she did, "Michel wouldn't listen to me. I told him that getting the book into the market at the beginning of the summer would leave us more time to promote it before the peak fall book season. I had several interviews lined up for him and if he hit the best-seller list with this book, it would be three in a row! Do you know what that would've done for his career? It would have ensured a successful launch of his restaurant, too. I only did it to help his career. I'm his agent and it's my responsibility to grow his career."

Another thought occurred to Simon. A successful book launch and restaurant would also inflate his agent's bank account. A few minutes after they ended the call, an email arrived from Camille Scott, listing two more names that Simon added to a suspect list. One plaintiff lived in France, and the other lived in Lake Pines.

CHAPTER 80

Tanya's mouth dropped when Simon slid the printout from the court filing across the counter. Flour dusted the tip of her nose and the front of her apron, and the scent of cardamom filled the air. But at that moment, the warm, welcoming kitchen felt more like an interrogation room.

"Why didn't you tell me about this?"

Tanya's lip quivered, "It was a long time ago. I filed it the first summer I worked for him." Tanya lowered herself into a chair and wiped the side of her face with the back of her hand.

"Why did you sue him?"

"I was hired to stock his entire cottage. The list was ridiculous, but I thought it would be the chance of a lifetime to work with the great Chef Lalonde." Tanya wiggled her fingers in the air and rolled her eyes in a mocking gesture. "The items he wanted weren't even sold in Lake Pines. I had to order them online and there's no buy now-pay later plan. I couldn't afford to carry the cost on my credit card for an extra month, so when he refused to pay, I filed the papers in court."

"What was the reason for not paying you?"

"He said that he didn't need all the things I bought."

Simon narrowed his eyes, "Then why ask you to buy them?"

"He didn't," Tanya said. "His agent is the one who hired me and sent me the list of items to purchase. From that point on, he said he'd email a pre-arrival shopping list himself."

"Why didn't you mention this?" Simon asked.

"Honestly, I really didn't think it was important."

"You were one of the last people to see Michel alive and you had sued him for thirty-five hundred dollars," Simon explained.

"He settled the lawsuit within a day of being served papers," Tanya said, defensively. "He said he didn't want any trouble, and he cut me a cheque to cover the initial claim and my lawyer's fees. I don't even think he told his agent about it."

"But why continue to work for him?" Simon asked. "I wouldn't think you'd have a good working relationship with someone you tried to sue."

"The money was too good to pass up, plus, he apologized and asked that we put everything behind us."

"But you didn't have a good relationship, did you?"

Tanya shook her head, "I planned on quitting at the end of this summer. My catering business had made enough money in the last year to cover the cost of going out on my own." She paused and then with some genuine sadness in her voice she added, "I really thought I'd learn some cooking techniques from him."

Although most of the chef's life was steeped in secrecy, one thing was becoming exceedingly clear. There were a lot of people who had an axe to grind with Chef Lalonde.

CHAPTER 81

The sound of Peter's approaching footsteps in the hall came at a slow, plodding pace. Kerry's pulse quickened as each tap of Peter's heel on the linoleum tile signaled his approach. Even though she knew in her heart that telling Peter the truth was the right thing to do, she couldn't help but fear the outcome of their conversation.

Kerry prepared Simon that she might face criminal charges and at the very least they should expect that she'd lose her job.

Until now, she never could have imagined a scenario where Peter would have a reason to fire her. She never entertained the idea of another profession. Even as friends and neighbors planned secondary careers as they neared retirement, Kerry always imagined that she'd work well past the typical age of retirement.

But now? Now, she not only had to face her impending forced removal from a job she loved, but every case file she touched would be open to review. Court cases would be re-examined, and insurance companies would jump to re-evaluate life insurance claims for anyone who died with a large policy.

Family members would have to relive the trauma of losing people they cared about, as rules would dictate that everyone would need to be informed of what was happening.

Jean offered to fly into Lake Pines and stand by Kerry as she told Peter what she had done. But this was something she had to do alone. After all, she falsified the evidence in the Vivienne Strong case of her own volition. This was the music she needed to face.

Peter tapped on the glass, turned the handle, and walked into Simon's office.

They had agreed to meet at the police station since the hospital basement and room 24B offered no extra room or privacy. At six-foot-one, with broad shoulders and an imposing stance, Peter filled a room the moment he walked in.

A nervous look reflected in Peter's eyes, making Kerry wonder if he was already aware of what she needed to tell him.

When the door was closed, they both spoke at the same time. Breaking the tension and the shared awkwardness with a laugh.

"Why don't we sit down?" Peter lowered himself into a chair and placed his hat on Simon's desk. "Is Simon alright if we use his office for a while?"

"He's out at Storm Island right now, searching for a document that might help him with a murder investigation. He said he'd be awhile."

"Good," Peter said, seeming more interested in having the room to use as opposed to Simon's work on the case.

"Why don't you go first," Kerry said. She knew he wanted to talk to her about her lab and her placement in the hospital basement.

The entire situation would be irrelevant after she revealed what she had done fifteen years ago, but it gave her the extra time to formulate the right words in her mind and calm her nerves. No matter how many times she went over what she wanted to say in her head, as she sat in front of Peter, her throat tightened at the thought of speaking.

"You know the department has been reworking the budget," Peter started, "the fire and the costs to rebuild your lab have forced us to reassess your position."

"Wouldn't insurance have covered the costs?"

"Part of it, yes. But anytime we build a facility there are new codes we must follow, and the machines are only partially covered because of their depreciation. The price tag on setting you up in a new facility would cut into an already tight budget."

"Then why send the assistant?" Kerry asked. She had been curious from the first day that Trisha arrived why her request to cancel her leave of absence had been ignored.

"Trisha?" Peter seemed caught off guard by the mention of sending Trisha Chen to work at the hospital.

Kerry folded her arms and waited for Simon to give her an answer. If she was being watched, she at least deserved an explanation, and she wanted an honest answer.

"Trisha was working as a floater replacement in the district when you put in your request for a leave of absence. Technically she'd been working without pay for over a year. It's part of a national program where the government and provinces work in conjunction with each other giving school and work opportunities to children who are victims of crime." Peter explained. "When we told her she'd be placed in Lake Pines, she was ecstatic. She heard a lot about you, and your office was her top choice for placement when she graduated. I didn't have the heart to turn her away and tell her you changed your mind about your leave. I thought you'd appreciate the help."

Kerry considered everything Peter had said. She thought about the extra work Trisha was putting into each job and the additional research she was doing without being asked.

A wave of guilt washed over her as she thought back to Sal's accusation that Trisha may have been placed in the hospital as a plant and that they were both being watched.

Then another thought occurred to her. Whether it was her heightened sense of paranoia or the years she worked alongside Simon she couldn't be sure, and the question jumped into her mind.

"You said Trisha was part of a program that was geared toward helping children affected by crime."

Peter nodded, "Yeah, the program has given many kids a chance at a better life."

"What was the crime?"

"Pardon?"

"How was Trisha affected?"

"It was really sad," Peter said, thinking back to Trisha's file when it first came across his desk. "Her mother was murdered by a co-worker." Peter paused and then widened his eyes. "You may have heard of the case. Her maiden name was Strong. Her mother was Vivienne Strong. She's from a small town just north of Montreal, and if I'm not mistaken, you just started working for Jean at the time."

Suddenly, Kerry felt a rush of anxiety wash over her.

As Kerry stood, her vision suddenly became blurry and she felt lightheaded. She stumbled forward, her knees feeling weak, and she reached out to grasp the corner of Simon's desk. Her heart raced and her palms grew clammy as she struggled to keep herself upright.

Peter reached out and guided her back to the chair, "Kerry, are you alright?"

The room around her spun, and she couldn't make out any distinct shapes or colors. She felt as if she were floating, weightless, and disconnected from the world around her. Her ears buzzed, and she could barely hear the sound of Peter's voice.

She took a deep breath and tried to focus on something solid and real, but it was like trying to grasp onto smoke. As the feeling persisted, she felt like everything was crashing down around her.

There were only so many coincidences she could take in at once. Especially with the note's arrival and the inference of her wrongdoing in the murder investigation for Vivienne Strong and the ultimate conviction of Paul Buchanan.

Before she lost her nerve, she needed to tell Peter everything.

As she sat there with her friend, who was also the man who fought to have her hired, she prepared to let him down. She explained that she had done the unthinkable for a person in her position. She falsified the evidence to ensure Paul Buchanan's conviction.

CHAPTER 82

Sal pushed through the doors of the police station just as Peter was leaving.

"Is Kerry here?" He asked with panting breath.

Peter pointed to the hall, "She's in Simon's office making a call. If you hurry, you can catch her before she gets on the line."

Sal shot his hand up in the air, in what only Peter assumed was a wave of thanks. He disappeared down the hall in a half limp, half jog and burst through the doors just as Kerry was reaching for her phone.

He fell forward, resting his hands on Simon's desk, and let out a deep, long groan. "My lord, I need to get in shape."

Kerry pulled out a chair and helped him into it.

"What's wrong?"

"I completed the tests you wanted me to run on the poison for the Jesper file." Sal leaned his head back and took a deep breath.

"And?"

Sal straightened his head and leaned forward, resting his forearms on his legs. "And the box contained your run-of-the-mill baking soda."

"That's what you ran all the way over here? To tell me you confirmed I made a mistake that may be responsible for an innocent woman being arrested?"

"No, I came to show you this," Sal pulled a piece of paper out of his pocket and slammed it on the desk.

Kerry lifted the report, reading again how she misinterpreted the test on the warfarin and dropped it to her lap. "I've seen this, Sal. It only proves I made a huge mistake."

"No," Sal pointed to the form number on the top right corner of the page. "It proves that this form is the most updated form used by the province. I double-checked with the administration office and confirmed that they didn't distribute this form until two weeks after Cody Jesper died. That was after you examined the pills and poison retrieved from his home and did a full autopsy."

The realization that the evidence box and the form had intentionally been altered and falsified hit her like a lead weight, knocking the wind out of her lungs.

"When I was retrieving the evidence box, I learned something else too," Sal explained, speaking more calmly after catching his breath. "Your name is in the logbook having gone into the storage room three days ago. The same day that Trisha had the Jesper file."

CHAPTER 83

After rolling away the mossy boulder, he ascended from the cramped cavern nestled beneath a dark cluster of pine trees. The space was small, damp, and dark, but it concealed his presence on Storm Island for almost two weeks. He placed his hands on his lower back and stretched out his spine. Until he began sleeping in the subterranean cove, Paul never imagined that the prison cot would be a more comfortable option for a night's sleep.

Clinging to the memory of who Michel really was, kept him strong through the years he spent in prison. Nothing could erase the horror of what he did to both his own family and Vivienne, but the thought of being able to see his son and apologize kept him focused on what he needed to do to get released.

He wouldn't be able to make up for the years of abuse and intimidation he had leveled on his wife. Even if a heart attack hadn't taken her life at such a young age, he couldn't make up for the day she pulled their son out of his bed in the middle of the night and fled to her parent's home in the secluded countryside.

Initially, he signed up for the prison therapy program to avoid being around his fellow inmates. His brash bravado set him at odds with his co-workers, his family, and his son. But that same bullying approach fell short of the toughness that truly hardened criminals brought to their prison sentences.

Paul soon learned that he wasn't capable of defending himself against the physical violence that was unleashed on the new inmates when guards looked the other way. But he suddenly realized the terror he caused in so many people's lives.

Guilt for taking Vivienne's life when she spurned his advances would rest with him for the rest of his life. It would be a permanent stain on his soul that no amount of regret or reformation could erase. He had to accept that fact and focus on what he could do, which was to repair the relationship with his son. He couldn't take back the murders from his past, but he could move forward by repairing his relationship with his son.

He still thought of him as Paul Jr., and although he was sad to learn he changed his name, after some reflective therapy, he realized it was the rebirth that his son deserved. There was no reason that his son should live with the guilt that his father was an abusive, manipulative man convicted of murder.

These were the thoughts that rolled through Paul's mind as he wandered the forest on Storm Island. Paul walked out of the shadow of the trees blowing in the wind and took a deep breath. He remained hidden on Storm Island before his son arrived, hoping to learn everything he could about him. After discreetly arriving in Lake Pines, he had convinced a local teen to take him to the island, and for fifty dollars, he promised to keep the transportation secret.

Watching him from inside the dense forest, Paul took in each mannerism. He realized that his son walked just like his mother. That he scratched the back of his head just like his grandfather, and how his distinct hairline resembled his own.

A forest of pine and birch covered storm Island, but its elevated structure allowed for natural cave formations on the ground. That's where he had remained hidden since his arrival in Lake Pines and that's where he had waited while several visitors arrived on the island. And it's where he was when his son was murdered.

The familiar tone of anger followed by the distinct fear in his son's cry for help urged him from the cave. By the time he reached the bottom of the stairs, his son was already dead. A squiggle of waves trailed behind a boat as it sped away from the island and disappeared from view. Paul briefly caught a glimpse of the bright red jacket just before the boat dipped around the end of the island.

He knelt next to his son, fell forward, and screamed. The cry rang out through the air and over the water as he yelled out his name. Not the name the world currently knew him as, but as the small innocent boy that he carried out of the hospital the day after he was born.

It had been a week since his son was murdered, and Paul still hadn't left Storm Island. There were several opportunities, but he couldn't pull himself away from the last place he saw his son alive. Repairing his life and relationship with his son was the only thing that kept him focused and committed to making a positive change in his life. And now it was all destroyed. Everything was gone and he had no way of getting it back.

His rage returned. Stronger and more primal than before he was sent to prison. Paul sat on the edge of the cliff on the opposite end of the island, far away from the cottage and the place where his son was killed. And far away from the sound of the police boat that was pulling into Haven Bay.

CHAPTER 84

Trisha took in the familiar surroundings, the route to Storm Island, and the large, private bay that looked up at the cottage, pretending that she didn't know where Simon was taking her.

Unexpectedly, Kerry stepped away from the office, passing all of her duties onto Trisha for the day. Which included accompanying Simon to Storm Island as he searched for additional information in the Michel Lalonde case.

"I'm still not sure what it is you think I can do to help you?" Trisha asked as Simon slowed the boat and maneuvered it alongside the dock.

"Kerry thought you'd want to see the police side of the investigations where coroner examinations can affect a case."

Simon reached out and grabbed the dock, steadying the boat as Trisha climbed onto the dock.

"If we already have the murder weapon which wasn't even found here, then what are we looking for?"

"Even though the weapon wasn't found here, the victim was. He was killed on this island after having a confrontation with his attacker. Outside of Mary McLean, who lives across the bay, no one heard or saw anything." Simon spoke as they walked toward the second set of stairs next to the boathouse. "But something happened that resulted in Michel's death. Whether it was an argument that got out of hand or something less personal, I don't know. But I'm positive that there's evidence of every person who was on this island."

Trisha stopped walking, "Everybody?"

Simon looked at Trisha and stopped beside her, "Are you alright? You look pale."

Trisha touched the side of her face, and she felt the warmth rise to her cheeks. "It must be the boat ride, I'm not used to the water."

Simon smiled, "You'll get used to it. Especially if you want to work in Lake Pines."

Before Trisha responded, a loud crash came from the porch.

Simon called out as they climbed the stairs, "It's the police! Is anyone there?" He pushed Trisha toward the boathouse and motioned for her to step inside.

Taking the steps two at a time, Simon bounded up the stairwell and jumped behind the pumphouse, taking cover from the view of the cottage porch.

Simon stood next to the pumphouse, his gun drawn, and he checked his stance as he shifted his weight over the uneven ground. Trisha moved forward and Simon waved her back, and she quickly complied.

Again, Simon shouted a warning, just as a thundering boom resonated as a shadowy intruder jumped off the porch and ran toward the forest.

Simon pushed him down to the ground and pulled his arms around to his back. Within a few seconds, he tightened handcuffs on the man's bulky arms and pulled him to his feet.

As he spun him around, he recognized the man's face from the Vivienne Strong murder file which also included an updated photo taken on the day of her killer's release.

"Paul Buchanan?" Simon said with some surprise. "What are you doing on Storm Island?"

Paul dropped his eyes and then as Trisha stepped out of the shadows he looked over Simon's shoulder.

"What are you doing here?" Paul stammered out with some difficulty as he looked into Trisha Chen's dark black eyes.

Simon spun around and recognized the look on Trisha's face. It wasn't the fear and shock she displayed when Simon pushed her into the boathouse. Instead, it was the glazed seething glare of hate, and it was aimed directly at Paul Buchanan.

CHAPTER 85

Information pamphlets, stuffed into cardboard holders, lined the front desk in the courthouse. Ineffectual signs, written with a thick black marker, invited visitors to 'take one'. Some information concerned the filing fees and rules of conduct in the courthouse, while others covered the health and safety procedures to be followed if visitors were symptomatic of an infectious respiratory disease.

Looking around at the empty hands of each person in the room, the pamphlets and their information were of little interest.

An altered copy of Michel's Last Will and Testament needed to be filed. Michel bequeathed his property, financial holdings, and copyrights to one person.

That was the purpose of standing in line at the courthouse. The moment the papers were filed there would be no need to remain in town, and the true heir wouldn't know the difference.

Being seen, or talking to the police, was not part of the plan, but then again, neither was Michel's murder.

The line moved forward and with only two people ahead, it shouldn't take longer than an hour before the messy business surrounding Michel's death would be over. There was no other choice but to patiently wait.

Outside, just beyond the rear of the building, the noise of the metal wheels grinding against the tracks reverberated through the building. A low rumble came from no discernable direction, as the cargo train rushed through Lake Pines. The sound grew louder and more intense, drowning out all other noise in the small room and the clerk had to shout his question at the woman standing on the opposite side of the counter.

From inside the old building, the sound of the passing train was deafening. The floor plate shook, causing small particles of dust and debris to rain down from the fiberglass ceiling tiles. Any level of conversation was almost impossible, and the stand filled with information pamphlets rattled in time with the train's movement. Eventually, the noise slowly receded, leaving behind a ringing silence that flooded the room for several moments before fading away completely, returning the awkward hum of the court clerk's computer.

The court clerk rolled his eyes as the elderly woman fumbled in her purse and searched for her identification when she finally realized what the clerk had been shouting under the noise of the train. She was mumbling something about having left her glasses at home and needing to empty her bag on the counter.

Eventually, the woman located her identification and submitted her grievance regarding her rent increase. The court clerk assured the woman that he'd file her complaint immediately, and considering the urgency, a judge would read it by the end of the week.

Relieved and exhausted, the woman thanked the clerk and stepped away from the counter.

The long, snaking line had been filled with people of all ages, each carrying their own grievance and handful of papers and looking just as impatient. Once the train had passed, the noise level was muted, with chatter and the rustling of bags and shifting feet. People jostled and bumped into each other as they tried to shift their weight and find a more comfortable position. Thankfully, it wasn't an environment that welcomed small talk.

A digital clock on the edge of the counter ticked through forty minutes while the line slowly moved.

The end result would be worth the wait.

The person in front stepped to the side and the young clerk smiled and asked how he could help.

The clerk smiled when a stack of completed forms, signed and properly notarized was placed on the counter.

He stamped the file along with the legal documents regarding the property transfer and attached the Death Certificate to the top.

"Is there anything else I can do for you?" The clerk asked. He was glad to help someone who had all the correct documentation that was signed and in the right order.

"No, thank you."

As the next person stepped forward, the clerk thought to himself that he wished all the plaintiffs and registrants coming to his office were as nice as the one who filed the paperwork today. Oh, how it would make the world so much easier.

CHAPTER 86

Simon reached into his pocket and extracted the key for the handcuffs. A muted click released the constricting cuffs from Paul's wrists. Simon grabbed Paul's elbow and guided him to a chair, and then instructed Trisha to sit several seats away.

The awkward boat ride back into town was made more bizarre by the tension between Paul Buchanan and Trisha Chen, who appeared to know each other.

Outside of trespassing, Paul hadn't committed a crime worthy of being arrested for and Simon was grateful that he hadn't put up a fuss about being handcuffed while he was being transported to town.

Having a convicted killer, even one out on parole, in the back of a boat with a young woman made Simon more cautious once he realized he'd have to drive them both back to town at the same time.

Simon recently learned that Michel Lalonde's birth name was Paul Buchanan Jr. The bulky, hardened man who was running away from Simon on Storm Island wasn't just connected to Kerry's past. He was the murder victim's father.

The interrogation room was in use, and even though this wasn't an official interrogation, Simon wanted some answers. He asked

Sally to clear the main lobby and soon Simon was alone with Paul and Trisha as he prepared to figure out which questions to ask first.

As interested as he was in how Paul Buchanan and Trisha Chen knew each other, he was immediately concerned by Paul's presence on Storm Island.

"Why were you on Storm Island?" Simon asked.

"I arrived a day before Paul. Sorry, Michel. I wanted to make amends for what I did when he was small, but he didn't respond to my phone calls or emails. I thought if I came here when he was on his summer break from work, I could convince him to speak with me."

"He didn't invite you?"

Paul shook his head and tears welled up in his eyes.

"Did you have an argument?" Simon wondered if he had inadvertently stumbled upon Michel Lalonde's murderer.

"I didn't even get the chance to talk to him. He didn't know I was on the island."

"My officers searched that island, but no one saw any sign of you."

"There's a cave about fifty feet from the cottage. It's pretty well hidden inside a clump of trees. I covered the opening with a moss-covered rock so it blended into the ground."

"You've been on the island the entire week?"

Tears morphed into heavy sobs and as Paul nodded his head, they rolled down his cheeks, trailing through a thin layer of dust. Streaking his face before spilling onto his light blue shirt. He dragged the back of his hand across the side of his face, smearing the tears and dirt along his jaw.

Simon lowered his gaze. The pain that surfaced in Paul Buchanan's eyes stood at odds with what Simon expected from the man who abused his son as a child and murdered a young woman.

The contradiction made him feel uneasy.

After a few moments, Simon continued in a lower voice, "Did you see what happened on the day Michel was murdered?"

"A lot of people were coming and going all afternoon. I had planned to speak with my son that afternoon. I had it all planned out, at least, I thought I did. Anyway, each time I approached the cottage, a different boat pulled up to the dock. There was a lady who arrived with some food and boxes of supplies, but she never left the boathouse. She unloaded everything and then was gone without speaking to Michel." Paul paused, wiping his tears with a tissue Simon offered him. "Thank you." Paul blew his nose and then scrunched the tissue in his fists. "After she left, a guy arrived with some lumber, but Michel wouldn't let him unload the boat. I heard them arguing that the order was wrong. There was also a woman, but I'm not sure when she arrived, I think she was there right after Michel returned from town. But I don't know why she was there."

"What about around the time Michel was murdered? Did you hear or see anyone?"

"Because there were so many people, I decided to wait until the evening to speak to my son. But I heard him scream, so I rushed down and saw him lying on the dock. I knew he was in trouble because it wasn't like a yell from a disagreement. It was the sound of someone who was frightened for their life."

"I guess you know all about that," snapped Trisha. Simon had almost forgotten she was there. She had sat so quietly the entire time that Paul was speaking.

"Trisha, would you feel more comfortable in another room? You can wait in my office if you want?"

Trisha stood and jabbed her finger in Paul's direction, "I'm not going anywhere. I want to hear everything this monster has to say."

Kerry turned the corner and walked into the room with Sal close on her heels. They came to a quick stop when they saw who Simon was talking to. Kerry held the report in her hand and tightened her grip when she raised her arm.

"Trisha!" Kerry exclaimed. "You have a lot of explaining to do."

Color drained from Trisha's face when she recognized the form in Kerry's hand. Kerry stepped forward, ready to launch into a tirade against the deceptive assistant when she recognized the man sitting in the chair near Simon.

Kerry's eyes widened, and her mouth fell open as she recognized the man sitting a few feet away. She stepped back, recoiling involuntarily at the sight of Paul Buchanan. He was older and slightly thinner than the last time she saw him, but Kerry knew without a doubt it was him. She blinked several times as if hoping to clear her vision and make sure that what she was seeing was real. She struggled to find the right words, her voice catching in her throat as she tried to speak. Her mind raced, trying to process the implications of what she was seeing.

Jean warned her that Paul had been released.

For several moments, she stood frozen, her body locked in a state of disbelief. Then, slowly, she regained her composure. Her mind raced with questions and possibilities.

With a sinking feeling, Kerry realized that the only person who could've sent the note was sitting in front of her. Paul Buchanan, the man who went to prison because of her lie.

CHAPTER 87

Simon placed Trisha and Paul in separate rooms. The complicated nature required them to be apart as Simon questioned them. Simon asked Sally to call Josh, "I'm going to need someone to question Trisha while I'm speaking with Paul Buchanan."

"He's out with Jamie on some tech-recon mission. He said he would be busy the entire day."

Simon decided not to ask what a tech-recon mission was and prepared to question both Trisha and Paul himself. First on his list was Paul Buchanan, considering his past legal issues.

Simon sat across from Paul Buchanan in the recently vacated interrogation room and placed an empty pad of paper and pen on the table. Simon offered Paul the opportunity to speak with his lawyer. However, he reminded him he wasn't being arrested for a crime.

"I just want to clarify what you saw or heard the day your son died," Simon said. "But why don't you start by telling me why you didn't call the police once you realized someone killed him?

"Considering the fact you slapped cuffs on me at the cottage and you're asking me questions in an interrogation room should be explanation enough," Paul said. "If the police arrived at Storm Island and found me standing above my son's lifeless body, what do you think they would've done?"

Simon knew exactly what would've initially happened, but he explained to Paul that would've been sorted out just like he was doing now.

"I'm interested in what you can tell me about Michel's murderer."

"As I said, I only heard my son scream. That's when I came running down to the dock and found him. When I was kneeling next to him, I heard a boat speed out of the bay. I looked up and saw the boat just as they went around the island."

"What do you remember about the boat? Anything. The color, motor, what was the driver wearing?"

"The boat was white with a blue stripe. The engine was black and I remember the person driving the boat was tall, and they were wearing a red coat."

"How do you know Trisha? You recognized each other on the island."

"I was surprised to see her there."

"How do you know her?" Simon asked again.

Paul folded his brows, narrowed his eyes, and tilted his head. "You don't know?"

Simon shook his head.

"Trisha is Vivienne Strong's daughter. The last time I saw her, she was at my Parole Board hearing with her husband. She was trying to convince the Board to deny my request. Her anger didn't surprise me, but the fact is, she didn't know how much remorse I felt because of what happened. Trisha wouldn't have cared, and to be honest, I don't blame her. I ruined her life and there's no reason for her to forgive me."

CHAPTER 88

Patricia Strong officially changed her name to Trisha Chen when she got married sixteen months ago. She was waiting in Simon's office while he spoke with Paul. Simon told Kerry not to ask Trisha about the report from the Jesper file. At least until he finished sorting out the confusion from earlier in the day.

The connection between Paul Buchanan, Michel Lalonde, Trisha Chen, and Kerry was eerily suspicious.

His conversation with Paul explained the connection between him and Trisha, but not why she was in Lake Pines and working for Kerry as her assistant. Kerry and Sal quickly filled Simon in on the falsified report that Trisha altered a few days ago. He took the report and slipped it into the folds of the pad of paper he was carrying.

Trisha stood when Simon walked into his office, and he asked her to sit back down as he walked behind his desk. It suddenly struck him how young she looked. Her petite stature had never given him that feeling before now, but seeing her thrown off kilter after she saw the man who murdered her mother upset her all over again. And he wanted to keep that in mind.

He placed the pad of paper upside down on his desk, shielding his notes from his conversation with Paul.

"Why don't you tell me why you're here, Trisha," Simon calmly said.

"You asked me to go out to Storm Island."

"I mean, why are you in Lake Pines?" Simon held up his hand, stopping Trisha from immediately answering. "And don't say Peter sent you because he's next on my list of people to call. I want to know with all the labs and offices to work for why you ended up here. In Lake Pines, and more specifically, working with Kerry."

Trisha's face froze. She had been prepared to explain her shock and surprise at seeing Paul Buchanan, but not why she targeted Lake Pines and Kerry Dearborne.

Simon leaned forward on his forearms, "I know your mother was Vivienne Strong. I didn't make the connection because your last name is different, but now that I know the connection, I'm wondering why you came here?"

"I chose this profession because of what happened to my mother. It was the forensic work from the coroner that put her murderer behind bars. I thought if I followed in that profession, then maybe I could help make a difference for other victims."

"What happened? Something changed if you concealed your identity from Kerry." Simon thought of the falsified report inside the pad of paper on his desk.

"During a work placement job in Montreal in my final year of school, I signed out the file for my mother's file. I know I shouldn't have done it, but I was curious about what happened during the murder investigation. When I read the file, I saw the report on the initial DNA evidence being excluded because the junior coroner didn't follow the correct regulations when logging the evidence. He almost avoided being charged for her murder." Trisha's voice increased to the point she was almost shouting.

"But he went to prison," Simon said. "I don't understand why you sound upset."

"The investigators miraculously found his DNA on the rock that was used to kill my mother. It didn't take a genius to realize that Kerry falsified the evidence. The forensic team examined the rock at the beginning of the investigation and found only my mother's DNA."

"Are you responsible for the note that was slipped under Kerry's door?" Simon asked. He recalled Kerry's comment about how the paper resembled samples at Michel Lalonde's cottage.

"I took the paper from Michel's cottage when I was there. I went by to see him and to tell him that I was getting close to Kerry," Trisha lowered her head. "And I sent the box with the rock. When I was working in Montreal, I was able to get into the evidence storage area and retrieve the evidence box for my mother's file. I loosened the bottom of the box and got the rock out without disturbing the security label. I wanted to prove to Doctor Dearborne that what she did was wrong."

Simon pulled the report out from between the pages of paper and slid it across the table. It took Trisha only a moment, and then she recognized the form.

"These files weren't used until after Cody Jesper died," Simon pointed to the alphanumeric number on the top corner of the page. "This wasn't the report that Kerry filed. Now, why don't you explain again what you were planning to achieve by making it look like Kerry made a mistake on her last file?"

CHAPTER 89

Kerry and Sal had returned to the hospital, knowing that their presence in the station would only make the situation with Trisha more puzzling.

Sal was confused about the link between Kerry, Trisha, and the newly paroled second-degree murderer. Kerry waited until they were in the privacy of room 24B before she explained the entire situation to him.

Patiently, he listened. Nodding intermittently as he connected the intricate pattern between Kerry's past mistake and the current murder investigation. He rested his right hand on the side of his face, balancing his elbow on his left hand, which was tucked around his body. The move reminded her of Jean, who did the same thing as he waited for a student to explain their findings.

"Trisha is the daughter of the woman who Paul Buchanan murdered?" Sal posed his comment as a question, but Kerry understood Sal was trying to make sense of Trisha's presence. In the short time that Kerry worked with him, she learned that Sal often repeated facts he was already aware of as a question. She put it off to his years as a researcher and double-checked several facts for accuracy.

Sal shifted his arms, releasing his right hand from the side of his face, and pointed a finger in the air. "But wouldn't she have been grateful to you for ensuring her mother's killer didn't get away with her murder?"

"I think she blames me for Paul not receiving a longer sentence. With the chain of custody being argued early in the investigation, Paul almost walked away from the murder charge. After that scare, the prosecution agreed to a shorter trial when Paul accepted a plea to a second-degree murder charge."

"You said she figured out what happened while she was a student," Sal said. "Why not just go to the authorities and report what you did?"

"If she did that, then Paul's lawyer would've found out and he would have been able to have his client's case reviewed. As angry as she was with what I did, she was more concerned with keeping her mother's killer behind bars."

Sal leaned back in the chair, looked up at Kerry, who was sitting on her makeshift desk and shook his head.

"She may have done more damage to her cause by targeting you."

"I thought for sure you'd chastise me for what I did."

Sal shrugged his shoulders, "I don't agree with what you did. That's not how we build trust in the justice system, but I'd be lying if I said I didn't understand why you did it." Sal explained. "I've seen enough of what you do here with the cases you worked in Lake Pines to know it's not who you are."

Kerry choked back the emotion and thanked Sal. "At least we know the Commissioner didn't send Trisha here to dig up dirt on us." Kerry joked, temporarily relieving the tension in their conversation.

Three low, quick knocks came on the door and Kerry stepped across the small room and pulled it open.

The woman was taller than Kerry and had an oversized purse slung over her shoulder. She looked over Kerry's shoulder, into the small room, and seemed confused about being sent to 24B.

"I'm sorry," the woman apologized as she glanced down at the small piece of paper with the room number and directions on how to get there from the main hospital entrance. "A security guard told me this is where I could find the coroner."

Kerry rested her right hand on the door handle, shifting her body slightly in the same direction. "You have the right room." Although, Kerry thought to herself, for how much longer is anyone's guess. "How can I help you?"

The woman pulled an envelope out of her purse and handed it to Kerry, "I'm here to arrange for Michel Lalonde's body to be transferred."

Kerry's eyes widened, "You're Camille Scott?"

They spoke only a few days ago, but with everything that happened, it seemed like months.

"I'm sorry it took so long to get here," Camille said. "I can see why Michel found it such a refuge for him on his island. It's so far away from everything out there."

Kerry nodded, "It definitely is."

"I wanted to arrange for his body to be released," Camille handed Kerry the name of a local funeral home. "I've already spoken with the funeral director, and he's aware Michel wanted to be cremated. I need your department to arrange for his body to be transferred."

Camille's glance drifted toward Sal and Kerry wondered if she thought Sal was the sole employee of her department.

"And if it's possible, I'd like to collect his belongings before I return home." Camille handed Kerry her identification along with a photocopy of Michel Lalonde's Will. "I recently learned that Michel entrusted me with coordinating his funeral arrangements. I don't know what documents you need since this is the first time that I've had to do anything like this."

"That's okay," Kerry took the paper from Camille's outstretched arm. "Come with me and I'll make sure that you have everything you need. Then I'll call the police station and let them know that you'll be picking up his personal belongings."

Kerry left the room with Camille Scott as Sal returned to the research lab to work on the samples he was examining before Kerry pulled him into the web of confusion surrounding Michel Lalonde's death. His eyes remained fixed on Camille as she disappeared around the corner with Kerry, feeling like he had seen her before.

He shook the feeling from his mind. He had become paranoid since Trisha arrived and began working in the anti-room next to the examination room. He was a doctor and not a private investigator, and his preoccupation with Kerry's problems drifted him away from the focus of his research.

Maybe with Michel Lalonde's body being transferred out of Lake Pines, Kerry would relax a little bit more and things would return to normal. But then again, probably not.

CHAPTER 90

Simon had reason to consider Paul Buchanan and Trisha Chen suspects, but something told him that as bizarre as their stories were, they were telling the truth. However, he was dealing with a murder investigation and until he could be certain that neither of them was involved in Michel Lalonde's death, he asked them to remain in the station.

Sally knocked on Simon's door, "I finished the manuscript."

"Did you learn anything from it?" Simon asked.

"Yeah. That chef had a dark life, you won't believe what I read. At the end of the book, Michel credited his connection with Vivienne's daughter for convincing him to write the manuscript."

"Trisha Chen?"

Sally nodded, "He reached out to her when he was eighteen. His mother died shortly after the police arrested his father, and his grandparents refused to let him read anything about the case thinking that they could protect him if they concealed what his father did. But when he was old enough, he went to the courthouse and read the transcripts. That's how he learned the details that his grandparents were trying to keep from him. He even mentions how he believes his mother died when she learned her husband was a killer."

"That explains why he wanted nothing to do with his father."

"And why he legally changed his name?"

"What prompted him to reach out to Trisha?"

"He felt he needed to apologize and let her know his father hurt so many other people, and if she ever needed to talk that he'd always be there," Sally said. "Over the years, they remained friends and kept in touch through emails. He also revealed that after his grandparents died, she was the only person who knew about his past. After his father applied for parole for the first time, they decided that the world needed to know the truth. They've been working on this book for years."

"This entire book was about Vivienne's murder?" Simon asked.

Sally shook her head.

She opened the manuscript to a section flagged with a yellow sticky and read, "*My heart raced as I looked at my father's picture, realizing with a sickening feeling that I was staring into the eyes of a killer. I had known him my entire life and had always thought of him as a decent person, but now I saw the darkness that lurked behind his eyes. Memories flashed through my mind, the pieces of the dark puzzle falling into place. I realized the little details that I had missed before. The lies, the cover-ups, the little hints that had been there all along. I tried to speak to my grandparents, but they ignored my questions. I felt a sense of betrayal and anger well up inside me. I not only lost my mother, but the only decent memories I had of my father. If the man who carried me on his shoulders and tucked me in at night was capable of murdering six people, what else was he capable of? The realization hit me like a ton of bricks, and I knew that I would never be able to look at my father, or my name, the same way again.*"

Simon took the manuscript from Sally and read the following entry that outlined the evidence that Michel and Trisha found. They believed Paul Buchanan was guilty of murder before he hurled his anger at Vivienne Strong, and they were intent on letting the world know for the sake of the other victim's families.

“That explains why his agent didn’t know about it. They must have been working secretly on the book.”

“Oh, but she did know,” Sally pointed to the page dogeared to the reference of when Michel revealed the manuscript to his agent, Camille Scott.

Sally waited while Simon read the four pages.

It was in those four pages that it became clear who had the most to lose if Michel Lalonde published the manuscript. His murder had nothing to do with Paul Buchanan or Vivienne Strong. It had everything to do with money.

CHAPTER 91

Following Kerry's directions, Camille drove straight to the police station and parked in the lot behind the building. She looked at the time. Factoring in the drive back to the airport and returning the rental car she should have enough time to make her flight.

Six months ago, when Michel took the train from Paris to London, it was under the guise of working on the plan for the launch of his upcoming cookbook. Camille recalled the excited fervor he exuded when they unboxed the first run of books.

She never tired of sharing an author's excitement at the publication of a book. The only problem she was finding in her business, there were too few authors interested in being represented by a small literary house.

Because of that, she put everything she had into Michel's career, and it paid off. Her commission hadn't dipped below high six figures and she was finally making a name for herself in the publishing industry.

One of the largest agencies in London had recently offered her a position on their team. They represented three of the current global best-selling authors, two in fiction and one in non-fiction, and they were looking to expand their roster of clients.

It didn't surprise Camille that a prime condition of her offer rested upon bringing Michel Lalonde onboard as a client of their agency.

For the first time in her career, Camille had the golden rings within reach. But the moment Michel unveiled the first draft of his manuscript, her world collapsed.

Besides ending his celebrity status after being outed as a fraud, Michel would drag Camille's reputation as a reputable agent through the mud.

She tried to convince him to wait until the end of his career before publishing a memoir. Michel hadn't been around long enough to survive the onslaught of bad press that would surface the moment the book hit the market.

He claimed to not want the celebrity that he eschewed from the beginning, and although he enjoyed the trappings of a successful career, Michel claimed all he wanted was to run the small restaurant in the south of France. Michel wanted a quiet life with no drama, after all, it was drama and the public press that caused his mother's untimely death and forced the mark of shame on his life.

He believed it was time for the truth to come out.

When Michel left London, his mind hadn't changed. Camille sprang into survival mode as she planned the next few months, hoping she could salvage her future.

If she was going to go down, then at least she'd have the best seat in the house.

The early release of Michel's cookbook was just one cog in her plan, the other was to stop the publication of his manuscript at any cost.

'*The End*'

It had seemed an odd title, but with what happened over the last week, it was surprisingly appropriate.

The clear sky had disappeared and gray clouds quickly rolled over the bay and opened a torrent of rain down on Lake Pines. Camille reached into the back seat and tugged the raincoat from under her purse and pulled it over her arms, awkwardly shifting in the front seat of the sedan.

Camille reached for her purse, pulled the hood over her head, and stepped out of the car. As she neared the station, she realized this would be the final phase in her plan of retrieving the manuscript. And although she was excited at the prospect of ending the threat that the manuscript presented, she missed Michel deeply.

Camille climbed the stairs, pulled open the door, and rushed into the station to collect the box containing Michel's belongings. Then, and only then, could she put the worst behind her.

CHAPTER 92

Kerry phoned Simon, alerting him that Camille was heading to the station to collect Michel's belongings. He filled Kerry in on the last few chapters of Michel's manuscript, which revealed who he thought was the person who had the most to lose by the publication of the book.

"So, his death had nothing to do with his father or Trisha?"

"I don't think so," Simon said. "Trisha and he were friends. They connected before Michel became famous and were each other's support network. Vivienne's death traumatized both kids, but for different reasons."

"Do you believe Paul was really in Lake Pines to make amends with his son?"

"I do, but I also know that Trisha opened a can of worms for you. Especially concerning Paul Buchanan's case. And now that there's the implication of more murders, I need to hold him here until I can sort out what the truth is."

Kerry let out an exasperated sigh, "I told Sal everything."

"That was brave," Simon said. "I never had the chance to ask you how things went with Peter?"

"Better than I would've expected. He's telling Commissioner Robertson today and I've planned to meet with them both later this week."

Despite being Kerry's biggest supporter, he knew Peter had to follow protocol once he knew what had happened. He also imagined that Jean would be called to testify and explain his actions in the investigation.

He prepared himself for the worst of the fallout but hoped for the best, and he encouraged Kerry to do the same.

With the manuscript locked in the evidence room, Simon headed out to the lobby to await Camille's arrival.

A clap of thunder shook the windows of the station, and Sally jumped in her seat. Simon smiled when he saw Sally's reaction, thinking about the time he calmed Dominique with the explanation that thunder was just bowling above the clouds.

Although Simon understood why Kerry wanted Oliver to keep their daughter away for a few extra days, he wondered if it was the best decision. Right now, seeing the hope and purity in their daughter's eyes might be what Kerry needs to see her through the next phase in her life.

As the rain intensified, a stream of water blurred the glass on the widow of the front door. A long red shadow grew in the watery haze that covered the door, and Simon glanced over just as a tall, dark-haired woman walked into the station.

Sally stared at the woman and then twisted her face toward Simon, who immediately recognized her.

They were looking at the image of the woman that Janus described to the sketch artist. The woman who he overheard arguing with Michel Lalonde on the day he died, and the woman who scared Janus into lying to the police. And she was wearing a bright red raincoat.

CHAPTER 93

As they sat in the small interrogation room, Camille fidgeted with the straps of her purse, avoiding the question for a second time. Her bottom lip quivered as Simon slid the printed image from Janus' description across the table.

She squeezed her eyes closed and shook her head, "I would never have hurt his wife. I was just desperate to make sure he didn't tell anyone that I was arguing with Michel."

"Is this because of his book?"

Camille nodded. "The moment he published that book, his career would've been over. There were people with a larger career who didn't withstand scrutiny from their past, but somehow Michel believed he was popular enough to weather the storm."

"You didn't think he would?"

Camille laughed, "God no. He was popular, but he hadn't built his career to where he was irreplaceable. No matter what I said, he was insistent upon publishing this book before his restaurant opened this September."

"We know you were on the island the day that Michel was murdered. Tanya, the woman you hired to purchase his supplies, ran into you as she was leaving. She recognized your picture when we showed her the sketch artist's image. But since she had only communicated with you through email she never realized it was you on the dock."

"I saw her as I was rushing to the rental boat I docked on the opposite side of the boathouse," Camille explained. "We didn't speak, and she didn't know who I was. I was so upset after I argued with Michel, that I just wanted to get away from the island. I went to Storm Island to apologize to Michel and to ask him to reconsider publishing his memoir."

Simon recalled the time Tanya said she left and when Noah claimed to have arrived, which put Camille's departure before Michel was murdered. That is if she was telling the truth.

"Can anyone vouch for your whereabouts after you left Storm Island?"

"The hotel manager where I was staying." Camille wrote the name of the hotel she was staying at along with the name of the manager, who signed for a package that same afternoon. "I went straight back to the hotel because I was waiting for a package to be couriered from London. I knew I had to take on a few new clients if I was going to survive Michel's book."

"Why are you still in Lake Pines?"

"Michel wanted to be cremated, and I wanted to arrange that and hopefully get hold of the manuscript while I was here. Once I get back to London, I need to track down Michel's sole heir. He left his entire fortune to one person."

"Who was that?" Simon couldn't imagine who Michel could have left everything to since they had so much difficulty finding a next of kin after he was murdered.

"She's a childhood friend. Her name is Patricia Strong Chen."

That only left one person who may have lost everything if Michel published his manuscript.

CHAPTER 94

Jamie pulled up Henri's social media account as Simon and Josh watched over his shoulder.

"I thought you said he was in Italy?"

"I also thought Camille was in London when I spoke with her on the phone, but she was at the Lakeside Inn waiting for the right time to reappear to claim Michel's belongings." Simon turned to Jamie. "Please tell me you can find something that proves he was here when Michel Lalonde was murdered?"

"I can do one better," Jamie said. "I can tell you where he is right now."

Jamie walked Simon and Josh through Henri Badeau's social media account. Images of rustic stone alleyways, colorful hand-painted bowls, and tantalizing dishes that Henri claimed to be enjoying while traveling in the Italian countryside in search of items for his new restaurant.

"The first thing that struck me is that he posted at the exact same time every day. Even if you are extremely organized and committed to posting regularly, there's no way that he would've been posting at the exact same hour every day." Jamie explained. "The only way he could do that is if he used a social media scheduling tool. Users upload their images along with text and voilà. They set the times and dates and then the program does the rest. A lot of companies use a tool like that to keep up with the regular posts they need to send."

"How does that tell us where Henri is now?" Josh asked.

"It doesn't, but it was odd enough that I looked at each post a little closer. Every post has a location tag for a rural village outside of Naples. Everyone except the last three."

Jamie increased the image and pointed to the location tag at the bottom of the picture. "He must have forgotten to turn off the roaming location feature when he sent the last few posts. And judging by the one he sent this morning, he's at the Lake Pines Regional Airport.

CHAPTER 95

Henri waited in the vacant parking lot, glancing at his watch every few minutes, wondering what was taking so long. He had spent enough time in Lake Pines and he wanted nothing more than to get out of there.

The unexpected storm delayed his flight, and he waited until the flight tower cleared the Learjet for takeoff. He stamped out the last embers of his cigarette and dashed out from under the cover of the awning and ran back into the building.

He hesitated to refer to the one-room building as an airport, but it obviously served its purpose. Three black faux leather sofas faced the large wall of windows that looked onto the tarmac. Although he couldn't imagine anyone lounging in the space to watch the news, a chair faced a flat panel screen hanging on the wall. Framed posters displayed the recreational offerings in and around Lake Pines. Commercials of fishing camps, canoe expeditions, cottage rentals, private yacht rentals, and more blared from the television. The one story that seemed out of place was the coverage of a large fish statue that was being renovated after a storm had damaged its hull. When the colorful fish flashed across the screen, the two employees at the check-in desk launched into an argument over the renovations.

Henri checked his email for the fourth time, wondering how much longer it was going to take. He was about to interrupt the two attendants behind the counter when he noticed his plane was making its way toward the building.

Finally, Henri thought.

He reached down, grabbed his small black satchel, and walked out to his plane. The gleaming white paint finish always amazed Henri. The hours of flight time, through storms and ice hadn't dulled the finish. Although it wasn't his. It belonged to the main investor in the restaurant and he insisted Henri use the plane to travel to Lake Pines and change Michel's mind about publishing his book.

At first, Michel was glad to see Henri when he appeared on his dock in the middle of the afternoon. His excitement grew when he believed Henri was there to plan the opening of the restaurant and it was all Henri could do to stop Michel's chatter about menu plans and regional accessories they could add to the restaurant.

It wasn't until Henri mentioned the manuscript that Michel realized the real reason for his surprise arrival in Lake Pines. It was by a haphazard mistake that Henri even learned about the proposed book release. Both Henri and Michel had the same black satchel, a gift from their investor at the beginning of their talks regarding the new restaurant.

Late one evening, Henri grabbed the wrong bag on his way home and hadn't noticed until he unclipped the latch and Michel's belongings tumbled out. Henri spent that entire evening reading the book, and he learned about his future business partner's secret past.

He was sympathetic toward Michel's experience and commended him for overcoming the tragedy and pain. However, when he shared the information with his investor, everything changed.

Experience taught the financier that tantalizing news may work for some celebrities, but Michel hadn't amassed a loyal enough following to assume he'd be forgiven for deceiving them from the beginning of his career. And the investor who was putting up the funds for the new restaurant refused to be associated with Michel Lalonde on any level if the book was published.

"It's the money for the restaurant or Michel's book," his investor screamed. "It's your choice."

The choice was easy but when his attempt to change Michel's mind failed, Henri ran down to the boat. After a few moments, he panicked. He grabbed the oar inside the boat and ran back up the steps to confront Michel. He would try to scare him into changing his mind, but somehow everything spun out of control. In a fit of frustration tinged with desperation, he struck Michel with the oar.

Henri watched as Michel tumbled backward on the wooden staircase and landed with a thud on the dock.

He started walking toward the cottage to search for the manuscript when he heard the rustling of the branches in the dense forest to the side of the cottage. He couldn't be caught with a bloody oar and the battered body of Michel on the dock.

Henri rushed down to the boat, tossed the oar on top of the seat, and drove out of the bay. He rushed away from the island just before a scream echoed over the water.

Someone discovered Michel's body, but Henri counted on the fact that by the time they figured it out, it would be too late.

There was no news report of the bloodied oar being found in the damaged fish statue, and Henri smiled when he learned they had completed the renovations. Sealing the murder weapon inside the oversized fish statue, never to be found.

The door of the Learjet hissed as it folded forward and lowered the small staircase. Within a day he'd be back in France and far away from Lake Pines and he could put the horrible issue with Michel Lalonde behind him.

But as Henri walked up the stairs, a flash of red and blue reflected in the gleaming white paint on the side of the plane. The siren's wail echoed, growing in intensity as the patrol car pulled up next to the plane, putting a stop to Henri's departure and closing the case on Michel Lalonde's murder.

CHAPTER 96

The sun shone brightly, reflecting the mood in the crowd that assembled below the covered statue. Unusually clear, the sun's rays warmed and comforted the crowd gathering near the park. The atmosphere was bright and vibrant, alive with colors and sounds that appeared more vivid than the days before.

An orange tarp covered the renovated statue as hundreds of people gathered around the base. Some spectators sat on the small hill while others watched from the comfort of their boats in the bay.

Revealing the renovated statue should have been a celebration. Instead, mixed reactions from the crowd brought a feeling of unease to its debut. The pomp and ceremony seemed out of place to some residents, while others celebrated the pride of their small town.

Everyone congregated in groups according to their chosen allegiance toward the project. Crowds of smiling supporters and sulking dissenters filled the lawn on the small outcrop of land.

Colorful signs and banners dotted the hill, welcoming the new version of the long-standing icon. Posters drawn by young and old leaned against lawn chairs when people grew tired of waving them. Possibly because waving a sign supporting a fish embarrassed them, or because their arms were numb.

A group backing the taxpayer's coalition was less social than those in favor of the renovations. They stood with folded arms, shaking their heads and complaining to the small circle near where they stood. Their presence in the crowd was reminiscent of black-and-white films with undercover police trying, but failing, to fit into a parade.

Lisa handed out small cookies, baked in the shape of a curved fish. She decorated each one with white icing and sprinkled them with candy flecks, festively celebrating the unveiling.

Oliver and Elin returned with Dominique and Lucia the day before the unveiling of the town's refurbished icon that would welcome visitors into the area.

The girls munched on cookies as they waved their miniature fish cut-outs over their heads. Raven slumped against Oliver's legs when he grew tired of the jeers and screams from the crowd and fell asleep despite the noise. As Oliver and Elin shared a private joke, Josh and Kerry watched them, happy that they had found each other.

"How's Thomas doing with his mother's new boyfriend?" Kerry asked with a wink.

"I'm not sure. I think we'll keep an eye on him for a while before we decide." Josh snapped a photo of the girls as they twirled around, waving their signs. "How are you doing with Peter's decision?"

Kerry wasn't sure how to reply. On one hand, she was prepared for a quick, decisive end to her career. It would've been within Peter's right to fire Kerry because of what she did. On the other hand, she was also ready to be charged with interfering in a murder investigation, but thankfully that didn't happen.

What she wasn't prepared for was to be placed on probation while Ontario and Quebec authorities reviewed each case she worked on. Whether her reports were involved with cases of a suspicious death, death because of natural causes, or when evidence she uncovered resulted in a conviction, everything was under scrutiny and required review.

"I know I'm lucky, considering what happened, but I'm not sure where I fit in anymore." Kerry glanced at Dominique. "I want to make sure whatever I do, that Dominique is proud of how I conducted myself. I won't hide the fact that I did something wrong at the beginning of my career, but it's going to be a painful conversation to have with her."

"That's a long way off," Josh said.

"So was Vivienne Strong's murder, but her daughter was so full of anger that she plotted her revenge against me. Even though what I did put the man who killed her mother behind bars."

"Simon told me that Doctor Varanus has to supervise every file you work on. How do you feel about that?"

"Surprisingly alright," Kerry smiled. "He's turned out to be a good guy, after all. Who knew Sal would turn out to be my ride-or-die?"

"I'm glad to hear that because after your probation is over, you both are going to share an office," Peter had walked up behind Kerry and Josh, overhearing the final part of their conversation.

Kerry turned around, "What?"

"I just returned from a meeting with both provincial heads and they agree that considering your work history, combined with Paul's admission confirming that he killed Vivienne Strong, you deserved leniency with this case," Peter said. "The Commissioner also said that Josh's work on the identification thefts was useful in stopping several groups on both sides of the border. In addition to moving you and Doctor Varanus to your own building, he's approved additional funding for police resources in Lake Pines."

"How are they going to afford a new building? I thought that was a huge roadblock after the fire in my lab?"

"It was, but someone stepped up and donated the building supplies and labor for the structure," Peter pointed to Thomas who was standing a few feet away talking to Lisa. "That just leaves the equipment, which fits into our budget."

Simon walked up and shook Peter's hand, "I didn't know you were going to be here?"

"How could I miss such a momentous inauguration?"

A loud roar from the group of teenagers rolled over Peter and Simon's conversation, muffling their greeting, and reminding Kerry of the close bond several people in the community had to each other.

Kerry turned away from the laughter, shielding the uncertainty that clouded her eyes.

She hadn't decided if she wanted to return to her job as the town coroner and now wasn't the time to bring it up.

It took a long time for Kerry to admit that finding justice might mean never knowing the entire truth and that had her questioning her entire career.

A bell rang out, silencing the crowd of revelers, protestors, and supporters. Felicity gave a brief speech, thanking the individuals and government officials who raised the funds for the repairs.

"Without further ado, I give you," Felicity reached up and tugged on a rope, releasing the large orange tarp that had concealed the statue.

Adding dramatic flair, the mayor waved her arms up in the air and shouted, "Lake Pines Larry."

Laughs, whistles, and shouts rang out as those supporting the renovation celebrated their win.

While anyone who opposed the expenditure offered claps and smiles in a good-natured manner. Supporting their friends and neighbors with Lake Pines' characteristic warm reputation.

With mixed reviews on the painting design, the landscaping, and the new name, the residents retreated from the public park, returning to their homes and businesses.

In the end, everyone welcomed Lake Pines Larry.

Regardless of anyone's position, the passion they displayed during the controversy connected them. But above all, they were bound by the love of their town - which ultimately brought them together in the shared pride of the small lakeside place they called home.

THE END

Did you enjoy this book? You can make a difference.

Reviews are the most powerful tools in my arsenal when it comes to getting attention for my books. And I have something more powerful than a New York Publisher. I have you – my reader.

If you've enjoyed this book, I would be very grateful if you could just spend five minutes leaving a review (it can be as short as you like) and it will help bring my books to the attention of other readers.

Thank you very much.

About the Author

L.L. Abbott is the author of the popular Lake Pines Mystery Series, The Anna Ledin Spy Thriller Series, and many standalone novels, spanning several genres. She makes her online home at www.llabbott.com, where you can find links to all her books.

Free Books, Downloads, and Contests

Go to www.llabbott.com/Contact to join our reading community.

Manufactured by Amazon.ca
Acheson, AB